CATTYWAMPUS

Ash Van Otterloo

THIS BOOK IS DEDICATED TO WITCHES OF ALL AGES WITH HOMEMADE WANDS. YOU ARE GOOD ENOUGH AND STRONG ENOUGH.

Copyright © 2020 by Ash Van Otterloo

This book was originally published in hardcover by Scholastic Press in 2020.

All rights reserved. Published by Scholastic Inc., *Publishers since 1920*. SCHOLASTIC and associated logos are trademarks and/or registered trademarks of Scholastic Inc.

The publisher does not have any control over and does not assume any responsibility for author or third-party websites or their content.

ISBN 978-1-338-56160-9

10 9 8 7 6 5 4 3 2 1   22 23 24 25 26

Printed in the U.S.A. 40
This edition first printing 2022

Book design by Baily Crawford

CHAPTER 1
DELPHA

THERE WAS A SWEET SPOT IN DELPHA McGILL'S week, between the hustle of school and the hard work during the weekend, that had no floors to sweep, no leaky faucets to tighten, no homework to riddle, and no lawn to mow. It was her time, and she fully intended to spend it in a blissful expanse of quiet, working on a secret whittling project in her bedroom. *Finally.* She started up the staircase in the hall, taking two steps at a time, careful to avoid the bad spots in the wood. A leaky roof meant rotted steps, and fixing shingles wasn't something she'd worked up the courage to tackle yet.

"Delpha, darlin'?"

Delpha winced at her mama's voice, her fingers clutching the worn bannister. A crack in the ceiling blinked out a tear that splattered her nose as she froze in place. *She can't know you're fixin' to make a wand*, Delpha reminded herself. *She can't read minds.* "Yes, ma'am?"

"Go into Mamaw's closet and bring out the three flower garden quilts. Careful not to get 'em dirty, please."

Delpha's stomach instantly churned. She had avoided her grandmother's room since Mamaw passed away a month ago, even though they needed the space.

It wasn't the smell. It wasn't even the sad memories. It was the *quiet*. Mama knew danged well why Delpha didn't want to go in. Delpha had enough depressing empty spots in her life, and ignoring this new one seemed like a good idea, no matter what Mama's bedside copy of *Embracing Loss* claimed. "Do I have to?"

"Yes, and you'd best watch your tone! Thank you, darlin'."

Delpha sighed, then held her breath and darted into the shadowy room, rushing past the empty bed and her grandmother's walker to the closet. She scowled. Her mother planned to sell the quilts to the Hearn family's Appalachian Culture Museum near downtown Howler's Hollow, where tourists would coo over the intricate stitchwork and fork over their cash. Mama had put it off for days, and Delpha had secretly hoped she wouldn't go through with it. It was like they were trading a part of her grandmother away. But she and Mama needed the money to keep the lights on, especially after paying for the funeral.

Just get it done, Delpha told herself. *Don't overthink it.* She yanked the string for the closet light and stood on her tiptoes, reaching for a stack of folded quilts. As she eased them from the shelf, something heavy and brown slid off the top of the stack and clocked her senseless, right across the forehead.

Delpha lay dazed on the wooden floorboards for a moment, constellations swirling before her eyes. A tender spot throbbed just above her hairline. She muttered dark things under her breath and pushed herself upright. *What was that?*

"Delpha?" her mother called. "Everything all right in there, baby girl?"

"Yeah, fine," Delpha replied. She reached up and tested the tender spot. A furious bump the size of a sparrow's egg greeted her fingertips. "Be even better if Mama would use her healing magic for once," Delpha muttered to herself. But that was out of the question. Magic was strictly forbidden in the McGill household, bruises or not. It had been ever since her mama's siblings had been killed decades ago in a spell gone bad. Delpha's grandmother had whispered muddled stories to Delpha about "the old witchin' days" sometimes when Mama wasn't listening.

But Mamaw was gone now. People got old. They got dementia and died, even old witches. If there was one thing in the world reliable as rain, it was that everybody left eventually. Delpha breathed deep, feeling the tight clamp of sadness in her chest. It was just her and Mama.

Presently, she twisted around this way and that to find what had fallen on her head. Crackled with age, a thick leather book lay splayed open beside her like a bird shot from the sky, mid-flight. Delpha's brows furrowed. She squatted and gathered it together, her tight bootlaces creaking. Flipping it right side up, her heart jittered in her chest.

In neat letters, tooled into the leather cover, were the words *Macgeil Booke o' Spelles*. Delpha blinked in disbelief.

"You had it all along, Mamaw, you old devil," Delpha whispered. She'd spent dozens of afternoons combing her grandmother's bookshelves when she was little, looking for her family's book of spells, curiosity burning a hole in her. Magic had sounded exciting. Forbidden magic had been even more tempting. She'd even sneaked up to scour the moth-riddled attic once, though the rafters of the old cabin were as unstable and off-limits as McGill magic. And now the spellbook was here, in her lap. Leave it to crafty Mamaw to put it somewhere casual, knowing Delpha would never look any place so boring.

The book called to her now, and every atom of Delpha's body thrummed back in response. This book knew her. She knew *it*, too. It lived in late-night arguments between her grandmother and Mama, atop the laps of grim, sharp-eyed old crones in yellowed family photographs, and—most powerfully—in the lonely corners of Delpha's own imagination. Passed down from firstborn to firstborn, the book kept record of the homemade charms and hexes of cousins, aunties, and sisters across several centuries. Delpha's long fingers trembled as they traced the binding.

The McGill spellbook.

"Delpha? If we don't carry those quilts to the Hearns' museum soon, it'll close! Shake a leg!"

Quiet as a deer, Delpha slid a threadbare pillowcase from the linen trunk and nestled the spellbook inside it. She gripped it in her hands a few seconds, wishing she could read it *right then*.

If she could study magic on the sly, things might start looking up for her and Mama. Maybe Delpha could fix things up around the house with magic. Maybe there were even spells for money! They might have plenty, for once.

"Comin', Mama."

The weight of Delpha's secret tugged at her gut, promising to rearrange her life nine ways to Sunday if she'd let it. Delpha slid the wrapped book back onto the shelf and cracked her knuckles. "I'll be back later tonight," she promised the book in a low voice.

She gathered the quilts up neatly, then hurried out to Mama's rusty old Buick.

CHAPTER 2
KATYBIRD

KATYBIRD HEARN THANKED THE STARS THE BATHROOM counters at her family's Appalachian Culture Museum were sturdy—because she was standing atop one. Katybird's mother hummed as she stocked shelves in the gift shop outside the bathroom, calling for Katy's help every so often. Just in case Mama came looking for her, Katy had locked the door for good measure.

Tugging her iPhone from her pocket, she clicked it on and held it up toward the skylight window next to the ceiling. In exactly this spot, she could connect to the neighbor's Wi-Fi and use the internet. In private. And today, privacy was important.

She pecked out *hands glowing magic* into the search engine.

After a minute—the neighbor's Wi-Fi was slow as molasses—Tumblr links for Wiccan spells popped onto the screen.

"That ain't it," Katybird sighed. Maybe she needed to be more specific. She started the search over: *witch hands glowing stuck.*

This time, the internet treated her to dozens of buy-links for glowing Halloween witch decorations. Katybird deflated like a balloon. No one in the world could help her. She clicked the phone off, her heart sinking. A tingle prickled at her fingertips. Katy glared at them as she climbed off the counter.

It was happening again. Why couldn't her magic be easy? Why couldn't anything be easy, just this once? Her hands had been glowing like lightning bugs on and off for a week, filling Katy with an uncomfortable buzzing that reminded her of an electric cattle fence. *The magic is trying to happen, Katy*, she told herself. *Maybe you can work with it.* She thought of her favorite Roald Dahl book and stared down the paper towel dispenser with her best Matilda face on, willing it to shoot out napkins or burst into flames.

But of course, it didn't work. Instead, eerie light glowed around her fingernails, then crept up both her hands. Her fingers looked bizarre, like electric-lime Jell-O. The glow wasn't soft blue and flowing, like her mama's. Katybird held her hands out, afraid to touch anything. They weren't giving off heat, but they grew brighter by the minute.

"No, no, no," she whispered. Her hands were shedding sparks now—dad-blasted sparks.

Fighting the impulse to holler to her mother for help, Katybird ran for the sink. She slammed the stopper into the marble basin, slapped the faucet on, and plunged her hands into the growing pool of cold water. Tiny green comets sputtered from her fingertips and chased one another around the sink like radioactive tadpoles. Katybird chewed her lip, tears welling. This wasn't how her magic was supposed to start, all of a sudden and weird.

There were rules. In the Hearn family, your gift showed up early and slow, unless you were a late bloomer like Katybird. Or you refused to use it, like Katy's cousin Echo. Katy was Echo's opposite. She longed for her magic to work, but instead it stayed trapped inside her, useless. Katybird nibbled a strand of cherry Kool-Aid–colored hair, staring at her own wobbling reflection. "Your conjure gift cannot be rushed, and when it shows, we keep it shushed," she whispered.

She'd learned the silly rhyme when she was three years old. Lately her mama always followed it with, "But you might not even have to worry about it at all, darlin'."

Those words cut Katy like a hot knife through butter. Katybird wanted to yell, "You mean because I'm different, Mama, so I might not be a witch. You can say it, if you think that's why!"

Instead, Katy smiled and answered, "Fine by me!" That's what Mama and Nanny wanted to hear Katybird say, so they could pretend having a non-witch girl in the family wasn't a bitter disappointment. But their too-big smiles and nervous chuckles told Katy it did matter. She couldn't blame them. It mattered to her, too.

Unlike most girls, Katy'd caterwauled her way into the world with a pair of XY chromosomes instead of double X's. But her body hadn't had much use for hormones like testosterone—the chemicals that give people whiskers and let them sing bass in church choir.

In fact, Katy's body converted them straight to buckets and barrels of estrogen, even before she was born. At nearly twelve, Katy didn't shave her legs, because she didn't need to. Her friends from swim team called her lucky. Katybird never got zits, either, which was pretty handy for an almost-popular girl in seventh grade. She was impeccably, fabulously Katybird. But that one Y chromosome haunted her still, for one pesky reason: Her family's magic craft—witch's magic—was passed from mother to daughter.

Katybird was a daughter. She was, wasn't she? *She was.* Her heart knew that. But as she hunched in a sad ball over the sink, doubt ran circles around her mind. *If I ain't a good witch*, Katy thought, *does that mean I'm not a girl?* Or maybe it was the other way around. Either way, things were knotted up and complicated.

In the sink, the sparks dwindled. Mascara-black tears dropped and spread like ink through the water. She kicked the pipe beneath the sink with her purple sneaker. One thing was for sure: This wasn't the sort of "magic" she wanted to show off to anyone. Her family's safety rested on keeping their conjure secret. People in Howler's Hollow were good folk, but they were scared of magic. They politely pretended not to remember that a few generations back the Hearns had been witches. And Katybird's magic, if you could call it that, seemed weird at best—freaky Day-Glo hands weren't a great advertisement for normal. She pictured the pity in her family's faces, too, and knew this had to stay secret until she fixed it.

Katybird pulled the stopper, and the water spiraled down the drain. Trembling, she muttered her favorite Elizabeth Taylor quote, "Put on some lipstick and pull yourself together." Then she pulled a tube of peach sparkly gloss from her pocket, coated her lips, and cleaned her runny eyeliner with a wet paper towel.

Time to go be Super Katybird, she told herself.

Plastering on a dimpled smile, Katy soldiered out of the bathroom, sleeves rolled back to help arrange shelves for another big tourist weekend. That was Katybird's job: smiling, being a good kid, and making folks proud.

Her spirits brightened when she heard voices from the gift shop. It was too late for visitors, but artists often came by to restock their wares after-hours. Katybird liked the way other people took her mind off her own problems. She hurried past the copper stills in the moonshine exhibit and around the corner.

Beside a set of rustic shelves stood a tall girl with a long pitch-dark braid. *Delpha McGill.* Delpha was striking, Katy thought, but in a grim way. Her jet-black eyes were solemn daggers, and Katy had known Delpha long enough to know that a tiny, lopsided smirk was more or less the extent of Delpha's smiling ability. Today, Delpha's straight eyebrows gathered like thunderheads. Katy shivered.

Delpha was the only other young witch in the Hollow, from the only rival magic family in the state, the McGills. Neither family did magic in public. There had once been bad blood between the two clans, and even now they maintained a polite distance, which Katy found silly. Sure, the McGills and the Hearns had thrown hexes and burned each other's barns to cinders and would have torched the whole valley if a truce hadn't been called a century ago. But traditions died hard in the hills, even if the tradition was acting plain old cranky. No one actually knew how their feud started—something about a stolen cow, or was it a jinxed washtub? When Katybird Hearn's relatives repeated the dusty family lore over sweet tea, only one fact stayed consistent: The McGills had started it.

To the non-magical folks in Howler's Hollow, it was the stuff of local folk legend—fish tales with a microscopic grain of truth. Katy's family did magic at home now, just for fun and away from prying eyes. She figured that's what the McGills did, too. Their herbs and advice were considered mountain wisdom now, not conjure. That left Katy and Delpha, last of their magical lines.

Across the room, Delpha stood motionless, staring at the folded quilts in her arms. She looked even more serious than normal, and Katy remembered Delpha's grandmother had passed away several weeks ago. Katy bit her lip. She wanted to say something nice to Delpha. They could forget their families' prejudices, couldn't they? Before she lost her nerve, Katy cleared her throat and stepped forward. Delpha tensed. She shot Katy a sideways scowl, then slid her quilts into an empty place on the shelf, fingertips lingering on the perfect stitches. For a hair's breadth, Delpha's lower lip trembled. Katy remembered how she'd felt after her own cousin Echo had died a year ago. Katy bit back a "Sorry." A person got sick of hearing that sort of thing. So instead, Katybird slid a cheerful smile onto her face. "Hey, Delpha. Haven't seen you in a while."

Delpha grunted. "Saw you yesterday at school, didn't I?" She hunched next to the cardboard box by her feet and removed half a dozen elderberry whistles, each with a neatly penned price attached.

Katybird's eyes flitted to Delpha's hands. Not glowing. Not even trembling. Delpha was rock steady. Katybird wished all the way to her toenails she could ask Delpha point-blank whether her magic had . . . *arrived*, too. Delpha didn't bother looking at Katy, keeping her sad eyes forward. Katy tried again. "You carved those whistles yourself, right? They're gorgeous."

Delpha sighed hard. "Yup. Got bored after about the third one."

"Oh, but tourists love 'em!" Katybird reassured her. "They fly off the shelves faster than anything! No one ever believes a twelve-year-old girl did 'em. Anyway, must be nice, havin' the pocket money." Katy recalled her own joy last summer, when she'd been paid for cleaning glass in the museum every week. New Chucks in her color of choice had been pure bliss. She wondered what sort of things Delpha McGill got joy from. Knives? Another pair of steel-toed boots?

Delpha's eyebrows raised. "Sure. Pocket money."

Suddenly, the fraying hem of Delpha's shirt and her well-worn boots stood out. One of Delpha's bootlaces was even broken and tied together in the middle. Katy looked away, cheeks burning, and berated herself for being so stupid.

She needed to change the subject, and fast. "Delpha, can we talk? About magic?"

Delpha's eyes widened. Before she could answer, the bell on the entrance door jingled, and both girls clamped their mouths. Katy withered as their chance to talk about magic evaporated. Tyler Nimble, a stocky boy with glasses, and his moms, Muzz and Honey, shuffled in, swatting off moths that tried to hitchhike a ride into the store. Tyler spotted the girls right away and grinned. Katy waved a half-hearted hello as Tyler helped his moms haul in crates of hand-turned wooden bowls, made by Tyler's uncle for the museum shop.

Tyler set down his last box and walked over, wiping sweaty palms on his shirtfront. "Hey, Katybird! Hey, Delpha! Y'all got big plans for the weekend?" He asked as if Katy and Delpha were sort of friends who might do things together. Katy toed a knothole in the floorboards with her sneaker.

"Nope." Delpha's gruff tone had no use for manners.

"How 'bout you, Katy?" Tyler asked.

Katy sighed. "Just Spring Fling, I guess. We're expectin' a big turnout this year. Are you going?"

Tyler repositioned his glasses. "I'm hanging out with my uncle on Sunday, so probably not." He lowered his voice and leaned forward. "But I'm going ghost hunting tomorrow night! It's gonna be a full moon."

Delpha rolled her eyes, and Katy suppressed a giggle. "Sounds exciting," Katy told him. She didn't volunteer more, guiltily wishing Tyler would go away. She needed time to wheedle magic talk from Delpha.

Katy's hopes vanished when her rosy-faced mama bustled out of the storage closet, breathless and carrying a basket full of blank price tags and pens. Delpha darted away and wandered toward the info booth. There, she glowered at a topographical map, as Mrs. Hearn and Katy helped the Nimbles shelve their bowls until Katy's arms were sore and sweat slicked her forehead.

When they'd finished, Mrs. Hearn offered Delpha and Tyler soft peppermint sticks from a jar on the glass counter. Tyler accepted several of the chalky sticks with an eager "Thank you, ma'am!" Delpha stiffened, then politely refused.

Mrs. McGill finished scribbling her paperwork at the desk, then checked her watch and waved Delpha toward the car. Mrs. Hearn saw them all out the door before pausing to slip a small brown paper bag into the pocket of Tyler's raincoat. "More stone root for ya, darlin'." Tyler mumbled his thanks.

Medicinal herbs, probably, Katybird noted idly. Mama's stalk magic was constantly at work behind the scenes, being useful, even when the people in the Hollow didn't know about it or appreciate it. Katy let a wistful sigh fly.

Tyler caught Katybird staring. Or he'd been starting at *her.* His bright hazel eyes flicked away, then back again. He gestured to the pocket of Katybird's white hoodie.

"Your cell phone's ringin' on silent, Katybird. I can see it glowin'." Katy looked down. Pea-green light shone through the fabric of her pocket. Her left hand thrummed with unspent power, and her right fingers began to tingle, too. She fought to control her panic.

"Excuse me, will you?" Katybird blurted, heart fluttering. Her magic couldn't be actin' up again! It had only been a little over half an hour!

A wave of dizziness hit her, and she hit the bathroom door just as her fingers began twinkling.

CHAPTER 3
DELPHA

TWO HOURS LATER, POISED ON A WOODED HILL near her cabin, Delpha shivered. The night air of early spring wound its tendrils around her, but she paid it no mind.

Nothing else mattered now but this: After Delpha's mama had left for work, Delpha had stolen the spellbook from her grandmother's closet. Her mama would tan Delpha's hide if she found out, which is why she wouldn't. Sometimes rules had to be shattered—'specially when you craved control so badly, you couldn't stand it, not for another minute. She sat alone outside, where she felt the most invincible, and prepared to cast her very first spell.

Delpha carefully opened her favorite carving knife—the one

with a handle in the shape of a howling wolf—and set about whittling the bark off a stick.

Clip, clip, clip went the blade against wood, slicing off neat little curls of bark. Her mind spun as the wand slowly took shape beneath her careful fingers.

Her mama had forgotten to hide the bills from Mamaw's funeral before she'd rushed off to attend a birth earlier that evening. Mama had also forgotten to hide the electric and water bills. Delpha had thumbed through them for a half hour, flabbergasted at how bad money was. Delpha would gladly yank out her own eyeteeth with pliers if it meant never feeling that helpless ever again.

She'd figured things were rough, of course, since they'd sold Mamaw's precious quilts. But if there were prizes for being in the hole, she and Mama were takin' home the blue ribbon.

There was food in the pantry, sure. Mama, a soft-hearted midwife, often let her clients trade canned vegetables from their gardens or new tires for service. Delpha couldn't blame her mother. Times were tough for everyone. And it was true that food and free tires *were* better than nothing. But you couldn't pay for a casket and house repairs with tires, could you? And all the canned vegetables in the world couldn't fill the loneliness that kept creeping through Delpha's soul. With Mama working around the clock and Mamaw passed on, she found herself wishing for more company, too. It'd all be easier if her father hadn't left . . . but she couldn't even remember what he looked like.

A murky memory rippled through Delpha's thoughts. Looking down, the wolf-handled knife wasn't in her hands right then, but in her hands long ago. *Sinewy, warm arms inside a denim jacket wrapped around Delpha's shoulders, and Delpha leaned back against a humming chest. Her father smelled like pine sap and coffee and chewing gum. His voice was deep and happy, and the tickling rumble of it made a giggle rise in Delpha's throat. She dragged the knife too hard over a knot in the wood. "Easy now," the deep voice instructed, guiding Delpha's tiny hands as she carved. "Always focus, and always cut away from your body. Elsewise, you're liable t' lose a knuckle. Lookythere! You're a natural!" Delpha's face beamed with pride.*

"No!" Delpha spat into the still night air. The word echoed in the ravine below, doubling the self-admonishment. Delpha blinked hard. She hadn't indulged that particular fantasy since she was six years old and soft and didn't yet understand how the world worked. Some people didn't stay. And when they left, you just made do with what you had. Her face grew hot. "There ain't no point in wishing after a stranger," she muttered. She'd have to help herself.

Delpha eyed the hickory wand with a critical eye. Satisfied with the result, she ran the freshly hewn flesh of the hickory grain across her lips. Smooth as silk. She spun it in her fingers, then nodded.

It was her first wand.

She'd use magic to find a way to pay the bills. Since Mama had strictly forbidden conjure, Delpha would figure it out without help. She pocketed her knife and gave a dark chuckle. Her father had left the knife behind the day he'd abandoned them, and it gave her spiteful satisfaction to use it for wand-making. She'd use the wand to prove she and Mama didn't need him, or anyone. Besides, the knife's handle had the inlay of a wolf—her favorite animal.

Delpha cracked her knuckles. Time to become a witch. "Here goes nothin'." She settled cross-legged on some pine needles, opening the book to a yellowed page with the title "Wytch Wake." She raised her wand, then cleared her throat and chanted:

> *"Awake the powers dark and deep*
> *That here betwixt these bosoms sleep."*

Delpha blushed at the word "bosoms" and self-consciously secured the top button of her flannel shirt, then found her place again.

> *"Let young'un join the ring of grannies,*
> *To kick my foes right in their fannies."*

Pursing her lips, Delpha threw a handful of feathers in the air, then spat into a circle drawn in the loamy forest floor. Her watchful eyes narrowed, muscles tense, but the end of her wand stayed dull as dirt.

Delpha waited a few moments, just in case the magic needed to brew for a bit. After all, it didn't need to be impressive. It only needed to work.

When nearly an hour had passed and her toes had gone numb, Delpha snapped the book shut in frustration and rubbed her aching forehead. The book didn't say what was supposed to happen when a young witch "awakened." Still, Delpha had expected a surge of power, or a blast of light, or some piddly something to indicate she'd succeeded. Anything but nothing.

She'd done the "Wytch Wake" spell exactly how the book had said. She'd collected the feathers from a chicken, a crow, and a dove.

The only other variable was her wand. It looked fine as far as Delpha could tell, but then again, she'd never seen the real McCoy, now had she? Not with Mama's contempt for all things magical. Frowning, Delpha pocketed her wand, slid the book into her leather satchel, and picked her way home through the dark woods, refusing to flinch at the occasional call of an owl or coyote.

Once home, Delpha scurried through the overgrown grass toward a small building at the back of her yard. The old shed had been an outhouse, once upon a time, but it hadn't been used like that in decades. Delpha and her mother had nailed new boards over the hole in the bottom and reshingled it, so it made a dry spot to store firewood in winter.

Just for giggles, Delpha waved her wand at the door, half hoping she could make it swing open. It didn't. Sighing, she grabbed the knotted rope that served as a handle and eased the door open. Leaning inside, Delpha slid the book atop the remainder of the winter's logs, then laid the wand beside it. "They'll be safe in here," she whispered to herself, then shut the shed door. She'd try the spell again in the morning.

Patting her hair smooth, Delpha tromped into the house looking like butter wouldn't melt in her mouth. This wasn't necessary, though, because her mother was still out. The house was cold and empty. Delpha brushed her teeth above the leaking sink. She told herself good night and, pressing her head to her pillow, drifted into a restless sleep.

Outside, a crimson light flashed through the moon-shaped peephole of the shed. Then, with a creak and groan, its stacked-stone foundation reshuffled itself into a set of granite legs. The shed disturbed a patch of weeds as it staggered into the woods, each clattering step threatening to send it toppling, tail over teakettle. The only living thing to witness this wonder was the bluetick hound on the porch, and he, being mostly blind, huffed a stream of air through his jowls and went back to dreaming of possums.

CHAPTER 4
KATYBIRD

IN A COZY BRICK HOUSE ACROSS HOWLER'S
Hollow, Katybird Hearn locked her bedroom door, careful to keep quiet. She didn't want to wake her family. After a few blissful hours of peace, her hands tingled with constipated magic. *All the better for what I'm fixin' to do,* Katy thought. A bundle of nerves, she shoved her chittering raccoon, Podge, off her shabby chic bedspread. He landed on the carpet with a squeak.

Katy winced as the animal's black eyes glittered at her in reproach.

"Sorry, Podge. Cozy down into your box with Fatso, okay? Mama's got somethin' to do." Podge snatched a crust from her neglected snack plate and retreated to his place under the bed, next to an enormous dozing tabby cat who used to belong to Katy's late cousin, Echo. Fatso was older than any feline had a right to be and twice as cranky. Podge gave a muffled chirp as the elderly animal hissed at him.

Katybird paused beside the bed, gnawing the glitter polish from her thumbnails and convincing herself that using her own homemade spell was a good idea. The Hearn women's magic ran in generational cycles of three: squawk, stalk, talk. This cycle had spun for a hundred generations from mother to daughter—Katybird knew because Nanny had repeated the stories since Katy was a baby. Squawkers could shape-shift into animals, like the Irish goddess Ceridwen, who could change herself into a hawk. Nanny was a squawker, taking the form of a cat at will. But not on command, no matter how much Katy and her little brother begged, insisting it was magic, not a magic trick.

Stalk-lovers like Katy's mama could coax any dying plant back to life and practically grow flowers from concrete, just by sweet-talking them into it. Mama made the gardens around the museum the county's pride and joy (not that anyone else knew the secret to her green thumb).

And talkers . . . well, if Katybird was one, she'd be able to speak with the spirits of the forest. To date, the only non-human Katybird could talk to was her raccoon, Podge, which didn't count, of course. Katy and Podge had an understanding, yes, but Katy was pretty sure proper magic spirits did more than hang out under people's beds eating stale cheese curls. Generations of links in a centuries-old chain of conjure women, and Katybird had managed to be the broken one. *But maybe not*, Katy thought, *if I can get this spell to work.*

She lifted a spiral-bound notebook from her desk and surveyed the scribbled words with a critical eye. Katy had no idea if her spell was any good—how could she? The older Hearns weren't big on spells, relying instead on their natural gifts. So, Katy wrote the words from intuition and what she'd seen Willow do in reruns of *Buffy the Vampire Slayer.*

Laying a big, frameless mirror flat on the middle of the bed, Katybird painstakingly arranged a circle of mismatched candles on the glass surface so their light would reflect upward. She'd even re-dyed her wavy hair to coordinate with their fading wax. It never hurt to be fancy. Her fingers shook, and she struggled to keep the matches lit. Closing her eyes, Katy took three slow breaths. Her hands steadied, and she lit the rest of the wicks. At last, a ring of glowing candlelight reflected from the mirror onto the water-stained ceiling, casting the shadow of her own damp strawberry-kiwi and grape Kool-Aid–streaked locks.

Katy set her wrinkled Sunday school Bible next to the mirror, for good measure. She stole one last nervous glance at her closed bedroom door, then shut her eyes in concentration.

"All right, magic. I'm Katybird—one of the Hearns. I've got

every right to be recognized, don't you think? Even if I do have one chromosome off from what you're used to."

A gust of wind rattled the windows. Katybird flinched and curled into tornado-drill position. Maybe the wind hadn't agreed with her. She wasn't sure she believed it herself. Her eyes caught her pale reflection in the mirror. *Try harder*, she told herself, squaring her shoulders.

"As mirror doubles candlelight, may my powers grow, too. Make me a real witch!"

Her hands began to glow. Still green, not blue.

Half a heartbeat later, a prism of smoke and shadow erupted from the mirror and tore through the room, knocking Katybird back on her throw pillows with a squeak. The candles toppled, and hot wax spattered Katy's foot in angry red droplets. Deep, guttural groans crescendoed, then filled the room so loudly, the shelf of knickknacks on the wall shook. Terrible silhouettes crouched and leaped, springing from wall to wall like enormous frenzied crickets in a fishing bait box. Under the bed, Podge growled a low warning and Fatso scrabbled around in a panic.

Katy crouched, heart racing, in the center of the mayhem. She tried to make sense of it. Were these forest spirits? The Hearn magic cycle wheeled through her mind: walk, stalk, talk. *I should say something to them*, she thought. *What, exactly?* She'd wanted results, but now she realized she was in miles over her head.

Katy sprang to her knees. "There ain't no call for that!" she ordered in a tone braver than she felt. "I'm on your side, can't you see?"

The shadows paused, considering her. Katy took advantage of the hesitation and planted her hands on her hips. She was meant to command them, so she took a desperate stab at it. "Like I said, we're on the same side, y'all and me. I'd love to learn all your names"—she managed a weak smile—"and I look forward to a long and, er, productive relationship!"

Instead of responding, all the shadows rushed at the bedroom window, exploding through the glass and shattering the mirror before vanishing into the darkness. Glittering shards rained outward, then . . . nothing. The forest spirits had gone. In shock, Katy stared at the droplets of candle wax hardening on her bedspread. No more spell. *And no more window, either*, Katy thought, groaning.

A muted hiss came from under the bed. Katy peered beneath the dust ruffle at Fatso and Podge. Other than prickly, on-end fur, the old cat looked unharmed. But Podge's bandit face was twitchy and hesitant, his body crouched. He looked wild and so unlike her Podge that, for a moment, she feared she'd lost his trust. What if Podge bolted out the broken window, too, never to be seen again? But then he rushed into her open hands, warm and trembling. "Mama's got you. I got you," she soothed. Katy pulled his shaking body to her chest, breathing in the comforting, dank scent of his coat as her tears landed in his fur.

There was a soft knock on her door, and then a drowsy voice called out, "Katybird LeAnn Hearn, I know it's not lights-out yet, but you best keep that racket down."

Katy's eyes flew wide. Scanning the broken mirror and smoldering wicks, she prayed her Mama wouldn't smell the smoke. Katy was lucky she hadn't set the house on fire. "Yes, ma'am. G'night!" Mama's footsteps shuffled away. Katy winced and grabbed a roll of colored duct tape and some poster board to cover her empty window frame. Her folks would not be happy about the broken window. Katy would have to think of an excuse for it tomorrow.

Worse than that, though, she'd failed again. The forest spirits had shown up, but they'd taken one look at Katy and decided she was too much of a dud to bother with. The word "imposter" seemed to stalk Katy, hanging over her life like a disappointing gray banner.

Her hands lit up with unspendable magic. Again. Katy flopped backward onto the mattress hard enough to shove the breath from her lungs, furious at herself. Swallowing tears, she tucked her knees to her chest and sucked back noiseless sobs late into the night.

CHAPTER 5
DELPHA

DELPHA WOKE AND BOUNDED TO THE WINDOW, eager to catch the first glimpse of the newborn sunrise as it inched over the mountains. She shivered, and a huge smile swept across her face—the kind she only wore when she was alone. The beauty of the morning wound straight around her soul like tender sweet pea vines around a garden pole, filling her with courage. She twisted her thick hair back into a tight braid, slipped her knife into her pocket, and stretched her body straight. Time to fix a big cup of coffee, grab the spellbook, and get to work.

But first, the bathroom. Walking the narrow hallway, Delpha deflated as she realized she'd forgotten to swing by the hardware store the day before. The danged toilet still needed a new fill valve.

And handle. She'd meant to fix it before Mama realized it was busted—last thing Mama needed was another thing on her to-do list.

Delpha was the only kid in the sixth grade who could change a fuse or fix a clogged pipe. When she was eight, kids had teased her after she'd bragged she'd mowed the lawn. *That's what dads are for*, they laughed, and Delpha's teacher had offered to have someone come out and do it as charity. Delpha's ears had burned, and she wasn't able to work out why no one was impressed with her accomplishment. Ever since, Delpha quietly checked out fix-it books from the library and kept her mouth shut.

But on pure-perfect mornings like this, Delpha sometimes wondered what it would be like to have a dad to fix the toilets. Or take her out for waffles at the diner on Saturdays, like Katybird's dad sometimes did. She tried to picture a home like that, and a hollow ache settled in her chest. For the second time in as many days, Delpha banished the featherbrained thought. *Naw.*

Why was she so feely these days? Probably, Delpha reasoned, she was just grieving her grandma. Maybe when she got her spells right, she could bippity-boppity-boo their leaky plumbing into behaving. For now, Delpha would pee in the woods.

After slipping out the back door for a quick trip behind an oak tree, Delpha washed her hands and whistled as the old drip coffee machine sputtered and warbled. She ate a banana and scrambled an egg. Wrapping both hands around a steaming mug, she kicked the screen door to the front porch open with her boot.

"Mornin'."

Delpha's gaze swiveled to the porch swing. Her mother sat humming to herself as she shelled dried peas into a metal bowl. She didn't look up. If it had been anyone else sitting there, Delpha could have remained cool as a cucumber. But since it was her mother, Delpha had the unnerving notion her carving knife was shining through the pocket of her denim shorts, giving away her secret intentions of carving another wand.

"Nice out, innit?" Delpha mumbled. She sipped her coffee and tried to look casual, but her eyes kept falling to the toes of her boots. *Snap out of it! You look guilty as a fox*, Delpha chided herself. She forced her shoulders to hang loosely, then tore her eyes away from the floorboards.

"Bit airish. Not bad, though. Spring's a-comin', and soon it'll be warm enough to get out in the garden. Good, too. I'm 'bout out of mullein and yarrow." *Creak, creak, creak.* The swing picked up speed, and Mama's voice sing-talked against the rhythm. "Noticed the old shed disappeared last night. Ain't been returned yet. Bit upsettin'."

Delpha's eyes flew wide at the mention of the woodshed. She managed to keep her mouth shut, but only just. Snatching a glance at her mother, she bit the inside of her cheek as guilt flooded her. Her goose was cooked. Then came a creeping dread. She'd hidden the spellbook inside the shed! Her breath caught at the realization: *If the shed's gone, the book's gone, too.*

Clink, clink. Peas landed in the bottom of Mama's bowl. "I'd guess it burned down, but there ain't no ashes," Mama continued. "The stack-stones were gone, too, with big ol' square tracks cuttin' right through the weeds, plumb into the woods. Almost like it went walkin' off by itself."

A vague, fuzzy hope seeped into Delpha's thoughts. Maybe the wand—and the spells she'd cast with it—hadn't been worthless after all. Had she somehow moved the shed? Heartbeat in her throat, Delpha blew on her coffee and decided to play innocent as a baby bird. "Wonder what happened? Think someone stole it?"

Mama gave her a sharp look. "Ohhhh, now I don't know. There's no tire marks, and it's a big thing to carry off. If someone's playin' a joke, it's a bad one."

The rocking chair creaked faster, and Mama's eyes flashed. Delpha finally noticed the frost that edged Mama's words. *She knows it was me,* Delpha thought, stomach dropping. This chitchat was the calm before the storm. Peas shot into the metal bowl like bullets. *PLUNK, PLUNK, PLUNK.*

"If we were in the old witchin' days, I'd almost say it was a con-jure gone bad. Maybe a conjure done by a young'un without any practice. But I don't need to worry about that, 'cause no child of mine is fool enough to mess with nonsense like that."

Delpha had to cough out the lie stuck in her throat. "No, ma'am."

"Any child of mine knows magic is a shortcut right off a cliff. Conjure can't ever replace hard work and common sense. It's poison." Mama's winter-sky eyes pierced Delpha from under her halo of dark curls. Mama never accused Delpha outright unless she knew she had the right to. But once she did know, there was always heck to pay. Mama usually brought down the hammer so hard over every piddly thing, she'd practically forged Delpha's independent streak into steel. Delpha was a model citizen at home, then spent most of her time hiking through the woods just to avoid having to deal with Mama's sharp-eyed scrutiny. And now, Delpha had gone and broken the McGills' first commandment, *Thou Shalt Not Do Magic*. So why weren't the sparks flyin'? *She can't tell if I did it or not*, Delpha realized.

"Maybe . . . it's the Hearns messin' around with magic."

"Hearns never had that sort'a magic. Back in the day, though, when both families were playin' at being witches, some McGills were puppet makers. They could make things move by themselves that ain't s'posed to. Rocks and trees. Sheds, too, I reckon. But spells like that could get a body killed. That doesn't sound too smart now, does it, baby?"

Mama's troubled eyes darted back and forth, studying Delpha's face. This unsettled Delpha. Her mother always knew things, and she especially always knew when Delpha was lying. But now Mama was looking at Delpha like she was trying to decide if Delpha was a rotten pea or not. Delpha felt a flush creep straight to the roots of her hair, and part of her wanted to tell Mama the truth. This was more than her mama had ever discussed magic in Delpha's life, and Delpha was hungry for more. But telling would mean her mother putting a torch to her plans, and they'd both keep plodding through life, shabby and small.

Delpha said the only thing she could. "No, ma'am." She twisted her braid, digging her toe into a souring porch rail, then blurted, "Before she died, Mamaw told me you used'ta have healing magic. Don't see how that could hurt anyone. Seems like you could even get paid for it."

Mama's face hardened as she hesitated. She stared at Delpha for a long moment, then gazed out at the trees.

"First off, folks around here wouldn't trust it, even if it helped 'em. And they'd be right not to. Did I ever tell you what happened after that Hearn boy broke my sister's heart?"

"Yes, mama."

When mama's sister—a weather witch—was sixteen, she'd accidentally made the creek swell above the banks in a fit of sadness, and her younger brother had drowned. Mama's sister had died, too, after she'd jumped in and tried to save him. Delpha knew the story well.

"Did you know I tried using my healing magic to bring them back? When it wouldn't work, my daddy had to pry me away before

I drained myself dead trying. Magic is a lie, Delpha. If somethin' seems too good to be true, it prob'ly is, and some things can't be undone. Your mamaw never was the same again, rest her soul. She was swamped with grief."

Delpha swallowed hard. She'd known her mama's siblings had passed on, but she hadn't known all that. This was the most Mama had ever said about magic, besides *Don't do it*. Mama's eyes pleaded with her. Delpha half expected Mama to tear into her, to outright accuse her of magic and forbid her from leaving her room. *She don't want it to be true. She wants to believe I didn't*. Delpha steeled herself against the guilt. She couldn't give up magic now, not when she'd only just found it.

Shrugging, Delpha flashed a puzzled smile. "Why you tellin' me this? You ain't ever gonna catch me messin' with that garbage, Mama."

"Good." Mama exhaled and relaxed her shoulders, then turned her attention back to the peas, her copper ring flashing as she fished out the last of the stems. Business as usual. She shifted to stand. "Reckon I'd better go call the sheriff and let him know about the stolen shed, then. I'll be doing prenatals in the downstairs office until two o'clock, and then I've got to go do rounds. There's soup in the fridge."

"Yes, ma'am. Think I'll go hiking before it gets too hot."

"Don't go too far."

"No, ma'am." Delpha set her coffee cup on the porch rail meekly, avoiding eye contact. As soon as the screen door closed behind Mama, Delpha shot off the porch and into the woods, the ground a blur beneath her boots.

Cold wind whistled past Delpha's ears as she ran, making them ache deep inside, but she barely noticed. She followed a trail of crushed leaves and broken branches through the woods for several minutes, her body taut and alert. Like Mama had said, there were square-shaped tracks in the softer bits of earth, just the size of the shed's four-legged stacked-stone foundation. Her hands shook from the shock of lying right to Mama's face, never mind the nausea she felt at the thought of her secret being discovered. But after a while, as she ran farther into the forest, an ember of pride flickered inside her. Could Delpha really be a puppet maker? A tiny smile tugged at her mouth. It had a nice ring to it.

Still, Delpha hadn't meant to make the outhouse go running off. She'd only meant for it to be a quiet place to keep her secrets safe. The spell hadn't gone right, not at all under her control. This started her witch-hood off on the total wrong foot. Her mouth bunched up like a cat's behind, and she growled under her breath. Now she'd have to catch the stupid thing, and then figure out how to get her wand out of it.

And the precious heirloom spellbook.

Delpha wiped sweat away and doubled her pace. No one else in

Howler's Hollow (besides the Hearns, of course) even knew magic like Delpha's still existed. Both families would be in deep trouble if folks noticed Delpha's shed lumbering through the woods. Folks would get curious, then downright suspicious. They'd meddle and ask questions. Worry snowballed inside Delpha, until her heart seemed to skip every other beat.

Folks in the Hollow were touchier about magic than most, ever since the days of the Hearn and McGill witch feuds. Even though the stories were more faded than the McGills' wallpaper, their bones remembered, Mamaw'd always said.

Just last month, in the school cafeteria, she'd overheard a boy brag how his youth group had torched all their Ouija boards, old copies of Harry Potter, and their kid sisters' Monster High dolls in a bonfire. All this to denounce the "dangerous influence of witchcraft." The story had made Delpha's neck hair stand on end. She didn't like to think how folks might interpret *her* setting a whole shed loose with magic.

She had to catch up to it. Spurred on by excitement and fear in equal parts, Delpha gripped her side and ran harder through the woods.

CHAPTER 6
KATYBIRD

KATY SLOUCHED AGAINST THE KITCHEN COUNTER
and nibbled on a Pop-Tart, hoodie sleeves pulled over her hands to
hide any magical eruption from her family. She had managed to convince her mother she'd accidentally broken her bedroom window
trying to chase Fatso off the curtains with a broomstick. It hadn't
been hard—Mama hated Fatso.

When Mama looked up from making pancakes for Katy's little
brother, Caleb, Katy tried to look appropriately remorseful over
the broken glass.

"Don't worry 'bout it, baby girl," Mama sighed, glancing at her
watch. She leaned forward and spoke soft, coaxing words to a row of
orchids on the windowsill, the soft blue haze of her stalk magic

flowing over them from her fingers as she opened the blinds. The flowers perked and bloomed. "You can make it up to me by finishing these pancakes. An' teach Caleb his ASL vocabulary words, too. I'm runnin' further behind than a tick chasin' a greyhound. Gotta get my face on." Mama's hands flew in sign language as she talked until both sets of words garbled when she clicked open a handheld mirror and carefully applied ruby-red lipstick.

Keeping her hands mostly covered with her sleeves, Katybird flipped the pancake and frowned at its sad, anemic color. She tossed an oven mitt at six-year-old Caleb to get his attention. Spikey-haired Caleb, who sat on top of the kitchen table like a barbarian, stuck his tongue out at her. Katybird tapped a two-fingered "V" against her opposite index finger, signing the word "vocabulary" to him. Caleb, who was deaf from birth, signed back, "No way."

Katy shrugged. She would have been forced to uncover her hands, anyway, to teach Caleb his three new words for school. Not good, since her hands had already glowed twice since she'd woken. Katy suspected her anxiety was making the pent-up magic worse, so when she'd gotten dressed, she'd opted for her black hoodie instead of her more see-through white one. She didn't want a repeat of yesterday. Anyway, Caleb's vocabulary was already huge for his age.

"These pancakes look awful," Katy muttered to herself as she fumbled the spatula through her sleeve-mitts. "And I hate cookin'."

Mama walked toward Caleb, transplanting him from table to chair with a single parental movement. "First pancakes are always weird," she chirped, and signed, kissing Caleb's forehead and leaving a mark.

When his mother's back was turned, Caleb sprouted an impish grin and signed to Katybird, "First kids are weird, too."

Katy narrowed her eyes in mock anger, then pressed her lips together to quash a smile. Play-fighting was a welcome distraction. It was all affectionate posturing, since both would gladly kick in the kneecaps of anyone who looked at the other one funny. Katy slapped the pitiful cakes onto a plate, drenched them in syrup, and then slid them in front of her brother, sweetly. He stuck out his tongue again.

Katy's mother pushed a bobby pin into her strawberry-colored twist of hair, completing her friendly-museum-guide look, then took a sip from her sweating glass of iced tea. "I gotta be at the museum all day again. Nanny and Papaw are fixin' to clean the place top to bottom for the Spring Fling tourists tomorrow. City folks just love the mountains in April."

Katybird detected a request buried somewhere in that speech. She slurped some orange juice, then guessed, "You need me to keep an eye on Caleb? Can we stay home?"

Mama squeezed her shoulder. "We'll be there for a while, so you'll have to come, too. You're such a good girl." She heaved a happy sigh and cupped a hand under Katy's chin. "There's only one Katybird like my Katybird. If we do good this weekend, there's twenty dollars in it for you—how's that sound?"

Katy nodded without protest, mostly because her grandparents would be there, too. Every Saturday, the old couple scuttled around the museum with bottles of Windex, making sure bored city kids kept their grimy hands off the glass, vacuuming dust off hanging patchwork quilts and pottery, and generally being nosey toward anyone who "wasn't from 'round these parts."

Katybird's job was keeping Caleb busy and stopping him from drawing private parts on the murals of Scotch-Irish immigrants with his crayons. Babysitting would give Katybird time to brood about her magic next to the museum's well-stocked candy counter.

"I'm bringing Podge!" Katy gathered her pet and herded her brother to the car. They rode in silence, gazing out the window as her mother drove the familiar winding slopes to the museum. Other than emerald rhododendrons and pine trees, the colors of spring were still timid splashes here and there. Caleb kicked the back of Katy's seat in time to the occasional sight of electric-yellow forsythia or snowy patches of bloodroot.

Once there, Katybird let Podge curl in his bed in the break room, then settled on a bench behind the rustic welcome counter. Waving for Caleb's attention, she signed, "I can do more jumping jacks than you!"

Caleb, who was fiercely competitive, immediately started jumping, his little arms and legs flailing while his brow furrowed in concentration. Katy giggled.

Katybird used this ploy often. The trick was to let him go first, then, once it was her turn, do one less jumping jack than he'd managed. Then she'd flop onto the floor in exaggerated defeat while Caleb danced around gloating. Last time, he'd stopped at around eighty-six. The game usually bought her ten minutes of peace.

Katybird tucked her knees under her chin and covertly fished a bag of jelly beans she'd swiped from storage out of a drawer. A happy mood called for lime-flavored beans, thoughtful times needed root beer, and anger demanded cinnamon. Today's flavor was chocolate pudding, the flavor of soul-sucking misery. She commenced her brooding.

Why hadn't the forest spirits talked to her? Katy darkly mused that maybe she'd managed to break the centuries-old "walk, stalk, talk" Hearn magic cycle by inserting a pathetic "balk" into the pattern. Her belly churned, and she popped another candy to soothe it. A voice crept into her head like a cold front sliding its way down the mountain into the valley, turning her insides to ice. It was the voice of Doubt, her nonstop, clingy sidekick.

You know why it didn't work.

Katybird's hands trembled as she signed applause to Caleb. "Shut up," she whispered to the hateful voice in her mind. *Maybe I'm really powerful, and that's why my magic is being difficult*, she thought. Katy's heartbeat slowed as she rolled the idea around for a moment. Maybe bigger magic took more practice. Or maybe she needed to be a grown lady for her brand of conjure to pay her heed. She bit her lip, revisiting one of her least favorite memories from two years before.

Katybird shuddered as she recalled the crinkly, uncomfortable paper covering of the medical exam table and the sterile smell of the doctor's office. The place had felt about as hospitable as a bed of skunk-infested stinging nettles outside a funeral parlor. A monotone specialist had announced to Katy's mother that Katy was "androgen insensitive," meaning she had XY chromosomes like most boys, but that nature had knitted her body up using a more traditionally female pattern. That hadn't phased Katy much. She *was* a girl. That's all she cared about. According to the doctor, she also had a pair of internal testes (the doohickeys that made all that testosterone her body didn't use). No biggie. Katybird had yawned and swung her heels over the exam table, itching to go home. That is, anyway, until the doctor plopped this doozie into the middle of the room:

"We recommend surgery to remove her internal testes, in case they cause trouble later. When shall we schedule the operation?" The fancy doctors in coats had asked the question nice and easy-like, as if they wanted to know whether Katy's mama wanted pickles on a burger.

Cassidy Hearn had wisely asked for time to think. After spending two weeks furiously texting and emailing with an intersex support group, Katy's mama told them she and her daughter weren't interested in their hamburger pickles, thank you kindly. The evidence was clear: Her daughter was fine as is. The Hearns went home, baked a pound cake, and marathoned *I Love Lucy* reruns. After that, they'd been preoccupied with Caleb's hearing specialists and his adorable kindergartner charm. Katybird had continued to be the same old Katybird.

Except she wasn't the same, not really, at least not in her family's eyes. There was a question now. Katybird was a girl, obviously, but words like "internal gonads," "testes," and "Y chromosome" seemed to muddy the creek in their minds, as far as magic was concerned. Hearn magic had always been used by females. When her family talked about conjure now, Katybird always felt studied. She imagined them thinking, *Is she a witch or isn't she?*

Katy frowned and pulled a tube of peach lip gloss from her pocket, inhaling its tart scent. She startled as the glass doors from the pottery exhibit squealed open and the voices of two elderly people cut across the silence like squeaky cabbage on a grating board.

"All I'm sayin' is, if you'd just tote the ladder out yonder, I could water them potted ferns, Harold! They're droopin' somethin' fierce, and there's only so much magic your daughter can work without water."

Papaw's voice sang in a lazy twang, unhurried, unbothered.

"Woman, I'm busier than a one-legged man in a butt-kickin' contest. I'm plumb to my ears in Cassidy's to-do list. Doc says I can't go get these bunions fixed in the hospital till tonight, so it'll get done when it gets done. Keep yer feathers on."

"You won't have to kick your own hiney for long if you don't tote that ladder out t' th' porch. I'll do it for you," Nanny warned, playfully thwacking him on the seat of his overalls with a dustpan.

Katy scrunched her eyes closed in mock disgust, hiding a grin. "I'm here, you know. I can see y'all whackin' each other's backsides."

Nanny stopped just short of the counter, then clucked her tongue. "Hey there, lady. Chocolate-flavored bean candies, eh? That's too bad. You want a hug?"

Katybird bristled. She hated how Nanny always had near-psychic abilities when it came to Katy's emotional states. Like many grandmothers, Nanny could lock onto the scent of her family's upsets like a bloodhound. Besides, Katy always ate chocolate jelly beans when she was sad: a dead giveaway. Katy crossed her arms, not bothering to pretend she was fine. "I just wanna be left alone." Her tone was sharp, and she knew it, but there wasn't anything for it. She'd fall to pieces if she wasn't surly.

Papaw's interest was piqued, too, and all four hundred wrinkles on his deeply tanned face slid southward in an avalanche of concern. "What's wrong, Doodle Bug?"

Papaw wasn't as tough as Nanny, and Katybird hated to say something ugly and hurt his feelings. She cinched her lips and looked at her shoes.

In the end, she didn't have to explain herself, because a sweaty Caleb stopped jumping at sixty-two jumping jacks and began running victory laps around the rug while waving his hands in self-applause.

Nanny wasn't as fluent in sign language as Katy, but she still managed: "Caleb . . . go . . . with Papaw . . . Move the ladder . . . Papaw will buy a soda." Caleb whooped in delight at the prospect of sugar in the morning and dragged his bewildered grandfather out the door by the hand.

Nanny planted her feather duster on the counter with an authoritative *THUNK*. This was her version of throwing down a gauntlet. Katy would spill the contents of her soul or have Nanny stare them out of her. Katybird's guidance counselor at school would say Nanny wasn't very good with boundaries. He'd be right, too. Nanny had all the boundaries of a tornado determined to hug a farmhouse. And unlike a tornado, Nanny didn't know how to move on.

"I'm fine, Nanny."

"Oh? I noticed you didn't draw any of them raccoon rings 'round your eyes with eyeliner today. I reckon there's only one reason for that."

"I'm experimenting with a more natural look?" Katybird suggested, not making eye contact.

"It's 'cause you knew you'd be cryin' all day long. Why's my baby girl bawling so much? Don't worry, darlin'. It's just you and Nanny now—you can tell ol' Nanny." Behind her grandmother's glasses were sweet, magnified doe's eyes. She was laying it on thick.

Be strong, Katybird, Katy told herself. She decided to test the waters a little. "Maybe I did somethin' I shouldn't've."

"Y'ought ta tell someone about it, then." Nanny smiled broadly to show she was just the sort of person to tell.

Katy's hands began to tingle again, and she shoved them beneath the counter. She needed to know how to make her magic work without giving her predicament away. Katy decided to throw one of her cards on the table. *If Nanny freaks out*, Katy reasoned, *I can always backpedal.* "Maybe . . . I tried a conjure. Just a *little* one!"

Nanny's face folded with worry. And was that pity, too? Alarms went off in Katybird's head. *Backpedal, backpedal!* "I mean, not a conjure, just a prayer. Just a little good intention prayer, s'all."

Katybird peeked up to see her grandmother relax ever so slightly, but Nanny's eyes still crinkled in concern. And definitely pity. *Nanny doesn't think I'll ever do magic*, Katybird realized, heart plummeting. *She feels sorry for me and doesn't want to see me disappointed.* Or maybe Nanny was the one disappointed in Katybird.

Either way, Katy would rather die now than let Nanny know Katy's magic was tangled. Katy yawned and shrugged to show she didn't care. "Just prayin' for a wart to go away. You know how that goes. Only works 'bout half the time, right?" Nanny chuckled in relief, snapping into happy mode.

"Bless your heart! Got faith like a child, ain't ya? Let Nanny look at your wart, baby!" Nanny grinned a gap-filled smile, rolled back the sleeves of her checkered cotton blouse, and held out her hands eagerly to receive a wart-infested limb.

"It's okay, Nanny. It was more I just wanted to try it myself."

"How about Nanny gives you another tea leaf readin' lesson? It's a fine an' respectable tradition."

Katybird grimaced. Tea leaves were an interpretive art, not Hearn magic. "No, it's no big deal! It's just . . ." Katy teetered dangerously close to confessing the truth. For one horrible moment, Katybird thought she might fall into her grandmother's plump arms and tell about her glowing hands and her badly botched magic. But it wasn't normal. The thought jabbed Katy into silence, and she studied the floor.

Nanny's eyes clouded over with concern, and Katy realized why Nanny was being such a mother hen.

She's worried I'll get unhappy and run away like Echo. Last year, Katybird's nineteen-year-old cousin, Echo, had passed away in a car accident. While Katybird had been longing for magic, Echo despised hers, claiming it was a ball and chain keeping her in the backwoods. Nanny, who'd raised her, told Echo she'd gotten too big for her britches—meaning Echo was dishonoring her heritage.

Over the course of a few weeks, Echo had grown despondent, refusing to learn conjure. One day, after her shift at the grocery store, she'd driven onto the highway, away from Howler's Hollow. Then, just like that, she was gone. Katy had been crushed—she'd idolized her cousin—but Nanny had been heartbroken *and* wracked with guilt.

Now Nanny's old eyes worried over Katybird. Katy reached out and squeezed her grandmother's hand.

"Don't worry, Nanny. I'm okay. I promise."

Nanny beamed approval. The door squeaked open again and Papaw trudged in, mopping sweat from his brow while Caleb happily nursed soda suds from a newly popped can of Mountain Dew.

"You're never gonna believe what I just saw running t'yonder across the path!"

"Well?" Nanny demanded, hands on her cauldron-shaped hips. She was eager for a good morsel of gossip to lighten the mood, Katybird could tell.

"I just saw a shed run off the hikin' trail and across the lawn, quicker'n greased lightning! I ain't never seen nothin' like it! Looked like a big ol' wooden hog just busted out of the pen." Papaw's scruffy face was serious as a heart attack.

Katybird giggled. Papaw was famous for his larger-than-life tall tales. He was good at easing tension in a room. Cutting her eyes over to her grandmother, Katybird expected Nanny to laugh, too.

But Nanny's eyes flew wide. "Are you yanking my chain? There's things that ought not to be joked about." She mouthed the words *McGill magic.*

Her grandfather shrugged and shook his head. "Coulda been my eyes playin' tricks, I reckon. I'm hungry as a bear and need to check my insulin."

Nanny clucked her tongue and herded Papaw toward the museum's tiny kitchen area, and Katybird found herself wandering to the window to peer outside. Through a clearing in the pines, Katy could swear she caught a glimpse of Delpha McGill near the museum's hiking trailhead.

"I'm gonna go out for a little bit! Somebody else watch Caleb!" Katy hollered, pulse speeding. Without waiting for an answer, she shoved the glass door open and darted toward the woods.

CHAPTER 7

DELPHA

AFTER FIFTEEN MINUTES OF JOGGING, DELPHA
slowed to a brisk trot. She'd been hunting before, but only for things like mushrooms or walnuts. Being hot on the trail of a rogue woodshed was a first. Her feet ached, and her throat was dry, but she couldn't stop.

The shed's trail wound its way through the rolling hills, thankfully keeping its distance from cabins and trailers. Every now and then, Delpha spotted a piece of stray firewood. She combed the grass and dry winter underbrush with her eyes for the leather spellbook, in case it had fallen out, too. It was tedious work, and so far, she'd found a gigantic, steaming heap of nothing.

As the tracks wound closer to town, Delpha's temples dripped with sweat. If someone saw the outhouse stomping around, would she be able to convince them it was part of a robotics project? A vain part of her was mortified the woodshed still resembled its former life as an outhouse, moon-shaped hole and all. What if Delpha couldn't get it under control once she found it?

After half a morning of walking, her tongue clung to the roof of her mouth. Delpha chided herself for not bringing any water along. She'd have to hydrate or end up dizzy before she ever caught the blasted outhouse, which she was starting to think of somewhat fondly as Puppet. Through spindly pine trees, she saw a marker for the hiking trail that looped alongside the Appalachian Culture Museum. She could run inside, drink out of the bathroom faucet, and be on her way in ten minutes—less if she seriously hoofed it.

Skidding around a curve, Delpha managed to stay upright until she swung herself to a dusty stop by grabbing onto a sturdy pine bough. Righting herself and tearing down the next leg of the switchback, Delpha barreled directly into a wavy-haired girl with a worried face, causing her to squeak in surprise and drop what looked like a massive bag full of rat droppings into the red dirt at her feet.

"Watch it! You spilled my jelly beans!"

Delpha froze in temporary horror, then drew herself to her full height and leaned slightly away from the other girl. It was Katybird

Hearn. *Drat.* In turn, Katybird flushed as she recognized Delpha. Her mouth worked as if she were gearing up for a melodramatic speech of some kind. Delpha huffed a stream of air through her nose. She had no time for this mess. If she didn't catch the outhouse soon . . . "Bye," Delpha huffed and stalked around Katybird in a wide circle, careful not to brush against her on the narrow path.

"Wait!" Katybird jogged after Delpha, her shorter legs pounding double time to keep up.

"Wait, what? I ain't got nothin' to say to you."

"Slow down, will ya?"

"Can't."

"I wasn't tryin' to be rude last night when I said the thing about the pocket money. It was stupid, and I'm sorry. I know y'all are strugglin'."

Delpha clenched her fists and quickened her pace. "For the life of me, I can't figure how you keep friends, Katybird Hearn. You've got the social skills of a skunk."

"Delpha, wait! I . . . I need your help."

Something about the tentative way Katy spoke caught Delpha's attention. Delpha scraped to a stop and heaved a sigh. "What?"

"H-have you been able to do any, you know, magic?"

Delpha's jaw dropped in surprise. How did Katybird know about that? "Have you been followin' me?" Delpha growled. She glanced over her shoulder, making sure they were alone on the path. Her pulse roared in her ears and she felt suddenly naked. Delpha didn't even talk to her own mother directly about magic, much less Katybird Hearn!

Katy's chin quivered as she slid her hands into her pockets. "What? Of course not. I need to learn conjure, Delpha. I can't talk to my family about it, because I don't want them to know I'm bad at it."

Fire shot upward from Delpha's belly, and it took considerable effort to relax her fists. It'd been years since she'd gotten in trouble for hitting someone, but being asked point-blank to discuss magic triggered a caginess inside her. "You're sillier than a bag of cat hair, Hearn." Her boots found a quick rhythm on the path, jogging away before her temper got the better of her.

Crunch, crunch. Crunch, crunch. Delpha glanced back. Katybird trailed after her like a sad puppy, hands still crammed into her tiny pockets. Delpha quickened her pace to maximum dignified speed. In several minutes, Katybird was out of breath and gasping. Delpha slowed, rolling her eyes. Without turning, she called over her shoulder, "Why do you need my help, anyway? Don't your family have its own spells somewhere? Like in a book? If you don't want your mama to know, just use that."

Katybird clutched her belly, sides heaving. "We don't have one," she said between pants. "That's why I asked you. Wouldn't have bothered you otherwise."

Delpha turned and studied Katybird's face for a moment, then arched an eyebrow. "Even if I weren't mad at you for insulting me—"

"I was only trying to help!"

"—there's things you just don't jabber about in the Hollow. Money's one. Witchin' is another. Folks've forgotten about the Hearn and McGill magic. Best it stays that way."

Katybird swiped a thumb under her glittery lashes and swallowed hard. "My nanny won't teach me anything but tea leaf reading, Delpha. Tea leaves! Any fool can pretend to predict the future. You're the best shot I've got."

Delpha frowned. Katy's tears tugged at the tiny soft spot in Delpha's chest normally reserved for orphaned fawns and old people. She sagged. "We ain't supposed to be talkin' about this. My mama'd skin me alive if she heard."

Seeing her plea was having some effect, Katybird pressed on. "I'll do anything, Delpha. I'll pay you, if you want."

Delpha's empathy froze over. Typical. "Ain't everything for sale, Katybird Hearn. Not that your family would know it."

Katybird's blue eyes flashed. "Meanin' what, exactly?"

"Meanin'," Delpha spat, "magic is kinda like the 'homespun'

quilts and 'handmade' mountain furniture y'all sell in that fancy museum of yours." Delpha made air quotes as she said the words. "If folks have to buy it to get it, they're kind of missing the point. Unlike your people, my family has pride."

A scarlet rash crept up Katybird's neck. Delpha felt a puny twinge of remorse. She braced herself against a dogwood tree and stretched out her calf muscles, studying the sky. "Anyway, my mama won't teach me, neither. She'd kill me if she knew I'd found her . . ." Delpha's eyes widened, and her voice trailed off, realizing her mistake a hair too late.

Katybird gasped. "You found something! Spells?"

"Yeah"—Delpha stiffened—"but I ain't supposed to have 'em. Anyway, our book's not for you, Katybird. Trust me."

Katybird's voice neared a teakettle's shriek. "Are you, like, so insecure and worried someone else will learn how to—"

Delpha raised a palm and shook her head. "Nope. That ain't it. It's just . . . our McGill magic don't match your magic." She wracked her brain for a good comparison, then finally said, "Look—it'd be like puttin' diesel in a gas-takin' truck. It wouldn't go. Or worse, it'd tear you up."

Katybird's face crumpled, forcing Delpha to look away. "Does it say so in your book? That our magics aren't the same?"

"Nope."

"Then how do you—"

Delpha took out her knife, eyeballed a dogwood limb, and then cut it off in a deft movement. "I just know. You know how sometimes you just know which egg's gonna be rotten before you crack it, or when someone's gonna die soon? It's intuition. Some things you just know, and this is one of 'em."

"You should let me see the book, just to make sure."

"Nice try," Delpha snorted. She started walking, wood shavings trailing behind her with each soothing *clip, clip, clip* of the knife.

"Hey, where you goin'?" Katy called after her.

"Trackin' a woodshed." Delpha winced. Why did she keep blurting these things?

"Woodsheds don't move. You mean a woodchuck?" Katy's eyes twinkled.

"No, I mean like a shed made of wood." Delpha felt her cheeks blaze. "An old outhouse. I . . . brought it to life . . . with a spell, I think." Talking about magic openly felt so *wrong*. Delpha pocketed the stick and her knife.

"Y'all have an outhouse?"

"That's your question? It's an antique, all right? I did a spell, and then it ran off." Delpha left out the "accidentally." Her pride stung enough for one day.

"Mercy," Katy said, eyes wide. "What else can you do?"

Delpha thawed a bit at Katybird's admiring tone but didn't let it show. "Not sure. I have to catch the shed, though, before anyone sees it."

"Then I'm coming, too."

"Katybird—"

"Your outhouse could be hostile. Since it came from *your* magic, it's probably mean as a junkyard dog. You'll want help."

"Rude much?"

"Just sayin'."

Delpha considered taking off in a dead run. She could probably lose Katybird in a few minutes. The girl was short. But then, it might be smart to take someone with her, for practicality's sake. What if she needed help cornering Puppet? "Fine. Tag along. But that don't mean you're forgiven. I ain't done bein' mad."

Katybird shrugged. "Of course not."

CHAPTER 8
KATYBIRD

"I DON'T SEE ANYTHING, DELPHA."

"Shhhh!" Delpha put up a hand. "Quiet."

A rhododendron limb slapped Katy's face, coating her freckled nose in sap. She grimaced. A miserable, sticky afternoon of hiking later, she was in no mood to be shushed. "We've been tracking your shed for a million years. I'm startin' to think you're yanking my chain," she muttered, trying unsuccessfully to wipe off the sticky stuff with her sleeve.

"There!" Delpha hissed, pointing down the hill. "See those saplings movin'?"

Several yards below, teenaged cottonwoods quivered as something lumbered through them. A hulking something. "Black bear, maybe," Katy whimpered, pulse quickening. Black bears were shy creatures, but a mother with cubs was not something you wanted to surprise in the woods. Not if you liked your face. "We oughta make noise so it knows we're here, don't you think?" She cupped her hands and drew a preparatory breath.

"Wait! Listen!" Delpha lifted a steady finger. *Creeeeeeeak. Shriek, squeak, grooooooooan.* That was no bear. It was a noise like pine trees scraping together in a windstorm. Katy gazed wonderingly at Delpha, who winked back. "I think it's Puppet," she mouthed.

Katy blinked. "What's a puppet?"

"My shed."

"You . . . named your shed?"

"Yep."

To each her own, Katy thought to herself. *But this girl's a nut.* She was just about to tell Delpha so, when a small wooden building on stacked-stone feet staggered into the narrow power line clearing. Katybird let loose a frantic giggle.

"You—you actually brought it to life!" Katy stammered, her brain unable to wrap itself around what she was seeing. The thing's legs looked bizarre, like some rock troll's from a storybook. It was honest-to-goodness magic, and so different from her family's. This wasn't coaxing or communicating. This was grabbing reality by the reins and changing its course. The thrill of it covered Katy's whole body in a network of chill bumps.

"Yes, I'm aware," snapped Delpha, jamming a finger to her lips. "Quiet, you'll scare it off!" She scowled, but Katy thought she saw a twinkle of something else in Delpha's dark eyes, too. Was Delpha McGill proud? In most people, smugness would be off-putting, but in Delpha's stoic face, it made her seem more approachable—almost human.

Katy lowered her voice. "How're we gonna catch it?"

"Well, that's the question, ain't it? I don't even know if it can hear us. We better just sneak up, quiet-like, and see what happens."

Katybird nodded. The girls skidded down on feet and rear ends into the gully, then crouch-ran through the underbrush on soft feet. When the shed was fifty paces away, Delpha whispered, "All right— I'll creep in from behind, and you run around and cut it off. I'm gonna try to break the spell." Puppet's rumbling form paused, as if the shack were eavesdropping on them. Something in Katy's gut twisted. The air around her crackled with an unsettling energy. She grabbed Delpha's wrist.

"Don't."

Delpha's eyes swiveled sideways. "What."

"Don't trick it like that." Katy didn't know where the words came from, but they tumbled out with conviction. Something about this just wasn't right. Something about treating the shed like prey felt wrong, wrong, wrong.

"Have you lost your dad-blasted mind?"

Katybird's forehead beaded with sweat. Her thoughts were catching up to her feelings, finding words for them. "Maybe you don't have to break the spell. Pup"—she cleared her throat—"Puppet feels like a critter instead of a building now. It's confused. What if it's lonely?"

Delpha rolled her eyes heavenward. "I swear on my great-granny's whiskers, you are the aggravatin'ist human I ever—"

Katy's face grew hot, but she pressed on. "I don't care what you think of me, Delpha McGill. You can act as ugly as you want, but I'm telling you—not askin', TELLIN' you—to treat that thing with a little respect." Every hair on Katy's body bristled, as inexplicable anger welled inside her. *What's gotten into me?*

Delpha drawled in a patronizing voice, "What, then, do you suggest we do, Katybird Hearn? Not only is Puppet hexed, it's got a working wand inside it. And my family's spellbook. I think the wand must be keeping Puppet animated."

"The book's in there?" Katybird squeaked, eyes growing wide.

Delpha glared at Katybird, nostrils twitching. She was right, Katy realized. They had to get Delpha's spellbook out. How else would she stop Puppet?

Katybird swallowed hard. "I've got an idea. You run on ahead, and when I give you the signal, you sneak up, easy-like, and get your things out of it. Then we can figure out what to do with Puppet."

"And what do you plan to do?" Delpha demanded. "You'll forgive me if I'm not too keen on getting my head knocked clean off while you make friends with my shed."

"Puppet." Katybird pointed at Puppet and pleaded. "Trust me? I have a sort of way with living things."

Delpha arched a dark eyebrow, as if to say, *Oh really? Could've fooled me.*

Katy rolled her eyes. "Livin' things that aren't you. They like me."

Delpha gazed at her for a long, hard minute, then gave a tiny nod before stealing ahead into the trembling thicket. As soon as Delpha was out of earshot, Katybird called out soothingly to the shed. "You're a long way from home, ain't ya? That must be hard. You've been standin' in place for all those many long years. Then some witchling comes along and tosses conjure stuff inside yer belly. Poor darlin'. There, now."

Puppet shuddered, and Katybird remembered the time she'd found Podge under the porch when he was an orphaned kit. In a soft voice, Katybird began singing Podge's favorite country song as she approached, but Puppet didn't seem to care for it. It creaked and squealed, moving to stand. Katy's hand shot out and closed the space between them, gentling its wooden sides. The fiber was soft and weatherworn, almost like driftwood beneath her fingers.

"I reckon you've been a shed for a long time, huh? What's that been like?"

An odd chill spread from Katybird's limbs to her chest, and she stumbled back. She had an untethered sensation, like she was falling through space.

In front of her, strange shadows flickered around Puppet. The building itself stood, locked in place, but there was another, more shadowy Puppet there now, too. It was like an echo from the past, bleeding into Katy's present. The shadow sped in reverse, like a time-lapse movie. Dim figures in modern jeans, then overalls, then old-timey clothes went in and out of the shadow Puppet, until finally one un-nailed its shadow boards apart, then un-sawed them into a gigantic fallen tree, which un-chopped and erected itself into a massive oak with sprawling branches and deep roots. Green iridescent haze floated around the shadow tree, until at last it shrank to a tiny seedling. At the end, it vanished into glowing wisps of light. Katybird's breaths came in short bursts, like she'd just been doused in ice water.

"Katybird!" Delpha's voice whisper-shouted from the woods ahead. "Stop dingin' around!"

Katy's heart hammered, and she wiped cool tears where they'd collected on her chin. Delpha, apparently, hadn't seen whatever had happened, just Katybird. She put a shaking palm against the shed. "Oh, Puppet," she whispered. "This ain't who you are. You're a tree. You remember."

She picked a different song, a song as old as the tree, and began to croon softly:

> *"Oh, he led her over the mountains and the valleys so deep,*
> *Pretty Polly mistrusted and began to weep."*

Puppet settled back on its stack-stones, and Katy motioned for Delpha to hurry. Delpha was there in a moment. She frowned and eased the outhouse door open with her boot. The stacked firewood lay in a messy pile on the floor. "Keep singing," Delpha murmured. "It might take a minute to find the wand and the book under all this mess." Firewood sailed out the door and into the weeds as Delpha picked her way through the jumble. Katy inhaled and continued, beginning to wish she'd picked a more cheerful song:

> *"Willie, oh Willie, I'm afraid of your ways,*
> *The way you've been rambling you'll lead me astray!"*

"Got the book," Delpha called in a muffled voice.

"Hand it out here. I'll hold it." Katy thrust her open hand through the doorway. There was a pause, and then something leather and surprisingly heavy filled her fingers. A satchel, with the book inside, no doubt.

"I can outrun you, so don't even think about takin' off with it," Delpha muttered, then gave a triumphant chuckle. "Hey, hey! And there's the wand." Delpha lifted a roughly carved and battered stick, then slid it behind her ear like a pencil. Instead of stepping right out, Delpha paused to brush wood dust and bits of bark from her clothes.

Katybird pulled out the book and ran her fingers softly over the binding. No way in heaven or hell would Delpha McGill let her peek inside the spellbook, but Katy had to see it. Suddenly, she had a rare, wicked idea, one that took over her mind like jagged lightning steals a calm night sky. Nanny always said Katybird was like the girl from that one Longfellow poem: When she was good, she was very good indeed, but when she was bad, she was horrid.

She leaned against the shed and whispered, "Sorry, Puppet." Then, before she could talk herself out of it, she gave the outhouse an almighty slap on its behind.

Puppet jumped to life and took off, barreling across the gully. Delpha fell backward into the shed, heels over head, then came up for air, cussing and beet red. Hanging on for dear life, she gripped

Puppet's doorframe and leaned out, her dark eyes flashing with murder. She knew exactly what Katybird was up to.

"You . . . you CROOK! You're gonna regret this, Katybird Hearn! If you open that book, we're all done for! I'll find you and rip your fool arm off and beat out what little bit o' sense you've got with the bloody end of it! Then I'm gonna . . ." Her voice trailed off into a faint trickle of maledictions as Puppet disappeared into the dusky forest. Peace reclaimed the twilight.

Katybird shivered from head to toe, partly from shock over what she'd just done, but also from excitement. A faded rainbow of sunset glowed on the horizon, transforming the trees into stark, accusing silhouettes. What had she done? Delpha would never forgive her now. Her frozen breath shot out in erratic puffs as the valley chilled for the night. Soon it would be too dark to read. Forget reading—soon it would be too dark to see.

Staring into the distance, Katy whispered, "Sorry, Puppet."

She bit her lip.

"Sorry, Delpha."

CHAPTER 9
DELPHA

GRINDING HER TEETH ON HER WAND AS SHE AND
Puppet whipped through the woods, Delpha tried to take stock of her predicament. Her book was gone. More than likely, Katybird was getting blown to smithereens back in the clearing, trying to mess with McGill magic—if she lived, Delpha would have to even that score later. Her most pressing concern was keeping her teeth from chattering clean out of her jaws. She swiveled and pressed her back against one wall, ramming her feet into the opposite corners, then took her wand from her mouth.

Making up things on the spot was not Delpha's way of doing things. Delpha preferred having a good plan—laid out crisp and smooth—and taking every precaution to prevent loose ends. She liked being on the tops of things, not rattled around like a bug in a jar. Her arm jerked wildly, making her wand flail like a baton in the hand of a drunken orchestra maestro. Stiffening her biceps, Delpha steadied her focus, then floundered for the right-sounding words:

> *"Obey my voice 'n' heed my will.*
> *Puppet made from wood, be still!"*

No good. If anything, Puppet redoubled its efforts to run clear to the coast in one night. Delpha was jarred loose from her wall, and she dropped her wand while scrabbling to remain upright. When she finally succeeded at planting a foot beneath her, it landed on her rolling wand, and she tumbled to the floor. Her head hit the wooden door with a resounding *thwack*, and everything went dark and fuzzy.

As Delpha lost consciousness, so did Puppet. Tumbling over a flat, upright stone, the shed crashed onto its side and collapsed into a shattered pile of boards. The young witch inside was flung from its door like a rag doll onto a soft patch of early spring violets, her battered wand rolling to a stop at her fingertips.

CHAPTER 10
KATYBIRD

KATYBIRD DIDN'T EVEN WAIT UNTIL SHE GOT home. Her trembling fingers pried the cover of the McGill spellbook open right there in the woods. *Ka-thunk, ka-thunk,* said her heart. Katy licked her lips in anticipation, squinting in the lavender dusk.

The first yellowing page was decorated with mysterious symbols in fading ink, in words that looked like they belonged in a Shakespeare play. A sketch of a hand with a cauldron on its palm embellished the top right corner.

Leteth charm passeth from moth'r to daught'rs
With the wisdom of the bless'd goddess Danu:

The pow'r to sky the wat'rs deep

And compass life to thought that in imagination creeps.

Whatever that meant. Katybird shivered and tossed a guilty glance over her shoulder, feeling watched, before returning her attention to the stolen book. On the next page, she found a family tree of sorts, scrawled out by many different hands over the centuries.

> *Cerridwen mam Fionnghuala, mam Ceinfryn, máthair of Brigh, máthair of Saoirse the Snake, moth'r of Laughing Maura, moth'r of Maeve, moth'r of Fiona, mother of Catroina the Crafty, mother of Aine the Dark, mother of Dizzy Delma, mother of Bronwyn, mother of Lottie the Immigrant, mama of Mattie the Weaver, mama to Lynnette, mother of Wizey, mother to Eudaimonia, mother of Sharp-Tack Mina, mother of sweet Kathleen, mama to Delpha.*

The final name had been penned recently with a felt-tipped marker. All women's names, Katy noticed. Their magic, just like the Hearns', was passed along the matriarchal line. All mothers of daughters—a cycle Katybird wouldn't continue, even if she turned out to be magical. No children for Katybird, unless she wanted to adopt 'em someday. Katy shook out her shoulders and flipped to the first spell.

The "Findeth Thy Way Home" charm seemed straightforward: Run a twig through your hair, then float it on any water's surface while muttering some binding words. Then a golden strand of light would lead Katybird home. Easy peasy.

After locating a suitable puddle, Katy stumbled through the incantation. She got all the way to the line "wat'r moth'r, pointeth mine feet toward the placeth wh're I hangeth mine coxcomb and cloak" when the floating stick began to spin around like a top, and the puddle bubbled and steamed. A bit too late, Delpha's voice drawled from a murky part of Katy's memory: *McGill magic don't match your magic.*

A jet of filthy water nailed her right between the eyes. Katy gasped. Her skin began to crawl and ooze, and the world shifted shape around her. The puddle swelled to a lake, and the twig grew as big as a newly felled log. Katy opened her mouth to scream bloody murder, but all that came out was a belligerent-sounding *CRRRRRROAK.*

Besides being an oversized world, there seemed to be more of it, too—Katybird could see in nearly every direction with her bulbous eyes. Some azalea bushes behind her rustled, and out popped a familiar gray-and-black animal. Part of Katy's mind was awash with delight at the sight of Podge, but her newer, froggier half hollered in panic, "JUMP AWAY! PREDATOR!!"

Before she could escape, a grubby human hand scooped her up. A pair of thoughtful, gray eyes examined her with interest. *Caleb!* Had he followed Katybird all this way through the woods? Katy croaked and tried signing to her brother, but only managed a clumsy dance across his palm. Caleb's eyebrows furrowed. He sat and nudged Katybird onto his knee to free his hands. "Katybird, why are you a frog?" he signed. "Mama will be really mad."

Katy blinked one eyelid in response.

Caleb whimpered. "I brought Podge, but I'm scared. Can we go home? My butt's cold." His massive eyes welled with tears, and his bottom lip trembled. Katy felt terrible and wished she could scoop him into her arms. Unfortunately, human arms weren't among her assets just then.

A bug zapper glowed from a cabin porch through the trees. A cabin meant a safe place for them to shelter, at least until Katy could manage to turn herself back into a human.

Springing from Caleb's knee, Katy leaped toward the glowing blue light. *This way, this way, this way,* she thought with every jump, keeping her frog brain on task. Caleb tucked Delpha's book and satchel under one arm and began running after her. His footsteps shook the ground beneath Katy's webbed feet, and she half expected to be crushed at any moment. Instead, he caught her mid-leap with his free hand and kept running. To Katy's enormous relief, he didn't stuff her into his pocket, as he had with several unfortunate frogs in the past.

As Caleb climbed the wooden steps, Katybird's human thoughts mingled with a flurry of animal instincts. Bugs she'd normally shriek at suddenly looked as tempting as an order of french fries. Caleb pounded on the door, and some ghost of her human synapses warned against the urge to hide in the souring mulch of a potted fern.

The door swung wide, and a kindly, weathered face peered down at Katybird. It was Aunt Eunice, the old preacher's widow from the tiny Methodist church—though, far as Katy knew, Eunice wasn't actually anyone's aunt.

HELP! The word came out as a pitiful croak. The elderly woman glanced from the frog in Caleb's left hand to his frantically signing right one. "Sister, sister, sister!" Aunt Eunice dedicated a long, hard stare to the leather book under Caleb's arm.

"Well, bless my biscuits. You're little Caleb Hearn! The Hearns and the McGills are at it again, I reckon. Y'all better get on in here."

Scooping Katybird into her soft, wrinkled hand, Aunt Eunice hobbled to the kitchen. The room smelled of a thousand pots of stew and an age's worth of fried-bacon breakfasts. Hanging on nails were half a dozen checkered aprons and several iron skillets. Framed cross-stitch quotes peppered the walls with sayings like, "Bless This Mess" and "Praise Heaven and Pass the Potatoes."

"Cut the light on, darlin'," Eunice said, pointing and motioning to

Caleb. She gently transferred Katy to a lazy Susan on her freshly scrubbed table. Caleb flipped on the light obediently.

Scooting aside a vase of silk flowers and a pair of salt and pepper shakers shaped like pigs, the old woman retrieved a carton of iodized salt from the cabinet. She poured some in a neat circle around Katy the frog. Then she struck a match and lit a banana bread–scented candle.

"I'm a mite rusty, but we'll see how it goes. Hand the book here." She waved for the spellbook.

Magic? Katy blinked her bulging eyes in surprise. The McGills and Hearns were the only witches in the Hollow. *Who ever heard of a preacher's wife conjurin'?*

Caleb hesitated and eyed the old woman, having already witnessed his sister reading from *that* book and turning into a slimy pond dweller. Aunt Eunice grinned, exposing her gums.

"Don't fret, darlin'. I ain't plannin' to use it. I just want to see what needs undoin'. I was close friends with Delpha's great-grandma when I was a wee thing. Picked up a magical habit or two." Caleb considered her smile, then nodded, turning over the book as if he were surrendering an unpinned grenade. Eunice smacked her withered lips and muttered.

"So you're Katybird, huh? Messin' with McGill magic, I see." She clucked her tongue. "Y'all sure know how to make trouble. Guess you come by it honest. T'weren't a McGill or a Hearn who could stop from tanglin' with one another back when I was a young'un, even after the magic truce."

Katy croaked in shock.

"Yes, darlin', I know about that."

Eunice thumbed through the book casually, as if she were browsing a sales flyer for the Piggly Wiggly. Her thick halo of white hair, braided milkmaid-style, made the old lady look like an angel searching for Katy's name in the Book of Life. Chuckling to herself, Eunice continued talking to Katy as if chatting with a frog was as natural as passing wind.

"'Course, back then, the magic truce was still new, see. Both families were still goin' at it like cats 'n' dogs all the time, but in secret. Once, your great-grandma Fayrene, rest her soul, got her cornbread turned into a sack o' spiders by Eudaimonia McGill at school. Liketa made her wet her britches. Here now. I reckon this is the right spell."

Taking a few aprons from the wall, Aunt Eunice handed them to Caleb. "In case her clothes don't turn back with 'er," she explained, miming wrapping herself up, and pointing at Katy. Then she lay the open spellbook in front of her and winked.

"You shore you don't wanna hop around for a minute? Last chance to be a frog for a while, I suspect."

Katy croaked indignantly.

"All right. I ain't got any highfalutin magic words, but I'll do m' best." Eunice smacked her lips twice, then warbled, "The Lord works in mysterious ways. This young'un wasn't born to be a frog, now. By the po'wr vested in me by heaven and by the state of North Carolina, I now pronounce you human."

Katybird swelled suddenly into a human being, her legs raking across the tablecloth as the giant lazy Susan turned under her weight. She looked down and gasped in relief, grateful to be herself again . . . with all her clothes still on. Caleb grinned and clapped.

"I . . . I'd like to have a shower, if you don't mind," Katybird stammered.

"Down the hall. I'll give your mama a call and fix us a nice snack," Aunt Eunice advised. "After that, we can have a little chat."

Half an hour later, the golden aroma of buttermilk cathead biscuits wafted through the shower curtain as Katybird gave her skin a third scouring with a washrag. Turning back into a girl had been a surprisingly clean process. No slime or puddle muck. Still, the memory of being a frog made her shudder, and she reached for the bottle of cheap floral hair conditioner for one last go. Once out of the shower, she squeaked a clear circle in the mirror fog, happy to see her own face. Katy fixed herself with a level gaze.

"You turned yourself into a frog, Katybird Hearn." It was too ridiculous. And even though Katy stood alone in the bathroom, she couldn't help but blush with pride. Accidental magic still counted, surely, even if it was something she never wanted to repeat. No non-magical person would have gotten such powerful results. That meant something, didn't it?

Her doubts tapped her on the shoulder. *It coulda been Delpha's family magic jumpin' out of the book. You've got no business foolin' around with powerful hexes. You know deep down you ain't a real witch.*

Katy's jumbled emotions dredged up bad memories. As condensation wept down the sink mirror, Katy thought of last year, when she'd been invited to her friend Alexis Gann's "first moon party."

Alexis was the daughter of the Hollow's only hairdresser, who had moved here from California. Though Alexis's family was non-magical, Mrs. Gann often burned piles of incense on her porch and arranged expensive-looking crystals into complicated grids across her living room carpet while happily crowing, "We're summoning cosmic consciousness!" in her California accent. They were nice enough people, though. Katy'd gone for a few sleepovers.

When Alexis got her first period, her mother planned a girl's night, in celebration. Only two other girls besides Katy RSVP'd. Everyone else avoided the Ganns (probably because Mrs. Gann owned a pentagram wind chime). Katybird, having nothing against brownies and cult-classic chick flicks, had enjoyed the night immensely . . . right until girls started trading their own "Aunt Flo" stories around a bowl of queso dip. They'd all looked expectantly at Katybird. And Katy had shrugged and told them her doctors said she'd never have a cycle. It didn't bug her. It was a matter-of-fact part of being in her skin.

But Mrs. Gann had gasped and encouraged everyone to "send Katybird love and light, so Mother Earth will heal her body." Katy had wanted to curl up inside her oversized T-shirt and die. The gesture was meant to be kind, but it stung Katy to the core. Too embarrassed to yell "I'm fine!" her stomach tied itself in knots instead as her friends stared at her with wide eyes and muttered awkward little prayers in her direction.

Katy hadn't argued that she was *perfectly* herself, though she'd wanted to. Her uniqueness felt personal, private—not for sharing just then. Katybird wanted that to happen on her own terms, in her own time, and with the right people. Ever since then, the girls who attended the party would tell Katy she was "on their heart," presumably because they viewed her "poor" body as some kind of lemon. Word had gotten around, apparently, because two other friends had cornered Katybird in Sunday school and offered to put her on the class prayer request list. Katy cringed at the memory and wished she could burn it.

As if making babies was the whole point of me existing, Katy thought, grinding her teeth. *Or the point of any girl, for that matter.* They meant well. She'd been sweet to all of them, of course, but their unneeded pity had worn Katy's confidence to tatters for months.

Those memories tightened the stranglehold on the hairbrush Aunt Eunice had lent her. Katy glanced down and saw that her hands, which had apparently been glowing for a while, were starting to fade. Katy gasped. She hadn't even noticed. It was like she was getting used to her broken magic, the way a person got used to the hiccups. The brush fell and clattered around the sink, and Katy's shoulders slumped. *Maybe you* are *a lemon, Katy.*

"Shut up," she whispered at the mirror. Her throat was so tight, the word "up" ended in a strangled squeak. "You can't let ignorant stuff like that get to you." Katybird swiped her hand over the mirror, smearing the reflection into a watery blur. It was no time to wallow in self-pity. She had to look after Caleb. And as soon as she could, Katy knew she should go find Delpha, wherever Puppet had carried her off to, and make sure she hadn't been hurt. Katybird yanked on her clothes and hurried out to the kitchen.

On the stove, a pan of ham sizzled and popped next to a lidded pot that simmered and spat, filling the air with the scent of sweet pork and collard greens. Eunice smiled and waved Katy to a chair. Katybird muttered a quick grace at the table, then scooped two biscuits from the bread basket with quick hands: one for her and one for a hungry-looking Caleb.

"Called your mama and told her you're fine," Eunice said, fishing ham out of the pan with a fork. "She shore was happy to hear it. Sweet woman. Said yer car was havin' trouble, though. Told 'er you could spend the night here. I'll carry you both down to the Spring Fling in the mornin' to meet her. Your critter's in a box on th' porch."

Katybird relayed this to Caleb, who shrugged and grinned, stuffing his mouth full of biscuit and grape jelly. Soon, he collapsed in a contented puddle of six-year-old drool. While she nibbled ham, Katy watched the steady rise and fall of Caleb's rib cage inside his fading *Guardians of the Galaxy* T-shirt, grateful he'd found her. She felt a flash of guilt. She was supposed to take care of *him*, not the other way around. His fist rested beside his face—a habit he'd kept since his thumb-sucking days. Katy reached over and ruffled his hair. Her mama would not be pleased Katy had run off after Delpha instead of watching him.

Eunice hiked her faded nightdress and settled onto a chair. "Bless his little heart. He's wore out, ain't he? We'll carry him to bed in a minute." Idly, she gathered a pile of biscuit crumbs with her gnarled fingers. "So, what were you and the McGill girl tanglin' over?"

Delpha's angry face loomed in Katy's mind, and Katy frowned. "Oh, you know. Stuff. Normal girl stuff."

The old woman gave a throaty chuckle. "So, somehow you ended up with her spellbook? Ain't nothin' normal about y'all, child."

Katybird felt herself flush. "Meanin'?"

"Oh, just your family bein' cunning folk an' all."

"Cunning folk?"

"Magical. Not everyone can do what y'all can."

Katy steepled her eyebrows. "Folks aren't supposed to know about that. How come you're not upset?"

"Darlin', I'm about as old as the archangels. When you get this long in the tooth, you stop worryin' so much about rules and focus a darn sight more on helpin' folk. Holy is as holy does, I reckon. 'Sides, I was best friends with Delpha's great-grandmother."

"She taught you magic?"

Aunt Eunice cackled. "Pshaw, she showed me some of her magic. Y'alls magics ain't the only kind. I reckon there's conjure from every corner of God's earth, so don't grow a big head about it."

Katybird nodded meekly. Her "magic" wasn't anything to be proud of, anyway.

"Anyhow, I just nudged things around a bit. That spell woulda worn off eventually."

"So . . . you're not magical, then," Katybird asked slowly. "But you can work magic? How?"

Eunice cackled. "I reckon everybody's a little bit magical, even if they don't know it. I treat it like a yellow jacket. I don't bother it none, an' it ain't gonna bother me back, see? Sometimes, I can brush it off my shoulder without gettin' stung, because we're on good terms."

"Huh."

"But you Hearns are different. I reckon the yellow jackets are inside your souls, and you can't help buzzin' with 'em, bless your cotton socks." Eunice's chair creaked as she shifted her weight. "I was a midwife for fifty-two years, before I turned m' practice over to Delpha McGill's mother, sweet girl. You were the last baby I ever caught. I always was proud to end my catchin' days on one of the Hearn young'uns."

Katybird's fork clattered against her plate, and she leaned forward with interest. "You . . . were there when I was born?"

"Surely was."

"Did you notice anything special about me? Like maybe a sign of magic or anything?"

"You were as healthy as a horse. But no, you didn't glow like the baby Jesus. Can't tell a witch baby from a reg'lar baby."

Katy swallowed hard and proceeded carefully. "My family . . . they ain't sure I'm actually a witch. I'm kind of different." Katy didn't explain about her androgen insensitivity, the clumsy forest spirit spell in her bedroom, or her green Fourth of July–sparkler hands. Still, Eunice smiled a gummy grin, like she understood.

"Darlin', I wouldn't worry about it if I was you." The old woman said it with such surety, tears scorched the inside of Katy's nose.

"I think maybe . . . the magic might not want me."

"Well, now. I ain't no Hearn witch. I'm a preacher's wife who's better at casseroles than conjure pots. But I'll tell you one thing, Katy-lady. You were made for magic. To heck with bein' normal, whatever that is. Pers'nlly, I don't see how bein' different makes a flying lick o' difference. You gotta follow your own lights. Your soul is buzzin' with a whole swarm of wasps. I reckon that's why your magic is takin' its time. It's tryin' to protect you from yourself."

"Myself?"

"Well, yourself and Delpha, prob'ly," the old lady muttered, raising an eyebrow. "An' everyone else in the Hollow. Lots of folks who's against magic. Now help me tote your little brother to bed. It's gettin' late."

Katybird lugged her brother to the bedroom. Aunt Eunice went to bed.

But Katy tossed and turned, uncomfortable from the strange, lumpy mattress and the nagging worry that Delpha McGill was dead in a gully somewhere, making Katy responsible. Who knew where Puppet had run to, or whether Delpha had managed to stop it before it careened off a cliff? Caleb stirred in his sleep, whimpering from a bad dream, and for a minute, Katy considered crawling into bed with him. Blood was thicker than water, after all, and Delpha wasn't even exactly Katy's friend. But what if Puppet crashed? What if Delpha needed help? What if someone shot at the enchanted shed, thinking it was a trophy-winning deer?

Katybird slid out of bed, scribbled a note, and left it on Aunt Eunice's kitchen table: *Woke up early and walked to Spring Fling with Delpha. Caleb needs his breakfast cut up for him and doesn't like black pepper.* Then she sneaked outside with her phone and the McGill spellbook tucked inside Delpha's satchel.

CHAPTER 11
DELPHA

DELPHA DRIFTED TOWARD CONSCIOUSNESS LIKE A surfacing bubble. Light glowed directly overhead, but it was foggy and oh-so-far away. A worried voice called her name.

"Delpha? *Delpha?* Oh man, please don't be dead." A cold, clammy hand slapped Delpha's cheeks. Delpha blinked, trying to make sense of the world. The blurry suggestion of light focused into the harsh metallic beam of a flashlight. It was a boy's voice, and it kept on yammering. "If you're dead, go toward the light—think harps and clouds! Don't stick around and haunt me, okay?"

Delpha blinked and grunted, trying to orient herself. Crickets trilled. *How late was it?*

Finally, Delpha recognized the voice. Tyler Nimble. *Perfect.*

Nearly a hand shorter than Delpha, Tyler made up for his height in double helpings of hyperactivity and superstition. The kid's tongue was loose at both ends with a spring in the middle—that is to say, he rarely shut up. And because that wasn't unpleasant enough, he tended to ask questions. Delpha sighed, her battered ribs aching. Social norms dictated that she not slap him flat like a mosquito, so she growled a one-word greeting. "Tyler."

"Yeah," Tyler beamed, adjusting his glasses. "It's me!"

Delpha sighed. The boy was excessive.

"You're alive! Here—I'll help you up. Man, I knew somethin' was going on out here tonight. I had a dream about haints, an' of all the nights I've ghost hunted this month, something felt especially good about this one. You hungry? Want a sandwich?"

Before Delpha could respond, a bologna sandwich in a Ziploc landed on her belly, along with a half-eaten bag of chips. She sat up slowly, twigs and leaves crackling beneath her aching body as she tried to stand. Dizziness stole her balance, and Tyler reached out and steadied her. Kid was stronger than he looked, she'd give him that.

"Easy, there. Want a sip of Coke? Ghosts made you faint, huh?" He popped the lid of a sweating can and eagerly thrust it into her hands. "If you see one again, tell me. I'll be able t'see it, too, if I look over your left shoulder."

Delpha ignored Tyler's prattle and sipped the soda—too sweet for her liking—and stewed. Her anger toward Katybird Hearn crept into her bones like hot lead, and she squeezed the metal can until it dimpled under her fingertips. Tyler mistook her sour expression for indication she'd spotted a ghost and rushed behind her to stick his chin over her shoulder.

"Where? Where's the haint? I can't see!"

"There ain't any such thing as ghosts," Delpha said, shrugging him off. "I was out huntin', but not for ghosts."

"Then why are you here in the cemetery? Alone? Fainted dead away in a pile of old wood? That don't make sense."

"Nope. It sure don't." Delpha tried to stand again.

"Delpha, stop!" Tyler frowned and leaned into Delpha's face, tilting his head sideways. "Look into my eyes."

Delpha dropped her can of soda and bristled. "What?" she snapped. "Are you off your nut?"

Tyler blushed crimson. "Oh, mercy, not like *that*. It's just your pupils are all cattywampus. They're like, *whoo, whoo, whoo*," he demonstrated with his hands, making starburst motions. "You look dizzy. You should probably see the doctor."

"I . . . got knocked down," Delpha snapped truthfully. She didn't explain how. She had a vague memory of Puppet colliding directly into the side of something hard and the terrible sound of boards smashing around her. "Probably a concussion. Good thing you found me," she admitted.

She drew a slow breath. On the upside, she'd disarmed Puppet, if you counted smashing it to planks against the side of a tree.

Still, Katybird Hearn had stolen her book. Fumbling a shaky hand toward her back pocket, she discovered one of her wands—the newer one—had survived the crash. Stealthily, she tucked it under her shirt. The last thing she needed was Tyler getting all worked up over seeing *that*.

Tyler offered a hand. "Can you walk?"

Delpha waved him off. "Yeah, I can manage."

Delpha squinted into the trees. In the moonlight, a clear trail was visible where Puppet had bowled through the woods. That would make it easier to find her way back to familiar forest, at least. The cool night air soothed Delpha's nerves. It made her sharper. She straightened her flannel shirt.

"How do you feel about huntin' something horrible, Tyler?" She'd rather leave Tyler behind, but if she did have a concussion, it might be a good idea to have him along. It wouldn't do to pass out in the middle of nowhere again.

Tyler's eyes widened. "Which one? Mothman? Bigfoot? The Wampus Cat? Lizard Man?"

Delpha gave him an arch glance. "A thief. But first, we need to build a fire."

CHAPTER 12
KATYBIRD

KATYBIRD BLUNDERED HER WAY THROUGH A TANGLED chorus of night, spooking at every new noise—twigs snapping, coyotes wailing, and spring peepers chirping from nearby vernal pools. Her teeth chattered as she tripped through the shadowy blackberry brambles, the flashlight on her cell having long since sucked her battery dry. Why did the forest have to be so messy? She hadn't been in the woods at night since she'd dropped out of Brownies. She'd said camping badges were overrated then, and she hated the mosquitoes every bit as much now. Being lost as a goose didn't help matters.

Every thirty minutes or so, Katy's hands shone enough to illuminate her signature purple Chucks getting completely trashed as she plunged through funky-smelling mud. She could actually feel her wavy hair mushrooming out around her head in the fog. "If I could talk to the spirits of the forest, we'd be havin' some words about this humidity," she muttered. She whistled softly to Podge, who waddled behind her. "Keep up, buddy," she chided him, mostly because bossiness made her feel a shade less nervous.

Before she'd left the cabin, her plan had seemed so easy: Track down Puppet, make sure she hadn't murdered Delpha, and be back before sunrise.

But now, Katybird realized Delpha had made tracking look deceptively easy. Legs wailing with fatigue, Katy pushed herself to the top of a hill and tried to identify something recognizable on the horizon.

Podge, growing impatient, leaped from her shoulder and scuttled off into the shadows. Katy cried after him. Much like his mistress, Podge was mostly house raised and ill equipped to survive the forest. "Come back, Podge! You'll get eaten by a . . . somethin'!" Katy set off to find him, then realized after a few steps she had no idea which way he'd gone.

She stood frozen for several long moments, staring into the darkness. Katy wished she had a rewind button for this entire day. A now-familiar tingle crept up her fingers, and Katybird whispered into the night air, "How about now, forest spirits? Am I still not good enough for you? 'Cause this would be an awful nice time for you to make yourselves useful."

She remembered her vision of Puppet as a tree and felt a flicker of hope. Was that communicating with a tree? If it had been, maybe she wasn't a lost cause, despite her unique biology. She had nothing to lose if she tried again. Katy held her luminous hands out and tried to focus her thoughts on the forest. *Help me. I'm lost. Help me.*

After a few seconds, a small neon light floated out of the mist several feet away, then blinked off again. Katy barely dared to breathe and kept concentrating. *Help me. Oh, please*, she thought. The pulsing glow appeared again, this time closer. Then closer still.

Something small and buzzing collided with the side of her face, then tickled across her cheek. It was then that Katy realized her green-glowing hands were attracting lightning bugs, and she shrieked, swatting madly as another tried to land in her hair. It was like nature was laughing, and she was the joke.

Katy muttered a furious string of dark words. When that wasn't satisfying enough, she kicked hard at a rock but failed to make contact. Off-balance, Katy's free right arm pinwheeled as she tipped backward and hit the ground with an *oof*, then kept rolling, trying to cradle the McGill family spellbook with her left arm. She tumbled in a whirl of night sky, long grass, and flying limbs, bag careening after her, until finally sliding to an awkward stop at the bottom of the hill. Everything hurt.

Gingerly, Katy felt for Delpha's book and found it still intact. Through the drone of cicadas came familiar chirping, and a fuzzy raccoon tail brushed Katy's cheek. Podge sat on his haunches and eyed her in disapproval. *I could have died from a stupid temper tantrum*, she chided herself.

If she'd broken her neck, how long would she have lain there? She didn't have to try hard to imagine her mother's reaction, or her grandparents', because she'd already seen them after Echo's accident: wastebaskets full of used Kleenexes, wringing hands, plates of untouched casseroles brought over by the neighbors—Katy owed her family better than that. And besides, she owed Delpha McGill an apology, if she was still alive.

Probably, it had been Delpha's magic that made the vision of Puppet happen. And McGill magic again, when she'd accidentally turned herself into a frog. Fine. Delpha could have her magic book back. Katy was done with it.

Forcing herself up, Katy noticed a faint red flicker ahead through the trees. A bonfire, probably, not far off. Katybird gasped in relief and became suddenly aware of what a mess her clothes and hair must look like. She wrinkled her nose.

"C'mon, Podge," she murmured. "No runnin' off this time." Cringing at every snapping twig, Katy picked her way toward the light, Podge trotting at her heels.

After walking a good while, she drew close enough to hear the fire crackling. Katy's shin crashed against something solid. Her fingers glowed again, illuminating a low, rotting wooden fence. It seemed to encircle a big, round clearing in the woods. Katy drew her hands into her sleeves, ignoring their stinging, and scrambled over the broken fence. On the other side were small boulders, jutting from the forest floor and arranged in a sprawling concentric pattern. Leaning close to inspect one of them, Katy realized the rocks were pale, eroded tombstones, glowing a sickly mottled gray among the trees.

She shuddered and walked a bit farther. The fire was only a hundred yards ahead now, near the center of the graveyard. Who would come out here at night? The place had long since fallen out of memory and into disrepair. A thin veil of cloud peeled away from the moon, and on one of the tombstones Katy could faintly make out the words *El-zabet- McG-ll.* Her foot scuffed something slick. A grimy marble marker read *Wise Woman Cemetery: Journey in Peace.*

Katy frowned thoughtfully. "Wise woman" was an old euphemism for "witch." A few more steps revealed another tombstone with the name *Caroli- Hearn, 1809–1872.* One of Katy's ancestors. The breeze shifted, filling her lungs with acrid smoke, and Katy's focus returned to the bonfire.

Creeping forward like a clumsy cat, Katybird drew closer, avoiding stepping on the graves. Soon, she was close enough to make out two figures hauling planks to the smoldering fire. Katy recognized the boy, Tyler Nimble, first, and then her heart skipped as his tall companion turned. Delpha was still alive!

Katybird sighed and sagged against a headstone, relieved. But what were Delpha and Tyler doing? Dull thuds echoed around the tombstones as Delpha lobbed another heavy board at the bonfire. And Katy's heart plummeted as she realized who they were burning.

From the look of it, Delpha had started the bonfire with brush and was now collecting broken bits of Puppet to feed the blaze.

The memory of the beautiful sprawling tree flashed across Katy's mind, and she couldn't shake the feeling she was watching something alive go up in sparks.

Before she knew it, Katybird was tearing across the graveyard, screaming like a cougar. "Stop! Stop that!" Katybird hollered, shaking with rage. Delpha and Tyler gaped as Katy charged toward them and knocked the plank from Delpha's hands. "You . . . you rotten, no good, low-down . . . warthog!" Katy screeched.

Delpha tensed, her dark eyes flashing. "Katybird? You got a lot of nerve showing up again," Delpha growled. "Where's my book?"

Normally, Katybird would die from shame over what she'd done, and certainly she'd melt under Delpha's glare. But she couldn't help it. The idea of such a perfect, living creature going up in smoke wrenched her heart, and she glowered right back at Delpha.

"Why don't you pick on somebody your own size, Delpha McGill, instead of destroying something so helpless?" Katy swallowed hard and drew herself to her full height. "Don't you dare put another board on that fire!"

Delpha blinked at Katy like a calf staring at a new fence.

"Why the heck not?"

Katy scooped up Podge and glared. "Because it's murder!"

CHAPTER 13

DELPHA

PAIN SEARED DELPHA'S HAND AS SHE TEETERED too close to the flames. Sticking the offended fingers into her mouth, Delpha realized what annoyed her about Katybird Hearn: The girl had no respect for other people's plans. Instead, Katy popped up at all the wrong times, sidetracking Delpha and making her life a misery.

Delpha pulled her burned finger from her mouth and let another plank drop from her free hand. Sparks flew from the coals.

"Stop it, stop it, stop it!" Katy shrieked. She dashed forward and kicked the plank into the dewy weeds, where it landed with a hollow *thunk*, still smoking. "You're a murderer, that's what you are, Delpha McGill!" She spat out Delpha's name like a cuss word.

Delpha still couldn't get her bearings. This conversation, if you could call getting yelled at a conversation, wasn't making sense. *Murderer?* When she found her voice, she fought to keep it calm. "You liketa killed *me*, Katybird Hearn, spookin' the shed with me inside it. Who exactly am I 'sposed to be murderin'?"

"You're killing Puppet!" Katy sobbed.

Delpha's head still throbbed from the crash, and it wasn't helping her patience. "Puppet ain't alive. Puppet is a pile of boards, which I was lucky enough to un-hex before it rattled my head clean off, thank you kindly. Now leave my fire alone." Delpha tried counting to ten in her head, but Katybird's nonsense was working on Delpha's frayed nerves like a cat's tongue on a chalkboard.

To make matters worse, Tyler Nimble's ears had perked up at the word "hex," and now his mouth worked open and shut, squeaking like an excited catfish. "Hex? You mean, you're a w—"

"Zip it, Nimble," Delpha ordered, wincing at her slipup. Last thing she needed was the Mouth of the South chattering to everybody about her magic.

"You gave it a mind," Katy continued, apparently not caring their magical cover had been blown. Her bottom lip quivered. "You made it remember it was a living thing. An' now, you're killing it!"

Delpha started to understand. The silly girl had imagined Puppet had feelings like a person. Delpha snorted. Typical. That sort of kiddie fantasy was an outrageous luxury. Delpha had spent her whole life facing hard truths: Food costs money, dads don't stick around, life is hard work, grannies get sick, and the tooth fairy isn't real. Delpha's jaw muscles worked.

"If I don't burn this wood, how am I gonna make sure it doesn't cause any more trouble? What if some magic hangs around in the wood somehow? D'you want the whole town after us on a witch hunt? Or didn't your mama tell you that's how the truce started?"

Tyler bounced on the balls of his feet. "Delpha has a good point, there, Katybird. People in the Hollow don't love weird stuff. There could be torches and pitchforks and—"

"Nimble!" Delpha growled.

"Sorry," Tyler mumbled.

"You should have thought about that before you brought it to life!" Katy sputtered at Delpha. "You don't get to create something and then throw it away just because it don't make sense!" She stepped in front of the fire, blocking Delpha's way. The girl was bringing ten gallons' worth of passion to a useless argument, and Delpha couldn't make head nor tail of it.

"Hearn."

"It's Katybird! An' you did a terrible thing to that poor tree."

"It was a shed."

Katy reached inside Delpha's stolen satchel and pulled out the familiar leather spellbook. Delpha's heart lurched in her chest. She started to reach for it, but Katybird lunged toward the crackling fire. "If you don't stop burning Puppet . . . I'll torch your family's spellbook."

Despite the blazing fire, Delpha's body went cold. Behind her, Tyler sucked in a sharp breath.

"I'm not playin'." Katy lowered her extended arm. As Katy dangled the book over the dancing flames, her fair skin grew pink and her arm hairs curled and singed.

Delpha's self-control slid beyond reach as white curls of steam rose from the bottom edge of the book. All those spells—the entire history of McGill magic—were sickeningly close to the flames, along with Delpha's hopes of making her life easier for once. The wand was out of her pocket before she could think, her fingers tight as she leveled it at Katy. "Give . . . it . . . back. Now."

Katybird's eyes widened, but she doubled down. "Your book ain't any good to me." She lifted her pinky finger, then her ring finger, and then her eyebrows, as if to say, *Should I keep going?*

Tyler stumbled in between them, shaky hands lifted like he thought he was the witch whisperer. "C'mon now, y'all. You don't want to hurt each other!"

Katybird seemed to regain her senses a little, biting her lip. She didn't protest as Tyler nudged her elbow away from the licking flames. "Katybird, why doncha give Delpha her creepy ol' book back," Tyler soothed. "And Delpha . . . I don't quite follow what you did wrong, but—"

Delpha leaned over and snatched the spellbook from Katybird's trembling hand. "That's because I ain't done nothin' wrong."

Katybird gave a chilly laugh and lifted an accusing finger. "Delpha knows what she's done wrong. Puppet—"

Suddenly, the tips of Katybird's fingers shot lime-green sparks as her hands glowed all the way to the wrists. The air around Katy crackled with a chaotic energy that made Delpha's neck hair stand on end. It felt like lightning about to strike.

Tyler jumped back. "Uh, Katy . . . your hands?"

Delpha's survival instincts kicked in. She shoved Tyler away and hit the ground rolling, cradling her spellbook and letting her elbows take the impact. "Stay down, Tyler! She's throwin' a hex!" Scrambling behind a tombstone for cover, Delpha knelt in a patch of soggy grass. Tyler obeyed, wide-eyed.

Katy stumbled toward them. "It ain't what you think! Delpha, I don't want to hurt you!" Delpha glanced around the headstone and saw Katy's hands flaring brighter.

"Yeah right," Delpha muttered, one hand fumbling the spellbook open at the middle and the other yanking her wand from her pocket. "That girl's harebrained as a soup sandwich." Beside her, Tyler Nimble's eyes bugged.

"Maybe y'all don't have to fight," he whispered.

"Hush!"

Delpha peeked around the headstone to see Katybird's hands crackling electric green a few feet away, but Katy was attempting to conceal them inside her shirt. Her voice whined.

"Delpha, I never should've messed with your book. I just . . . when I saw you burnin' Puppet . . . Let me explain!" Delpha could feel the helter-skelter mess of Katy's power now, creeping in waves across her own skin and jumbling her insides. With a glance down at her spellbook, Delpha put a finger on the first hex she laid eyes on—one that read "Wend-to-War." It was careless, but she had no other choice. Her pulse thudded as her lips formed hoarse words:

> *"At which hour mine kin art dead an' gone*
> *And findeth me fighting dark forces all high-lone,*
> *I calleth up the spirits of those in the grave*
> *To cometh to mine own defense.*
> *Ariseth once more and wend to war!"*

A shock wave of dark energy mushroomed outward from Delpha, knocking her sideways several feet. As she landed hard, Delpha saw Katybird lift her hand reflexively against Delpha's oncoming spell.

Sparks flew from Katy's palm and littered the graves that encircled them in showers of cinders.

Delpha and Katy stared at each other, panting. Their magic battle had ended before it even started. For a few seconds, Katy sat with her legs sprawled, eyes wide as saucers, staring back at Delpha as the glow of her hands subsided. Delpha lay motionless, too, her ears ringing and her whole body one pounding heartbeat. Tyler, curled on the ground behind the tombstone, was the first to break the silence. "I may need a change of jeans," he groaned into the dirt. "Y'all need to learn to use your feeling words."

"Hush, Tyler," Delpha ordered, body tensing.

All was quiet, but the air felt wrong. Delpha looked over at Katybird, whose knees were pulled to her chest. Katy's eyes darted around them like something bad might come creeping out of the woods. Delpha sensed it, too. Death.

Cold dread trickled through her veins like creek water, and Delpha became sharply aware of her surroundings. The tombstones had been garden-variety markers a few minutes before, but now they loomed. They watched. It was a stupid notion, but Delpha couldn't shake it. She felt small and helpless, like prey. She gripped her spellbook close.

Something was happening out there in the darkness—roots were ripped from earth, and stone ground against stone. Delpha couldn't place the sounds of scratching and digging. The dirt under her hands shifted and bulged. Terror surged in her throat, filling her mouth with the taste of acid.

Grabbing Tyler's shirt, she was running before her legs could organize themselves. Delpha stumbled pell-mell toward the dying fire embers beside the pile of Puppet, and Katy followed suit. They huddled together. Katy felt less like a threat to Delpha now, maybe because she was shaking with fear, too. Then the strange noises settled, leaving only the breeze hissing across dry leaves.

Katy relaxed, and Delpha felt Tyler's grip on her sleeve slacken. But something still wasn't right. Katy cleared her throat. "Delpha, about my hands—"

Delpha hissed, "Shhh! Don't. Move." Her eyes scanned the dimly lit graveyard.

Beneath the chorus of crickets, Delpha's ears detected a weak hum. Nausea swept her gut. It wasn't the wind. This was a feeble, human moan. Like an old patient in hospice. Like a person hoarse from grief. Like the rattle of the dying. Somewhere behind Delpha, another gravelly voice mingled with the first. Off to the left, yet another joined in—raspy and grating. Delpha, Tyler, and Katy jumped at each new voice, forming a triangle with their backs pressed together.

The eerie humming crescendoed, each new voice clashing then

settling into a dizzy tornado of harmony, until it reached a volume that ran Delpha's chest clean through. Delpha felt Tyler and Katy whimpering against her shoulders but couldn't hear them over the din. Then the warm press of Tyler was gone, and he lay on the ground by her feet—fainted dead away. Katybird grabbed Delpha's hand, and Delpha, scared spitless, squeezed back.

Words bludgeoned their way through the night, and Delpha realized she recognized them—they were from "Idumea," a song that had always struck her as bittersweet.

> *"A land of deepest shade,*
> *Unpierced by human thought!*
> *The dreary regions of the dead,*
> *Where all things are forgot!"*

From the shadows, forms materialized. Ragged, skeletal figures staggered from all directions, clothed in overalls, threadbare aprons, and tattered dresses. Delpha swallowed a scream. Their faces were desiccated, shriveled, and misshapen beneath long-faded sunbonnets. Decayed women, young and old, brushed grave dirt from their skirts, gaping at Delpha and Katy with baleful eye sockets. A few had skeletal cats circling their ankles, growling to be petted, or shabby, dead-looking owls perched on their shoulders. One or two women had jaws tied shut by knotted strips of cloth or wands jammed into matted gray buns atop their heads.

All of them looked surprised to be standing there. They stopped singing. Delpha's knuckles ached from Katy's vise grip. She couldn't wrap her mind around what her eyes were telling her: The residents of the Wise Woman Cemetery had woken from their everlasting sleep.

Tyler sat up with a bleat of terror. "Delpha?" he whimpered, clinging to her flannel sleeve and pulling himself to his feet. "I thought you said ghosts ain't real."

"They ain't!" Delpha whispered fiercely, hoping to intimidate the world back into logical order.

"Well, they're standin' right here, so I guess they're a little bit real," Katy squeaked. "But they can't touch us. They're haints. Haints aren't part of the natural world, so they can't touch you." Her voice was prim, like she was reciting a memory verse for Sunday school.

The haint-things seemed cannier now, like they'd been released from a trance. *That can't be good*, Delpha thought.

"Oh God," Tyler whimpered. "It's all those graves we walked on. Pure bad luck. Quick! Show 'em something they've never seen before—ghosts get confused by new things!" Tyler began to perform the latest viral dance with frantic enthusiasm. Katybird let loose a manic, nervous giggle, squeezing the devil out of Delpha's wrist.

"Turn me loose, Hearn," Delpha growled. "Tyler, stop that. The only person you're scarin' is me." Delpha swallowed her terror. Someone needed to take charge, and it wouldn't be either of these boneheads. Locking her eyes on the *things* that inched toward the center of the clearing, Delpha fought to stay logical. There was a skinny gap between two of the creatures, just wide enough to dart through out of reach. Delpha licked her lips and motioned.

"Listen, y'all. We're gonna run for it, on my signal. One, two . . ."

Before Delpha could say "three," a tall haint with a basket let loose an earsplitting wail to Delpha's right. *"AAAAAAIIIIEEEE!!"*

Tyler fainted again. Katybird screamed back at the haint and kept screaming, only pausing every few seconds to fill her lungs again so she could scream some more. The ghost-thing followed suit, until a fat, stern-looking creature with a wand strode over and clunked the hollering one across the skull with a rotting broom handle.

"Imagine goin' on like that—a growed woman," the chubby thing rasped to the taller one. The orange glow of the embers cast a hellish light across her rotten face. "You was a jabbermouth in life, Sukie Hearn, and you're an even bigger one now yer dead!"

Sukie rounded on the chubby creature, reaching with skeletal fingers for a mouldering leather pouch at her waist and pulling out a ghastly-looking rat. The rat skeleton moved. "I'm gonna hex yer bones, Sowmarie McGill! I'm gonna turn you into a mudpuppy! Or stretch out your earlobes and tie your arms together with 'em! You ain't goin' to heaven as anything natural, anyhow, that's fer sure!"

Sowmarie battered Sukie soundly over the head again, dislodging her dentures, which she'd apparently been buried with.

As if on cue, fights broke out among the ghastly beings all around them, and as far as Delpha could tell, the ones with the wands were on one side and the ones with dead-looking pets were on the other. The wand corpses threw fizzling spells from mildewed wands, and the pet-owning corpses screamed like banshees, hollering curses in mountain accents and Scottish burrs. Delpha began to understand the pattern: The things with wands were McGills, the things with animals, Hearns.

Delpha and Katy stood dumbstruck by the fire, as haints hiked up their moth-eaten skirts and climbed tombstones to get clearer shots at their opponents, woolen stockings slouching around their withered ankles. The entire graveyard swarmed with Delpha's and Katy's ghostly ancestors, all intent on destroying one another. *So that's what the "Wend-to-War" hex does.* The truth of it didn't sink in at first, but when it did, it hit with the force of an anvil. Delpha swallowed hard, as cold sweat broke out all over her skin. She was in a hundred miles over her head now, and she couldn't fathom how to fix it. If Puppet's presence in the Hollow was a problem, this was a mile-wide F5 tornado.

Somewhere far away, Katybird yelled Delpha's name and kicked her squarely in the shin. Delpha turned to her, still in shock. "It's a dream," Delpha whispered in a flat voice. A nightmare. It had to be. She bit the inside of her cheek.

Katybird's breath was warm and close. "It ain't. We've gotta get out of here before these things realize who we are. Look how the two clans hate each other! Imagine if your kin realize I'm a Hearn . . . or the other way around!" Katybird blinked tears. "Besides, they ain't normal ghosts. Look! These haints can move things in the real world."

As if to prove Katy's point, one of the dueling witches managed to sheer off a tree branch with a sputtering bolt from her fingertips. The limb cracked and fell on top of her grisly rival with a sickening *thud*. The old witch struggled beneath it, neck twisted at a creative angle, and her moldered pet fox bared its teeth at Podge. Podge hissed, then scampered into the woods. Katybird let out a wail of anguish, clutching her sides and screaming Podge's name, too scared to run after him.

"Not ghosts. Zombies," Delpha whispered. Her senses rebooted. There were rules now. Rules were good. The zombies had bodies— real bodies that could do damage. Delpha hoped this meant they could be damaged, too. But there were over a hundred of them, which meant Delpha, Katy, and Tyler were sorely outnumbered and trapped in the center of the clearing. From the look of it, outrunning the zombies wasn't likely. Delpha opened her spellbook shakily.

"Podge is tame! He can't defend himself!" Katy sobbed, face streaked with snot and tears.

Delpha ignored her, tearing through musty pages for a suitable-looking hex. She wouldn't be so careless this time. There. Her eyes landed on a page titled, "Stayeth Put Hex (nay wand needed)." Ducking as a decayed owl swooped at her head, Delpha cleared her throat and muttered in a shaky voice,

"Do not leaveth, do not stray.
Evil, in this circle stay."

As she spoke the final word, Delpha crumpled to her knees. Around the edge of the clearing, a dark ring formed in the grass. A pair of dueling zombies who ventured near it bounced backward from it and howled in pain. Delpha smiled grimly and struggled to her feet. She turned to Katybird. "I did a hex to keep 'em here in the grave-yard! Don't know how long it'll last, though."

Katybird already had an unconscious Tyler draped over her shoulder in a fireman's carry. "He fainted, and he won't wake up," Katybird wheezed, staggering. She turned to the spot her raccoon had ran off and hollered. "Podge! Podge?"

Delpha searched for a break in the whirlwind battle. Her gaze drifted to the pile of broken wood beside the fire coals. *Puppet.*

"You're not gonna like this, Hearn, and I can't believe I'm doing it, but . . ." Without pausing to explain, she yanked out her homemade wand, focused on the pile of rubble, and tried to will it to be Puppet again. Nothing moved. Delpha struggled to remember the way her mind had felt when she'd done puppet magic by accident. It was like trying to recall a food she'd tasted only once. Her mind folded inward, straining hard. Nothing. Instead, she tried using the sort of concentration she used while whittling something complicated. A cool, clear sensation.

The edges of Delpha's vision darkened as the half-charred boards of Puppet clattered and whirred into place. In front of her, Puppet teetered on stack-stone legs, impatient to do her bidding. A trickle of warm blood left Delpha's nostril as she stumbled to the outhouse, kicked open the door, and flopped inside, waving feebly for Katy to follow. Katybird bit her lip and balked. "But Podge!" Several zombies with dead pets pointed at Delpha and leered.

"Look at 'er wand! A McGill witch! Quickly, sisters, spill 'er blood!" Their sagging jaws gaped, and a rasping sound of pure evil poured from their throats, making the hair on Delpha's neck rise.

"Come *on*, Hearn!"

Katybird balked, even as a fireball hex sizzled over her head.

Delpha shook with strain and fear. "If Tyler gets hurt," she hissed, "it's gonna be your fault! At least get in to save *him*."

That did it. Katybird heaved Tyler inside Puppet and crawled in after him, sobbing. Just as Delpha slammed the door shut and latched it, undead hands began clawing at the outside of Puppet's walls, trying to find their way inside. Delpha slumped against the wooden wall and concentrated as Katybird blubbered. "We could have stayed longer! We could have found Podge."

"*Thanks, Delpha, for saving our backsides*, you mean." Delpha reached for her puppet magic again. Her head weighed a thousand pounds. Gritting her teeth, Delpha pounded Puppet's floor and croaked, "Go, Puppet, RUN!"

Puppet lurched toward the woods with Delpha keeping it under her control just by the skin of her teeth. A few tenacious zombies howled in protest, surprised to find themselves clinging to the sides of a moving shed. The last one flew away like a bug from a windshield as Puppet crossed the "Stayeth Put" circle.

As they careened into the forest, Delpha went down her mental checklist, her breathing fast and ragged.

Get her spellbook back: check.

Dismantle Puppet: check, then uncheck.

Figure out how to get the undead Hearns and McGills back in the ground?

Nigh impossible.

CHAPTER 14
KATYBIRD

KATY HAD ALWAYS BEEN THIS WAY: IF LIFE EVER
scared her spitless, she got along by looking after someone who was
an even bigger mess than she was. And right now, life had scared her
mouth drier than a box of Q-tips, and she couldn't stop shaking. Even
miles after their screeches faded into the distance, the zombies'
awful, gaping faces leered in her head, making the baby hairs on her
arms stand on end. So, whimpering, Katy braced herself against
Puppet's rocking floor and threw herself into reviving the limp and
unconscious Tyler Nimble. "Tyler! *Tyler!*"

Tyler woke with a flailing start, rubbing his eyes. When he realized his head was resting on Katy's knobby knee, his face went redder
than an August tomato.

Suddenly, Katy realized her fingers had been protectively clutching Tyler's head to keep it from bumping around the tilting floor. She yanked her hands away and wedged them behind her back, looking at the ceiling with her mouth pursed. Tyler struggled to sit up, but couldn't keep his balance. "Are we in . . . a closet?" he squeaked. His ears blushed, too. Katy shook her head wildly, not sure where to start explaining. She half hoped the chatty boy had amnesia and wouldn't remember her and Delpha fighting, or the magic, and especially not the zombies.

Delpha cleared her throat. Her back was pressed so far into the corner, she seemed to be trying to slip clear through the wall like Kitty Pryde from X-Men. Before speaking, she tossed Katy a dirty look, as if all this were Katy's fault. As if Katy had cast that stupid hex and raised a whole graveyard. As if Katy had almost gotten them all killed.

Katy wasn't done being mad at Delpha, not by a long shot. She tossed her hair sideways so Delpha could see her glaring right back.

"Where . . . where are we?" Tyler blurted, tugging his shirt down to cover his belly paunch. "Katybird? Delpha?"

Katybird tensed, looking to Delpha for a cue and then hating herself for doing it. Delpha raised her jaw and shook her head. *Don't tell him.*

Tyler groaned. "Y'all aren't fightin' again, right? 'Cause that's one of my least favorite things, right next to fried chicken liver and my math teacher figuring out I never learned my sevens. Even if my moms are fussin' over which way the toilet paper goes, it's video games for me till the air clears. Anyway, the last time y'all fought . . ."

Memory flooded into Tyler's hazel eyes. "The . . . the graveyard! With the zombies! And the *abracadabra*!" He waved an imaginary wand in an imitation of Delpha so funny, Katy would've laughed if she weren't so mad and scared. A dopey grin spread across his face, then faded back into a crimson fluster. "But how'd we get away? How'd I get here?"

Again, Katy found herself glancing for Delpha's direction. Delpha opened her grim mouth as if she might say something, but then clamped it shut again and gripped her wand till her knuckles went white, giving her head a firm shake. Tyler looked hurt.

Katy rolled her eyes. "We have to tell him, Delpha. It ain't his fault he woke up before we got him home." Katy's voice came out clipped and forced, and her knees bounced in agitation. Why did she keep waiting for Delpha's approval? *For mercy's sake.* "We're in a bewitched outhouse," Katybird explained.

"Woodshed," Delpha corrected.

Katy rolled her eyes again. "Anyway, Delpha hexed it so we could get away from the zombie witches. It hasn't exactly been a smooth ride, either."

"Wait—y'all didn't kill the zombies?" Tyler pressed his eye to a knothole in the side of the woodshed, clutching his stomach. Katy peered through a crack, too. Weeds whizzed beneath them, giving the uncomfortable sensation that the closet was floating through the woods. "Where are they now?"

"Delpha cast a hex to keep them in the graveyard," Katy muttered. A flare of envy made her glare at Delpha again.

"How'd . . . how'd I get in the shed?"

Katy stopped glaring at Delpha but didn't bother wiping the sour look off her face before telling him, "You fainted. I carried you."

Tyler blanched at this news, looking like he might cry. "Oh man. I'm real sorry about that."

"It isn't your fault, Tyler. We wouldn't've had any faintin' or carryin' if a certain someone hadn't gone and done out the nastiest spell in that awful book . . ."

"The awful book you stole? Stop yapping, Hearn. We're almost there," Delpha muttered. She sniffed hard, bracing herself against the doorframe with one hand as she squinted out a moon-shaped hole in the door. Delpha's movements had a deliberate sort of grace about them, like everything she did was part of one long, calculated dance: nothing extra. She didn't talk extra, either, and was putting out a serious *don't ask questions* vibe. Which was a good thing, since Tyler was bouncing on his heels like he wanted to ask a dozen more.

One look from Delpha, and he stopped. It pestered Katy, the way Delpha could do that. Even so, Katy found herself begrudgingly hoping Delpha had some sort of plan to get them all out of this mess.

The outhouse jarred to a stop, and Delpha suddenly collapsed to her knees, forcing Katy and Tyler to opposite sides of the shed. She was sweating and looked almost green, like someone just getting over a round of the flu.

"You all right, Delpha?" Tyler asked, putting a hand on her shoulder.

"Get out," Delpha wheezed, knocking the door open with a limp hand. Pale rays of early-morning sun streamed in. "We're a coupla minutes away from your house."

"You know where I live?"

"It's the Hollow. Everybody knows where everybody lives. There's not that many houses. Now, out. Katybird and I"—Delpha swiveled her pupils around like daggers—"have *things* to do."

"But . . . but!" Tyler exclaimed, crestfallen. "There's an army of undead grannies runnin' 'round the graveyard like beheaded chickens. If you let me try, I might could help somehow!"

"Nope. Out. Quick! Hearn and I have to go."

Where will we even go? Katy wondered incredulously. She should go straight to her mama and nanny, but she was overcome with shame for having any part of the mess they'd just left in the graveyard.

Maybe they could put it right, after a quick peek in Delpha's book. Katybird pursed her lips, looking Delpha over. *No way can Delpha drive Puppet again, weak as played-out catfish.* "Delpha, you look like something the cat dragged in."

"Manners, Hearn. Try 'em sometime."

Katy tried to push down her anger. "What I mean is, looks like your magic is sappin' you dry. My nanny says Hearn magic is all about convincing nature to do what we want, not forcin' it. That's why it don't cost our bodies when we do it. Looks like McGill magic runs a little different."

A dark look crossed Delpha's face, and she rubbed her forehead with her fingers. Then her stomach growled so loud, Katy winced.

"I am hungry," Delpha admitted. "*Real* hungry."

Tyler seemed to sense his opportunity. "Well, why not come into my house? I can get you food. And water. And all kinds of other stuff, if you need it. Salt and dried parsley and oregano—"

"You gonna feed us or cook us? What do I need parsley for?" Delpha spat.

"You know, for castin' witch spells!" Tyler grinned. "C'mon! I'll go to the front door, and y'all hide behind the azaleas. When the coast is clear, I'll sneak you to my room through the back door!"

"Fine. But just for a quick bite."

Katy stared at Delpha in surprise. She'd barely put up any fuss. *She must feel even worse than she looks*, Katy thought, frowning. Delpha swiveled her eyes toward Katy.

"Then we'll look through my book real quick and figure out how to fix those zombies."

Delpha sounded so certain, Katy brightened. Maybe they could fix this stew they'd gotten themselves in before their parents found out.

Maybe Delpha *can fix it, you mean. Your magic is still broken*, Doubt reminded her. Katy's cheeks grew hot.

"All right. Lead the way, Tyler," Katy said, forcing a smile. "Let's get Delpha fed."

One by one, they dropped from the shed onto the dirt trail and followed Tyler through the dense trees. Katy couldn't stop herself from jumping at every cracking branch, half expecting to see a zombie at any moment. *They're spelled inside the cemetery*, she told herself. She hoped with all her heart Podge had gotten away from them. Her vision blurred with tears just as they came up on a cluster of bushes covered in red and pink buds.

Tyler turned, swallowing hard. "Y'all hide here." His face was almost as white as it had been in the graveyard, and Katy peered through the branches toward his house. Rust-red wind chimes filled the air with pentatonic wonder as they jangled in the breeze. An old station wagon was parked in the gravel driveway. Tyler grinned and wiped his sweaty palms on his hands before tromping across the yard and up the porch steps.

"I'm home," he called meekly through the fraying screen door, which swung open before his hand touched the handle.

Katy squinted. Tyler's mother Muzz towered in the doorway, box braids swinging, and eyes lined with worry. She clutched a walkie-talkie to her heart, eyeing him up and down.

"He's in trouble," Katy whispered.

"We're *all* in trouble, case you haven't noticed," Delpha muttered.

Muzz lifted the walkie to her mouth and pressed the talk button. Her voice was all ferocious tenderness as she said, "He's home, Honey. He's alive, but don't worry. I plan to kill him."

Katy felt Delpha tense against her shoulder.

Muzz punctuated every word with a glossy crimson fingernail, talking loud enough to be heard clear across the yard.

"You are in a heap of trouble, Tyler Jonas Nimble. I thought we talked about you not goin' on your little ghost hunts without tellin' anyone! It's seven in the morning! Your mama and I were torn up worryin' about you all night. You're grounded. Forever. What if you-know-what had happened, and someone saw you?"

Tyler flinched, looked over his shoulder, and hissed something

Katy couldn't make out. She felt embarrassed for Tyler, and wondered if she ought to plug her ears.

Muzz pursed her lips. "I'm sorry, did I say I was done talkin'? What were you thinkin'?" She raised her eyebrows. "No, hush. I'll *tell* you what you were thinking. *You weren't thinking.* Did you even take your herb capsules? And did you have your inhaler?"

Before he could answer, Muzz yanked him into a bone-crushing hug, swaying gently the way mamas do. Delpha rolled her eyes, but Katy suddenly missed her own mama desperately and wished Tyler would hurry.

Tyler pulled away from Muzz. "I'm sorrry. I guess I'll just go to my room now," he said a little too loudly.

Gravel sprayed as a National Park Service jeep tore down the long wooded driveway and skidded to a stop in front of Tyler's house. *Slam!* went the door as Tyler's other mom, Honey, charged across the yard. Muzz went inside. *Oh, mercy. Poor Tyler.*

Honey's red ponytail swung as she bounded up the porch steps in her khaki ranger uniform, cheeks flushed. "Lord 'a' mercy, kid, do you want to give us a heart attack? You had no business being out in the woods by yourself."

Muzz reappeared in the doorway with a suitcase. Delpha glanced at Katy, raising an eyebrow.

"We won't have to cancel our plans, now we know you're not

dead in a ditch. I've stocked the fridge with a potpie for lunch. Your uncle Clement will be here sometime after noon. Can you manage to keep out of trouble for that long?"

Tyler practically shouted, "Okay! Don't worry about me. I'll be real sure to lock *THE BACK DOOR*."

Delpha poked Katy. "C'mon, Hearn," she whispered, clutching her spellbook. "He's tellin' us to go around back."

They waited behind the house for several minutes, not talking, until Tyler yanked open the tattered screen door, out of breath and arms teeming with snack cakes, a jar of pickled okra, beef jerky, and a glass of sweet tea. The tea dripped down the sides, as if it had been poured in a big hurry.

"Here ya g—"

Tyler had barely opened his mouth when Delpha snatched up several of the snack cakes and tore into the cellophane wrapping with her teeth. Katy stared bug-eyed as Delpha bolted the food down like a starving animal, barely pausing to breathe before guzzling the tea.

"Delpha, you'll get sick eatin' that fast!" Katy exclaimed, grimacing.

"I feel better," Delpha gasped finally, thrusting the empty wrappers into Tyler's hands. "Loads better. All right, Katybird. Time to go."

"Go?" Tyler exclaimed. "You just got here!"

"The less you know, the better," Delpha retorted. "This don't concern you. You ain't magic, and you'll just get in the way."

Tyler's face fell. Katy's stomach twisted hard at Delpha's words, too. If Delpha knew Katy was just spare luggage, too . . . Well, she was about to find out soon, wasn't she?

Katy shot Tyler a sympathetic smile. "But thanks for the food! That was real nice of you." She glanced at Delpha, who was already trudging off through the woods toward Puppet, then turned back to Tyler. "Don't say anything to anyone about all the the you-know-whats back at the you-know-where, all right? Keepin' this stuff secret is really, really important to our families. We don't mean anyone any harm. But you know how folks are."

Tyler pressed his mouth together and nodded. "Don't worry. I'm good at keepin' secrets."

CHAPTER 15

DELPHA

BY THE TIME DELPHA MANAGED TO STOP PUPPET in front of Katybird's house, the sun roared over the tops of the trees and early spring birds chittered a dawn chorus.

For a minute, Delpha let herself collapse back against the rough wood of Puppet's wall, head pounding as the world whizzed around her. Her stomach gnawed itself again like she hadn't eaten in weeks, and a drop of red landed on the leg of her good jeans. She touched her nose. It was bleeding again. Lifting her wand weakly, she let Puppet rest, collapsing its stack-stone legs back into a foundation.

Katy pulled out her dead cell phone and used the black screen as a mirror, wiping tear-streaked dirt from her chin. "Why are you wavin' that dumb stick around, anyhow?" Katybird spat, chin quivering. "Mountain witches don't use wands."

"This one does. And all the McGill zombies do," Delpha muttered, rubbing her pounding forehead. "And I thought being nice was your thing, Katybird. You're cranky."

"Ya THINK? You set a cemetery full of zombies loose, and Podge is gone," Katy said, voice cracking at her pet's name. "And Puppet . . ."

"Not this again," Delpha growled and tilted her head back, pinching the bridge of her nose. "For the last time, Puppet's a shed, not a tree. And it ain't like I had a choice."

Katy nestled her head between her knees, not seeming to hear. "An', anyway, Podge is lost. Or dead! I never should have taken him with me!" Her words choked off in a sob.

Delpha frowned hard. They didn't have time for this. They needed to find a way to kill the zombies. She crawled gingerly on hands and knees to the shed door and twisted herself down to the ground, her head throbbing as her feet hit the grass. "C'mon. We've gotta sort this out before those things get loose."

"But Podge—!"

Delpha started toward the house. "Things leave, Katybird. Stuff dies. That's life."

"That's . . . that's a heartless way of seeing things."

Delpha was already on Katy's porch and thumbing through her spellbook, ignoring the deep sting of Katy's words. "Better heartless than thoughtless. What if some innocent person wanders into that graveyard full of zombies? We gotta fix this."

No one was home inside the Hearns' house. Katy explained that her dad was on a truck run and her mama was busy setting up a booth downtown for Spring Fling. She fished a key out of the flowerpot by the door, and the girls let themselves in.

The house was creepy-quiet except for a fancy mechanical fountain that burbled in the entryway. Delpha craned her neck to gawk at the vaulted ceiling, then stopped herself as Katy waved for her to follow. The Hearn kitchen was cheerful, with orderly bundles of sage drying above the sink and dozens of elegant orchids on shelves that spanned the picture window. The smell of blueberry muffins hung in the air, and Delpha's belly rumbled.

Katy sniffed. "Smells like Mama made breakfast before she left. Want a muffin?"

Delpha shrugged, not wanting to seem eager. Katy kicked off her sneakers and skated across the slick tile in her socks. She pulled a handful of oversized muffins from the microwave and a bag of jelly beans from the cabinet. Delpha settled at the high counter and flipped through her spellbook, snatching glances around the kitchen when Katy wasn't looking. The fridge was covered in photos of Katy as a little kid: on her daddy's shoulders, snaggletoothed and eating ice cream here, and riding the teacup ride together at Disney World there. She stared at Mr. Hearn's smiling face with something akin to fascination. Delpha's memory of her own father's face had blurred long ago, after her mama had cut him out of the McGill photos.

What's it like, livin' that way? Delpha couldn't remember a time in her life when she'd ever been that carefree. In her twelve years, Delpha'd had plenty of opportunities to feel envy over things like new shoes or beach vacations. That was okay. Delpha could transform her longing into plans—plans that magic would help her accomplish.

But as Delpha gazed around Katy's house, she ached with something deeper than envy. This . . . this was missing a faceless person or having a sad song like "Blue Bayou" stuck in your head, bringing you down all day. It was emptiness without a bottom to it. Delpha tried to shake the maudlin feeling.

Still, a hazy idea of a man in a worn denim jacket and the smell of peppermint gum wormed its way into her thoughts, and a fiery stab of *something* shot her heart clean through. Delpha shoved the pain away and tightened her jaw. That memory was a little girl's daydream, nothing else. Her daddy hadn't been around like that long enough to matter.

Delpha jumped as Katy dropped a muffin in front of her, then brushed the crumbs off her spellbook before tearing into its sweetness. After she'd downed three muffins back-to-back, Delpha paged through the spellbook as fast as she could without ripping the delicate binding. When she'd found the page, she read the fine print below the "Wend-to-War" hex, which she'd overlooked in the graveyard.

> *Terms o' th' hex: Th' undead army will wage war against th' castin' witch's opposing clan (in addition tae murderin' anybody what stands in thair wey) fur eternity, or till th' Reverse-Curse is cast.*

Delpha shuddered, more relieved than ever that she'd managed to contain the zombies to the cemetery. She kept on flipping. There were spells to make a lover true, a "Getteth Lost" spell for banishing, and itch hexes for annoying nosey neighbors.

Finally, Delpha's eyes screeched to a halt:

> *If ye'r daft enough t' cast th' Wend-to-War, this is how ye undo her, provided th' undead haven't murdured ye yit.*

Delpha's heart leaped, her eyes scanning the text greedily. The spell appeared to be penned by two different people, one with neat and fluid handwriting and the other writing in a haphazard sprawl.

"Hearn, listen up! Here's the page we need!" Katy padded around the breakfast bar and leaned in. "It's a two-part spell," Delpha explained. "I do one half, you do the other."

"Why should I have to do it, too?" Katybird asked, chewing her lip. "You're the one who threw the hex, not me."

"The hex only wakes the ancestors of the caster, to form a zombie army. For feudin'. Both the McGill witches and the Hearn witches rose from their graves. I think the hex bounced off you and worked for your family, too."

Katy's eyes darted as she scanned the page. "So everyone from the cemetery will just keep fightin' forever?"

Delpha nodded, her throat tightening. "And they're probably after all the Hearns or McGills, too, not just the dead ones. You, me, our families. We *both* have to undo this. And fast."

"I'll try my best."

Delpha sat up tall. "Here it is."

> *"Two witch spell. (Prob'ly the ones what done it in the first place.) Best to choose a crafty miss what's full of vinegar and ~~piss~~ wits."*

Here, the word "piss" had been clearly crossed out and replaced with "wits" by a witch with better penmanship. Delpha smirked to herself and kept reading.

> *"An' best t' make her counterpart a lass what's kind an' soft of heart."*

Katybird whispered, "That'd better be me, I think."
Delpha nodded in agreement and continued:

> *"(First witch)*
> *With cunning mind an' strongest will, I call the hex of war to still.*
>
> *(Second witch)*
> *Love like hearth with coals aglow, my open heart makes magic grow.*
>
> *(Speak together for this part, with feeling)*
> *These balanced pow'rs make evil quake.*
> *Together, watch the curses break."*

"That's it, then," Delpha said, shoulders sagging in relief. *Not too bad.* She felt a smile tug one corner of her mouth. "We do the Reverse-Curse and the zombies die. You ready?"

Delpha looked up at Katy and startled. Katybird stared at her with swollen eyes, chewing a wad of buttered popcorn jelly beans. She wore two giant oven mitts, no doubt in a vain attempt to hide the fact that her hands were glowing.

But even if Delpha hadn't seen the green light edging up Katy's arms, her own skin had already begun to crawl with the God-awful sensation she'd had when Katy's hands had glowed in the graveyard. It was a claustrophobic, knotted-up sensation. Delpha grabbed for her wand, pulse thumping in panic.

"No, Delpha, wait! Listen, will you? My magic's broken. I'm not trying to make this happen. It just *does*. My mama don't even know, and I wouldn't be telling you, either, except"—she slid off the oven mitts to reveal firework-sparkler hands—"I don't know how I'm gonna do my half of the Reverse-Curse."

Delpha frowned and considered Katy's face. Her feelings softened. Katy was dead serious. She seemed embarrassed, almost. But surely Katy saw how real her power was, even if something was clearly haywire with it. "Hogwash. You're practically leaking magic all over the floor. Now sit down, and let's do this Reverse-Curse before that 'Stayeth Put' spell wears off and all those zombies get loose."

"But—"

"But nothin'! Sit!" Delpha flipped her braid and commandeered every ounce of her focus. The muffins had restored some of her strength, along with most of her confidence. Delpha wasn't about to let on to Katybird, but the way magic zapped her energy scared her. It made her feel like a lightbulb filament about to burn right out. *This'll be the last spell today*, she promised herself. Then, rest. Everything would be set right again.

She looked down at the spell and curled her lip. "I'll go first, and then you do the 'soft of heart' bit." Delpha glanced to make sure Katy was following. Katybird nodded. Delpha began.

> *"With cunning mind and strongest will,*
> *I call the hex of war to still!"*

Katybird hesitated, and Delpha swiveled on her stool and shot her a hard look. Katy took a trembling breath, then recited, *"Love like hearth with coals aglow, my open heart makes magic grow."* As soon as she said it, Katy's hands hissed and spat cold sparks several feet into the air. Her eyebrows shot up in alarm. Delpha suppressed a growl of annoyance and tapped her index finger on the final lines. *Keep going.*

Together, Delpha and Katy chanted, *"These balanced pow'rs make evil quake. Together, watch the curses break."*

For a split second, Delpha thrilled as an eddy of ionized wind whirled around them, lifting Katybird's curls and tickling the back of Delpha's neck. Then Katy shrieked as a large stoneware fruit bowl on the kitchen table exploded, showering them with broken shards and bits of apple and orange.

Delpha's heart skipped as she swore, and Katy's face crumpled to quash a sob.

"I told you I couldn't do it," Katy shouted. *"I told you!"*

"You . . . you aren't tryin' hard enough," Delpha found herself insisting, swabbing orange pulp from her cheek with one of the oven mitts. She'd gone dizzy with panic, but she didn't let it show. "Let's do it again."

"My magic is stuck, Delpha. I can't control it, believe me. I've tried." Katy's hands were fading to normal, no longer shedding sparks. She jumped from her chair and started for the back door. "I need to go out and look for Podge before something bad happens."

Anger flashed inside Delpha. So far, Katybird had done nothing but knock her plans off course, and now Delpha's dreams were bobbing out of reach. She couldn't let the zombies run loose around the Hollow. She'd be forced to ask for Mama's help, and the spellbook would disappear forever once Mama got her hands on it. *No more magic.* A blob of apple fell from the ceiling onto the book, besmirching the words "watch the curses break." Delpha hastily wiped it off with her thumb and stalked ahead of Katy to block the doorway.

"Listen!" Delpha wracked her mind for the words to convince Katy. "Can you imagine if we don't do the Reverse-Curse? Who knows how long that 'Stayeth Put' hex lasts. Zombies could get out of that cemetery, Hearn. They might go downtown! Folks'll get hurt. People will remember about our families being magical. You know the Hollow's history! Our families feuded until they came after us with pitchforks. You think they've really gotten more understanding in the past hundred years? You think they'll congratulate us for being so special? There's more at stake here than your trash panda!"

Katy's chin wobbled and her bright blue eyes blinked back tears, but she took her hand off the door handle. "I think my magic's probably a waste of time."

"But?"

"I'll try."

CHAPTER 16
KATYBIRD

THE MOST ANNOYING THING ABOUT STRESS EATING, Katy realized, was that sometimes the room in your stomach ran out, but the stress didn't. The next most relaxing thing was using a glitter atomizer and lip gloss, which is exactly how Katybird indulged herself for five minutes while blinking back tears in her bedroom. Next, she combed out her hair and changed her muddy socks, until she felt more human, bit by sparkly bit. She winced at the duct tape and cardboard covering her window, reminding her of her epic failure with the forest spirit conjure. *Think positive, Katy.* She sniffed her shirt. The only smell was the faint remains of her melon-honeysuckle body spray (an upside of being androgen insensitive—Katy didn't have to fool with deodorant often), but she changed it out for her favorite yellow T-shirt anyway before replacing her hoodie.

Her fingers started lighting up like E.T.'s again a few minutes later, just as Delpha yelled through the bedroom door that they needed to "find a new strategy to fix your magic and do the dad-gummed Reverse-Curse already." Katy drew a ragged breath and opened the door into the living room, the light creeping up her wrists.

Somehow it made Katy feel a tiny bit better to know Delpha McGill could get rattled. The smear of dried blood on the back of Delpha's hand reminded Katy that Delpha's magic wasn't effortless, either. It made Katy want to try again.

Delpha paced behind the recliner, wand behind her ear, nearly stepping on Fatso the cat as he waddled in from the hallway. Delpha studied Katy, steepling her fingers. "I can't believe I'm asking this, Hearn, but when you try to do your magic, how do you feel inside?"

The world's absolute worst magic therapist, thought Katybird. She picked at her cuticles. "I don't know. Worried it won't like me? With people, you can tell what they want from you. Then you can kind of, you know, chameleon."

"Chameleon?"

"Change the way you act. Fit people's expectations. Butter 'em up a little. Morph."

"I have no idea what that means."

"Work the room. You know, be charming."

"Huh."

Katy petted Fatso so hard, he hissed. "But I don't know what the magic wants! How'm I supposed to figure out how to communicate with something that isn't people?"

Delpha put a fist to her forehead and growled. "Hearn, the zombies . . ."

"I know!" Katy snapped. "How do *you* feel when you're doing magic? What makes it cooperate?"

"Seems like it's part of me. I'm part of it. Same way as nature. Just be one with it."

"Neat. You should start your own yoga channel," Katy muttered. Despite her family's nature magic, Katy had always considered sleeping with her windows open the most valid form of camping. She liked the nice bits of creation, like waterfalls and sunsets, but nature in North Carolina was also responsible for nasty things like flying wood roaches big enough to require their own license and registration. Rude.

"I'm just sayin', s'all. You're part of magic. Stop treating it as somethin' separate."

I don't know how to be "part" of anything, Katy realized. *Not deep down.* Not with nature, her family, magic . . . maybe not even with herself. She'd worn her helpful face for so long, sometimes she even forgot who was holding the mask up. On the outside, she was who people expected her to be: sunny and charming. Inside, she was a swarm of pieces that didn't go together: a magical dud in a family of accomplished witches, popular among peers who didn't understand the first thing about her. Delpha's advice sounded good, but it couldn't seem to find a place to land inside Katy.

"Let's try the Reverse-Curse again," Delpha's voice cut in.

Katybird swallowed hard, nodding. Delpha recited her half without looking at the page. Katy tried a confident tone this time, but her hands started to sting as the sparks flew, making her stutter through the part she and Delpha said in unison.

Through clenched teeth, she growled out, ". . . curses b-break!" and the lights in the fixture above dimmed and blinked. At the same time, hot knives of pain cut from Katy's fingertips to her elbows, making her yelp in pain before falling to her knees on the carpet, nerve endings throbbing. Katy couldn't speak until the pain slacked off.

"Magic," Katy said between gasps, "may go . . . poke a long fork . . . into an electric socket."

One corner of Delpha's mouth slid up at this, but the deep furrow between her dark eyebrows didn't relax. Her whole body was taut, like she was still waiting to see if Katy's magic might come through. Katy sagged. "Delpha, the Reverse-Curse isn't workin'." She bit her lip. "I hate to say it, but we should ask someone for help."

"No."

"Delpha . . ."

"No. Nope-covered-no, dipped in more no. We made the zombies, so we're handling it ourselves."

Katy opened her mouth to explain why her own magic might not *ever* work, then snapped it shut again. The yellow jacket feeling attacked inside her hands again, and Katy massaged the sting from her fingers. The hand-glowing episodes had gotten closer together since she and Delpha had begun attempting the Reverse-Curse, Katy realized.

Delpha huffed and stalked around the room, shoulders stiff. "Rest a minute," she muttered. "Then we can try again."

Katy made a nasty face behind Delpha's back and leaned back into the soft couch cushions.

Delpha paused in front of the Hearn's curio cabinet, her face reflected in its mirrored back. Her worried eyes glanced across the shelves, and Katy noticed a strange look slide across Delpha's features as she studied the contents of the cabinet: fancy old wooden spoons, faded needlepoint on hoops, jewelry boxes, and old family photographs in sepia. Katy's family treasures, passed down from one Hearn witch to another. As Delpha's lips shrank into a hard line, Katy thought of the times the McGills had brought antique quilts or hand-turned wooden bowls into the museum shop to be sold. Had they come from a curio like Katy's? Heat crept into Katy's ears as Delpha caught her staring.

"Is that what I think it is?" Delpha pointed to the top shelf, where a tight-packed disc of multicolored feathers the size of a pancake rested. All the fuzzy down pointed in the same direction, whorling in a flat spiral.

Katy nodded. "Prob'ly. It's a death crown." Death crowns—considered precious mementos in Katy's family—could be found in feather pillows of magical folks who are about to die. Or had already died, in this case. The one Delpha was pointing at had belonged to Katy's cousin, Echo, Fatso's original owner. Katy's mother had carefully cut apart Echo's pillow after she'd died, discovering the feathery omen. Since then, the crown had rested in the curio, untouched, to honor Echo's memory. It and Fatso stayed at Katy's house instead of Nanny's, because their presence made Nanny too sad.

"We burn ours," Delpha said softly, her breath fogging the glass. "Out of respect for the dead."

Katy shivered at the word "dead." She tried not to think about how her family's departed—her beloved witch ancestors—were now battling it out eternally in the cemetery, desecrated and corpse-y. A chill of nausea swept through her body as she realized this new, horrible layer of what she and Delpha had accidentally done. Surely, her mama and nanny would never forgive her if they found out. Katy's heart crumbled under the awfulness of it. She found herself agreeing with Delpha, for once. They had to figure out the Reverse-Curse alone, without help.

"Um, Hearn?"

"Hmmm?"

Delpha took a step back from the curio cabinet, letting her fingertips slide off the glass, gulping. "Are death crowns supposed to spin?"

Katy leaped to her feet and squinted. Inside the cabinet, the feather disc was whirling on its glass shelf. Katy blinked hard, thinking it must be an optical illusion. But there it was, spinning and gaining speed. The temperature around the cabinet plunged a dozen degrees. Fatso sprang from the couch and paced back and forth in front of the curio, arching his back. Katy's heart stuttered beneath her hoodie. *What in the world?*

The death crown became a gray blur, and Delpha staggered backward as the cabinet door rattled, causing the lids of the teapots inside to jar and clatter. The glass panes of the cabinet spidered, then cracked. Delpha clutched Katybird's arm, snatching a blanket from the sofa and covering them both. Seconds later, shards rained against the fabric as the curio's glass exploded outward. Katybird shrieked, and Delpha curled into Katy's side, head tucked as they landed on the couch.

Wind from nowhere whipped through the living room, and the blanket was torn from the girls' grasp. Fatso, heavy for a cat but still quite light compared to a human, clung to the carpet with all four paws, hanging on for dear life.

The death crown rose slowly from the shelf and floated out of the cabinet, breaking apart in the center of the room. The wind died to a soft, circular breeze, creating a whirlwind of downy feathers. The down arranged itself into the vague form of a woman. A soft groan escaped its lips. Fatso purred, trying in vain to lean against the thing's insubstantial legs and falling instead into an ungentlemanly sprawl.

"Lord 'a' mercy," breathed Delpha. "Impossible."

"Now that's a real haint," Katybird whispered, voice quavering. She rose from the couch and held out her hand toward the mesmerizing feather ghost, then took a trembling step. Delpha gasped as Katy edged toward the haint, but Katy couldn't stop herself. *Was it friendly? How could you tell, when the thing's face was made of feathers?* Delpha grabbed Katybird's sleeve and growled from the corner of her mouth.

"Hearn! You can't go touchin' every haint you meet. Stranger danger."

But Katybird's heart melted and her eyes widened. "This ain't no stranger, Delpha. I—I think I know exactly who this is."

The feather-formed haint floated toward Katybird. Its head quirked to the side in a jerking movement—one, two, three twitches to the left side, followed by a wild toss back and forth. Its shoulders were slight and its long mane of feather hair floated in a cloud. "Echo?" whispered Katybird.

Jerk, jerk, jerk, shake, shake, shake. The haint reached and brushed its feathery fingertips across Katybird's cheek, sending a shudder down Katy's sides. The haint spoke, but only one word was loud enough to understand. "Katybird." It was barely an echo.

"This is my cousin. She don't mean any harm," Katybird whispered. "Maybe she needs help crossing to the . . . the beyond."

"Fine." Delpha let go of Katy and snatched her spellbook from the coffee table. She flipped through it, eyes zooming across lines of text. "Let's help it, so it'll leave."

"What's the book say?" Katybird asked after a few seconds, gaze locked on the floating form. Friendly or not, the idea of letting it out of her sight gave her the willies.

"Not much. The McGills don't believe in ghosts," Delpha spat testily. "Chicken pox cures, wealth spells, baldness hexes . . . Not a word about haints."

"Help," the haint pleaded. Fatso tried again to lean against the spirit's legs, and Echo's hand reached to stroke the cat's side. Without warning, every bit of orange fur flew from the cat's skin and into the air, joining the feathers in creating a tangible form for the ghost. Katy yelped in horror, and Fatso, surprised to find himself suddenly naked, retreated behind the couch. The haint stood more solid now, her features distinguishable. When she spoke, her voice rung hollow and distant, like a person hollering down a long hallway.

"Poor Fatso. It's pure torture, being away from him."

"Why are you here, Echo?"

"Katybird, I've come to help you."

Delpha's book thumped shut. Katy stepped closer, and a painful lump gathered in her throat. "I've missed you so much, Echo, ever since your funeral. Can you . . . can you stay?"

"I can't. I ain't got much time—I'm breakin' the laws of nature, see. The pillow feathers and Fatso's hair—they still have a touch of my mem'ry in 'em. It's why you can see me."

Katy nodded and reached out to touch Echo's hand. Her own hand passed right through, the feathers and fur parting and regathering around Katy's touch. A cool tear slipped down to Katy's chin. "How can you help me?"

"I know what's happenin' to ya, Katybird. Why your hands are sheddin' sparks. Because it was happenin' to me."

"You couldn't work your magic, either?"

"I could. But I didn't want to. Nanny tried to teach me, but I didn't want no part of it. I hated having my future laid out for me like church clothes. Besides, the idea of talkin' to nature spirits scared me silly. But the more I refused to use the magic, the more my hands glowed when I didn't want 'em to."

"Is that why you ran away?"

Echo shook her head. "Naw. A guy at work saw my hands light up blue while I was ringing up groceries. I ran, but he followed me outside, trying to record it with his phone. I ran to my truck, but he and his friends chased me down the highway, whoopin' and hollerin'. 'Dirty witch!' they kept yellin'. I was so upset, and my truck started to fishtail." Echo's voice trailed off, and she shook her head. "And I slammed into their car. That's all I remember."

Katy's mouth formed a quiet, "Oh." What else could you say to a person who had died in such an awful way? Down and fur began drifting to the floor. Katy's chance to ask questions was slipping away with each passing second.

"So, your hands glowed at weird times, too. Because you held your power in?" she pressed.

Echo nodded, shedding feathers. "It got worse and worse. I think if I'd let it dam up any more, it might've killed me anyway. I had nightmares about exploding from the inside out."

It might've *killed* her? The words clobbered Katy's heart with a fresh fear she hadn't considered. She'd been scared of failure, sure. But death? As if on cue, her fingers began to tingle, then throb, and Katy slipped her hands into her pockets.

"Let me help you, Katybird. 'Fore it's too late," Echo's ghost pleaded. "I think it's how the Hearn magic goes. Use it or die."

"It ain't like I'm unwilling! I *want* to be a witch, no offense. What can I do?"

"I reckon," Echo sighed after a thoughtful pause, "you could drink some of the water from the old Hearn well. Great-Granny used to say it had power to strengthen magic. Nanny called it fiddlesticks, but Great-Granny swore by it."

Katy's heart leaped. That sounded easy enough. "Is that all? Just find the old Hearn well?"

Feathers and cat hair formed a small pile on the carpet now, and Echo's voice weakened as she hurried to finish: "You'll need a bond, too. It's the only thing that helped my hands. My fur—"

Before Echo's ghost could finish, the kitchen door swung wide. A gust of warm morning air scattered fur and feathers around the room, swirling the haint's form into oblivion. Frantic, Katybird wailed, "Echo, wait!" She tried to snatch the downy pieces, but she knew there was no point. Her cousin was gone. Someone wheezed loudly.

Both girls turned toward the open doorway, feathers and fur settling around them. Tyler Nimble scrambled inside without being invited, slamming the door behind him and collapsing against it. His sweaty hair was matted to his face above wild hazel eyes, like he'd been running from the devil himself.

"Hey, y'all," he wheezed, clutching his ribs. "I got bad news."

CHAPTER 17
DELPHA

DELPHA'S ANGER SPUN LIKE A TOP. SHE COUNTED back from ten, trying to keep her mind straight. "What in the name of creepin' black mold are you doing here, Nimble?"

Tyler coughed and grimaced at the disaster that was Katybird Hearn's kitchen. Fair enough. It *was* a mess. Feathers still floated through Delpha's vision, and in the corner a naked Fatso mewled with a traumatized glow in his yellow eyes. Slivers of glass crunched and squished together with bits of exploded fruit under Delpha's boots. Tyler frowned and righted himself.

"Cows," he croaked between panting breaths. "And stone, and, and—"

"Do what now? Start at the start."

Tyler wrestled an inhaler from his pocket and took two long puffs. "I thought y'all might change your mind about needing help. And on my way over, I heard somethin' out in the field between my woods an' Katy's. A real loud screech. I went out to see what it was, an' I saw these . . . people. They were cacklin' and walkin' funny, which seemed weird, so I hid. An' then"—Tyler paused to remove his glasses and dry his swollen eyes—"an' then, one of 'em pulled out a wand like yours. It put a hex on this poor mama cow. They turned it to stone, Delpha. It's just standin' out there like a cement lawn ornament. It's . . . dead, I think."

"A wand?" Katy said, sniffing and wiping her nose on her sleeve. "No one in the Hollow but Delpha has a wand."

Delpha's stomach began to churn.

Tyler shook his head, chin wobbling. "As they left, I got a good look at 'em in the sunlight. They looked like mummies. It was your zombies from the graveyard."

"What?" Delpha screeched, reaching across him to deadbolt the door and pull down the shade. "Why didn't you say that in th' first place??"

"The 'Stayeth Put' spell must not've lasted long," Katy groaned, settling into a chair shakily.

Delpha winced, her insides tying themselves into knots. They were in trouble. "The book said they'll murder anyone who gets in the way of their war."

"They can turn animals to stone," Tyler mumbled to himself. He almost looked angry. "If they can do it to a cow, they can do it to people. That ain't cool. Couldn't y'all just . . . undo whatever you did?"

His words were obvious, but the look on Tyler's face cut Delpha to the quick. Tyler Nimble was judging Delpha for screwing up badly, and, worse, he wasn't wrong. She'd been flat-out reckless and lost control of the situation. Delpha shot Katybird a meaningful look. Not a nice one, either. She knew Katy couldn't keep her magic from going haywire, but Delpha's fear kept souring to anger. If Katybird had just left Delpha's book alone in the first place . . .

Katy bit her lip and studied her fingernails. "I . . . I can't do my half of the Reverse-Curse. My magic's kinda messed up."

Tyler's face softened. "What about your mama? Can she help fix it?"

"No," the girls said in unison.

Tyler frowned. "O-kaaaay. How can I help, then?"

Delpha rocked on her heels. "We have to fix Hearn's magic. Seems we need some water from an old well, and to get her a 'bond,' whatever that is," she grumbled, waggling her fingers to make air quotes. Her to-do list was stretching longer by the minute.

Katy sniffled loudly, then did it several times more, until Delpha growled at her to go get a tissue. Katy made a face and left for the bathroom.

As soon as she left, Delpha grabbed Tyler's arm. He flinched but seemed to understand now that this wasn't some fun game. She needed to make sure. "Pay attention," she whispered. "Katy's magic's about to blow her up or something. She's workin' hard to control it, but if we don't help her fix it . . ."

"What do you mean, blow her up? You don't actually mean . . . explode, right?"

Delpha nodded. "Her dead ghost cousin sure thought so. Seems like it runs in the family or somethin'." Delpha told herself that she was just relaying the facts—that she wasn't actually worried about Hearn—but a twang of pain shot through her belly anyway.

"Dead . . . cousin?"

"Don't ask. So, if I let you help us get what Katybird needs for her magic, do you promise not to get in the way?"

Tyler hesitated. Then, chin wobbling, he nodded. "I'm in. Whatever you need."

Their conversation halted awkwardly as Katybird reappeared, red-eyed. Her wavy, pastel-streaked hair was back in two matching turquoise barrettes, and she wore a baby-blue Tar Heels jacket with the sleeves rolled back. She looked ready to work. Good.

"All right, then," muttered Delpha, blowing a feather off her nose. "If the zombies are out, we need a plan. We need to find the old Hearn well."

"I think our family property used to be downtown," Katy offered. "They sold it off to the city for the park a while back and used the money to open the museum."

Tyler clapped his hands together, sounding a hair too cheerful. "What are we waiting for? Let's go find the Hearn well!" Delpha nodded and began to pack her spellbook.

Katybird wrinkled her nose. "We?"

"Delpha says y'all could use a pair of hands," Tyler said. "And I'm pretty quick on my feet."

"In the cemetery you weren't on your feet much at all. Hearn had to drag you," Delpha drawled, somewhat enjoying the horror that spread across his face.

"If it happens again, y'all can leave me to the zombies, no hard feelings! I brought a bag of water bottles and some good luck charms, too, just in case. Sea salt, a horseshoe, and—" Tyler stopped talking as Katybird let loose a yelp of pain. Yellow jelly beans rolled in every direction across the floor. "Katy?"

CHAPTER 18
KATYBIRD

KATY FELL TO HER HANDS AND KNEES, FRANTIC with pain. Her fingers had gone translucent and bright as fireflies. Whimpering through pressed lips, Katy looked to Delpha for help. Delpha only shifted from foot to foot, frowning and tugging the end of her braid.

Tyler squatted beside Katy and wrapped an arm around her shoulders. Katy could feel his heart thudding and skipping out of rhythm. *My messed-up magic is scarin' him*, she thought. *It's scarin' them both.* Her hands started shedding sparks. It was happening more frequently now, and more intensely, too. Katy butted her head against the wall as searing pain tore through her wrists.

"Katybird," Delpha mumbled above her in a hoarse voice, "it's . . . gonna be all right. Easy, now."

After a few long minutes, the sparks stopped flying, and Katy relaxed. Tyler let his arm fall away awkwardly, relieved.

"It felt like my arms were crawlin' with fire ants," Katy gasped. Her eyes stung with frustrated tears. "Dang it, Delpha. I'm scared to death!"

Delpha's forehead furrowed. "Don't blame you." She stalked to the window. There, she pulled out a pocketknife and began etching patterns into her wand. Tyler's jaw dropped at Delpha's coolness, and he turned to Katybird. Katy shrugged weakly. *What'd you expect?*

"Are you . . . okay?"

"Fantastic." She pointed feebly at her half-empty bag of jelly beans on the floor. "Hand 'em here?" Tyler snatched them up, tossing them to her, sheepish.

"Dumb question, I guess."

Katybird tilted the bag and dumped the candy directly into her mouth. She chomped them to a yellow sludge, telling herself not to cry again. It wouldn't fix anything. After a minute, she let out a ragged sigh. "We gotta fix my magic. Fun as that was, I don't wanna be greedy about it." She didn't add that she was starting to feel lucky every time she made it through a flare-up alive.

"Okay. We find the old Hearn well, like Echo said." Delpha took the reins. "Somewhere downtown. In the middle of Spring Fling. Without getting caught. Before the zombies get there. And before anyone sees them." She lifted a finger as each new point occurred to her.

"No big deal," groaned Katybird, rolling her eyes.

"I have an idea," Tyler realized aloud, grateful to have something to add. "My uncle knows how to dowse for water. He lives a little way up the ridge. He's kind of a weirdo, but he can help us." Tyler slung his bag over his shoulder eagerly.

Delpha sucked in a short breath, and her dark eyes roamed the floor uneasily. "Don't think we have any other options. All right. Let's go."

"Sounds good," said Katy. "But how're we gonna get there?"

Delpha pocketed her knife. "I'm driving."

Katy winced. *Fabulous.*

Checking that the yard was clear, the three hurried from the house. The screen door banged shut, and Delpha jogged to the woodshed. Katybird jammed her hands down into her hoodie, trying not to feel useless.

"Everything's gonna be fine. Uncle Clement's a good guy. He'll show us how to find the well."

"Sure. We'll be fine as frog's hair," Katy muttered, then groaned. "Did I say that?"

Tyler grinned. "Yep. You're, like, eighty thousand years old."

Delpha hollered across the yard, "You two, stop jabberin'! I'm trying to help you, so if you'd let me focus, that'd be nice." Katy ground her teeth. Delpha flicked her wrist, but Puppet didn't move. Delpha's ribs expanded with a deep breath, and she staggered a few steps sideways on the lawn. Katy winced as a trickle of blood escaped Delpha's nostril.

"Think we might should climb inside first?" Tyler suggested.

"Shed's not that sturdy anymore, after crashin' in the graveyard. Better not climb in until after I spell it good, so we don't"—Delpha grunted and winced—"fall through the loose floorboards."

"Hey, Delpha, go easy—"

"Can't. Ain't time to wait around." Delpha's neck muscles strained, and Puppet rose upward with sluggish momentum, creaking and groaning. Delpha smiled a tiny smile, then shoved open Puppet's door and waved them over. "C'mon, Katy. We'll give you a hand. You don't look s'good."

Delpha looked green around the edges herself, but Katy didn't point that out. Katy stepped into Tyler's hands, letting him boost her into the shed, then frowned as Delpha swayed.

"Delpha?"

"I'm fine," Delpha muttered, bracing herself on the doorframe.

A split second later, a guttural screech split the air, echoing off the side of the house. Katybird whirled toward the sound. Half a dozen decomposing witches stepped from the woods onto Katy's lawn.

The lead zombie's jaw hung at a low, crooked angle beneath empty eye sockets, giving her a ghoulish look of surprise. Two more were dried-out and withered, the skin of their legs crackling under skirts thin as spiderwebs. Another was gooey, and her foot twisted sideways with every step. Horror rose in Katy's throat, and she fought not to retch.

These zombies had wands. McGills. The leader of the pack moved first, and the rest followed, fast closing the gap between the woods and Katy's house. The zombie in charge was near enough now for Katy to hear her speak as she waved her wand. "Says right there on the mailbox, *The Hearns*!"

Suddenly, in terrible unison, the zombies swiveled their grinning maws toward Puppet, locking sockets on Delpha, Katy, and Tyler. The zombies changed course and sped toward the woodshed, wands lifted.

"Time to go!" yelped Delpha. Katy and Tyler helped Delpha into Puppet, and then Tyler tried to scramble up after her. Before Delpha and Katy could haul him in by the wrists, another group of zombie grannies emerged from the opposite end of the tree line, accompanied by skeletal cats and brandishing mossy rolling pins and garden rakes. *Hearn zombies.*

Tyler froze up and swayed like he might faint. "Tyler, don't you dare!" Katy cried. The girls pulled until their neck veins bulged, but Tyler felt like a two-ton sack of flour.

The McGill leader let out a demonic screech. "It's them dratted Hearns! Come over here, you daft besoms, and I'll turn you into hogs!" This sentiment was supported by a general inarticulate cry of "Aaiiiiiiieeeeeeeeee!" from the rest of the undead McGills.

The Hearn grannies jeered at this and let loose a string of profanity that would turn a coal miner scarlet. Then, to Katy's disgust, her undead ancestors lifted their blackened skirts and dropped bloomers, mooning the McGills in an impressive display of rotting, wrinkled hineys.

Tyler gagged and exclaimed, "That's nasty!"

The undead McGill leader spun around and grinned at him. With a low, purr-like growl, she crept forward, savoring his terror. Katybird screamed, and Delpha redoubled her efforts, yanking on Tyler's shirt. *He's going to die*, Katy thought. Blood roared through Katy's skull, and the bottom dropped out of her stomach. Delpha let go and raised her wand.

"Delpha, we can't leave him," Katy sobbed.

"Don't plan to," Delpha spat, sounding offended.

Tyler Nimble slid to the ground, landing on his feet with a *THUD*.

"I'm a good person. I'm a good person," Tyler whimpered.

He plucked off his glasses, then thrust them into Katybird's palm with a sweaty hand. Katy took them stupidly, confused. What was he doing? The zombie kept creeping forward, its squelchy growl growing louder by the second.

"Tyler, stop this!" Katy heard herself demanding. "Climb into the shed! Don't just . . . give up!"

"I'm a good person. I know I am."

"Tyler, of course you are, but the zombies don't care about that!"

"Nimble, move your butt!" Delpha barked, reaching down with her free hand and grabbing the back of Tyler's shirt. Katy followed suit, pulling with all her might. The zombie cackled and hissed, just yards away.

There was the loud *riiiiiiip* as Tyler's T-shirt lost the tug-of-war with gravity. Delpha flew backward, smacking her head against Puppet's back wall.

"I took my stoneroot herbs, I still have my right mind. It's okay . . . it's okay," Tyler babbled to himself, voice cracking, as he faced off with the zombie.

He's lost it, Katy realized with dread.

The McGill zombie lunged forward several more feet, a nasty rattle coming from the hole in its throat.

"GO AWAY," Katy screamed.

"Don't worry, Katy!" Tyler rolled his shoulders a few times, finding a new balance.

When he spoke again, Tyler's voice came out in a menacing roar. Katybird gasped at the rumbling sound and then again at the hair sprouting on the back of his neck and arms. *Oh my sweet buttered stars, his fingernails!* They'd gone long and black like some Disney villain's, and dug into his massive clenched fists with sharp tips. Katy looked at Delpha to see her reaction, but Delpha still lay on Puppet's floor, rubbing her head.

"Leave us alone," Tyler snarled.

The McGill zombie faltered, then screeched and hissed. "Unfair! We got no quarrel with the Snarly Yows. We must destroy all Hearns, and she's one of them! Her blood must spill." It leveled a bony finger at Katybird. Katy's blood ran cold. "The curse demands it."

At Katy's last name, Tyler growled—honest-to-goodness growled like a bobcat—and seemed to grow a foot taller.

The McGill zombie arched its rotten back and spat in hatred but came no closer. "Your friends can't hide from death forever, Yow," it rasped through a slackened jaw. "Eye for eye, hair for hair! So demands the curse!" With an angry yelp, it turned back to rejoin the rest of its group in battle with the Hearn zombies and their skeletal animals.

"Very heroic, Nimble. Now get your butt in this shed before those zombies change their minds an' throttle you," Delpha shouted, snapping her fingers impatiently.

Tyler turned around, but instead of his usual freckled, jovial self, there stood a massive, terrifying brindled dog.

Katy felt the blood drain from her face. She glanced at Delpha, who seemed totally unfazed, other than a telltale twitch in her left eye. *The zombies are gone*, she told herself. *And Tyler is . . . a what?* Her legs felt wobbly. This was weird with a beard. Too weird.

Delpha shouted, "Butt, Nimble! In the shed! *Now!*"

Tyler leaped inside, crashing onto the boards on all fours. As soon as he landed, he began to contort and change shape. It was hurting him, the pain written on his face, plain as day. That snapped Katy out of it. Whatever *this* was, it was still Tyler. She grabbed his shoulders. "It's okay. It's all right now. You're okay," she soothed. He collapsed against Puppet's wall, shaking.

By the time he was done shifting, Puppet was already running—to Delpha's credit, she hadn't wasted much time gawking at Tyler's bizarre entrance. Katy felt another jab of envy. The girl had more grit than a sandal on a dirt road. Delpha grunted in concentration as she steered the animated shed into the woods opposite the zombies and up the hill.

Both the legs of Tyler's shorts and his Trampled by Turtles T-shirt hung in stretched-out tatters around his body. The air was musty with the smell of dog, too. His chin trembled a bit, and he shot Katy a nervous glance as he sat up.

Katybird handed him his glasses and whispered, "You okay?"

Tyler blushed a brilliant crimson. "I'm so sorry . . . about that."

"What for? Don't be silly," Delpha spat, not taking her eyes off the cutout hole in Puppet's door as the woodshed veered left. "We got away from the zombies, and that's what matters." Katy nodded in agreement, biting her tongue to keep her questions from escaping. They all seemed, well, rude. But Tyler could read her mind.

"I'm . . . I'm a Snarly Yow. It's like a Celtic weredog." He twirled a shaky finger in the air in mock celebration, then shoved his glasses on miserably. "Surprise, y'all."

"Can't . . . can't say that I've heard of that before," Katy managed. She was working too hard to be polite, her voice too formal, but she couldn't help it. "Is that like . . . magic?"

"Kinda. My uncle claims his side of the family descended from the Irish shape-shifting goddess Morrigan and the hero Cú Chulainn. It's a kind of protective magic. It lets you change form when you need to defend something."

"You can change into anything?"

Tyler shook his head, cheeks still hot. "Just the one thing. A kind of werehound, like a guard dog. I'm not too proud of it, though. I'm more of a K-pop and *Great British Bake Off* kind of person. I don't like scarin' folks. Or hurtin' them. Makes me feel like some sort'a creep." He swallowed hard and shoved his hands under his armpits. His hair stood on end above his round hazel eyes, making him look more like a baby bird than a magical guard dog. Katy stifled a giggle. Compared to the horrors her fight with Delpha had unleashed in the graveyard, Tyler was about as creepy as a blueberry muffin.

"Well, I'm glad you did it. We owe you one."

"And you didn't faint," Delpha grunted.

Tyler's hundred-watt smile was back.

"Now what do we do?" Katy asked in a hoarse voice.

Delpha cracked her knuckles, nostrils flaring. "Stick to the plan. We learn how to dowse for Hearn well water. Then we Reverse-Curse the heck out of those zombies. Tyler, how do we get to your uncle's house?"

"You know the clearing atop Graystone Mountain? He's the only house up there."

Delpha thought for a minute, then veered Puppet to the right. "Yep."

They were back on track.

So why didn't Katybird feel better?

Beside her, Tyler chewed his thumbnail, deep in thought. The corners of his mouth turned slightly downward. When he caught Katy staring, he smiled and looked away.

Doubt hummed in Katy's ear. *Everyone here is doing their part. 'Cept you, of course.* Katy tightened her stomach and shifted uncomfortably on Puppet's wooden floor. She'd try extra hard. They'd find the well water, they'd find her "bond," and then Katybird Hearn would start pulling her weight. She'd find Podge, too, and soon enough, they'd be safe and sound in her bedroom, snuggled under blankets.

We'll see, Doubt responded.

CHAPTER 19
DELPHA

HAIR ESCAPED DELPHA'S BRAID AND CLUNG TO her damp cheeks in ribbons. Her throbbing head protested as she concentrated on Puppet's stacked-stone legs. After nearly toppling the shed a dozen times that morning, she was starting to get a feel for guiding Puppet across the uneven terrain with her magic. She had to feel the stones with her mind, then pretend hard they were magnets, attracting and repelling and never actually touching one another. It required total focus—one stray thought might send them cartwheeling over an escarpment or into a rocky gully. Clutching her wand helped. With it, her magic felt more focused. And way more drained.

This was taking a lot longer than she'd have liked. But she'd rest once they reached Clement's house. Tyler or Katybird could learn to dowse for water, and Delpha could lay down somewhere quiet and go over the Reverse-Curse again with a fine-toothed comb.

She was good at plans. The girl who didn't need anyone. That was Delpha McGill. If you had a good enough plan, being alone was easy. Even so, she wished someone could see her carving her way up Graystone Mountain with nothing but a wand. Katy and Tyler didn't count. Not Mama, either. Mama'd combust on the spot if she saw Delpha doing that forbidden thing they didn't talk about. Who did that leave?

Without meaning to, Delpha's mind flashed to the worn denim jacket again, and then to the wolf-handled knife in her pocket. Wouldn't her long-lost daddy feel foolish once he realized exactly *who* he'd abandoned? Or how little his absence had mattered? With a tiny thrill, Delpha pictured a flicker of regret in his eyes. As she did, her concentration flagged, and Puppet lurched violently to the left, and a low-hanging tree branch sheared several shingles off the outhouse roof.

"Dang it!" Delpha cursed at herself, heart still racing from the close call, and she reclaimed her focus. Up, up, up the mountain they went.

As Puppet neared the peak, a massive black cloud floated into their path—gnats! Delpha gagged as one collided with the back of her throat, and another stabbed her square in the eyeball. Through watery eyes, she saw a long dirt road ahead and veered onto it. Delpha clenched her teeth and dug Puppet's back legs into the dirt, like brakes. With a groan and a joint-crunching thud, Puppet flipped onto its back and skidded across the road, spewing stones and clods of red clay before grating to a halt.

Delpha couldn't breathe. Tyler and Katybird lay sprawled on top of her in a jumble, banged up but alive.

"Delpha McGill—tell me you didn't do that on purpose!" Katybird moaned. "How hard can it be to stop without crashing?"

Delpha licked her finger and fished the gnat from her eye, then slumped, hollow with exhaustion. "I stopped so we *wouldn't* crash."

Tyler's muffled voice reverberated against the wall. "Are we there yet?"

"I dunno. I hope so."

The three of them climbed out, groaning and massaging various bumps and bruises. Tyler glanced around. "Hey, nice work, Delpha! Clement's house is just up the way." He motioned along the sloping dirt road.

"Let's drag Puppet to the side of the road and walk the rest of the way," Delpha said. "In case anyone comes along."

Tyler and Katybird helped Delpha roll the outhouse into the ditch. Delpha released her spell on Puppet then, letting it collapse into boards. Tyler went behind some trees to change his tattered clothes, and then they all trudged up the road. The packed dirt beneath Delpha's feet swam, and she staggered with exhaustion.

"Want to lean on my shoulder, Delpha?" Tyler offered, frowning.

"Nope."

"How 'bout Katy's?"

Delpha shot him a look.

He wilted, then recovered. "Oh! Listen. We've gotta be polite when we go in to meet Clement."

"I'm always polite," Katybird protested.

"Not just polite. Like, we have to be extra gentle," Tyler insisted, with a pointed look in Delpha's direction. "Clement's kinda eccentric. Don't get me wrong—he's the nicest fella you'll ever meet. He's just diff'rent. People make him nervous."

"Fine. You talk to him. But don't tell him why we're dowsing for the well. Or about Katy's messed-up magic. Or the zombies, or any witches at all." Delpha sighed hard, rubbing her temples and ignoring her growling belly. *If you want something done right, do it yourself.* "Never mind. I'll talk to him. Y'all stay here."

A cluster of ramshackle buildings loomed ahead. Tyler hesitated, then pointed at a monstrous red barn with peeling paint. "He'll be in there."

Delpha stowed her wand and book in her satchel, then set off for the barn, careful not to trip over exposed live oak roots. Under her breath, she rehearsed how she'd make her request to Tyler's uncle. But as soon as she stepped inside the barn, her words vaporized.

The sweet, sharp aroma of hewn wood hung in the air, and the ground was littered with curled shavings and sawdust. In the back right corner were circular saws, jigsaws, and about every other kind of saw Delpha could dream of. Along the length of the right wall, row upon row of carving chisels dangled from hooks. Beneath them, on a shelf, wooden bowls with dogwood blossoms and strands of ivy etched into their sides gleamed beside an open can of linseed oil.

Delpha's hand darted out to touch one, and, finding it mostly dry, she raised it to the light to examine it, turning it slowly and looking for the telltale wobble of poor symmetry. A low whistle escaped between her teeth. It was almost perfect.

Someone coughed behind her, and Delpha nearly jumped out of her skin. She spun, feeling sheepish, but managed not to drop the bowl.

"I'm Clement. Can I help you?" Tyler's uncle looked flinchingly at the ground, hair falling into his face. His nervous sway put Delpha in mind of a sweet-natured dog that someone had kicked too many times. He still didn't look up.

"I'm a friend of your nephew, Tyler. He said you know how to dowse. I wondered if you'd take a minute to teach us."

"Sure, sure," Clement said, glancing up. He wiped his hands on his apron, even though they already looked clean. "Let me just, uh, let me just . . ." He shuffled in a circle. The wall behind him was plastered with dozens of maps. Unlike the rest of the tidy workshop, they'd been fixed to the wall haphazardly and marked with frantic circles and lines.

Clement raked his mop of fire-hued curls away from his face, frowning as if looking for something. It was the sort of long hair that wasn't long on purpose but had accidentally grown right past haircut day. Eccentric, like Tyler had said. Tyler's warning to be gentle rang in her head, but they needed Katy's magic fixed an hour ago.

"Listen, we're in a hurry."

Clement put a hand to his chin, like he might cry. "I'm sorry," he muttered. "Folks usually have appointments."

The clock radio on the worktable switched from songs to a cheerful report of "today's annual Spring Fling in our very own downtown Howler's Hollow!" No reports of zombies. *Yet.* Delpha breathed a sigh. There was still time, then. If she could only get this guy to calm down and cooperate . . .

"Um," Delpha blurted, pulling her own ornate carving knife from her pocket and waving it. "I like carvin'. Maybe I'll come back for a class sometime, and I'll make an appointment then. How's that? But today's sort of an emergency."

Clement gazed at her oddly for several moments, then brightened. "That's a nice knife you got there."

Delpha bit back her impatience. Tyler's uncle seemed to be calming down, at least. "I'm partial to it. Needs sharpening, though. Been carvin' a lot lately."

"May I?" He held out an open palm. "I could fix 'er up for ya."

Delpha hesitated, then handed her knife over, hoping to speed him along.

Clement took the knife and studied the ornate handle. He sucked in a long breath, glancing up at Delpha with nervous eyes. Then, with shaky hands, he unfolded the knife and studied the blade. He reached up to a shelf, took down a whetstone, and drizzled it with mineral oil, then set to work. "'S good to keep 'er real sharp so you don't cut yourself," he said in a soft voice, glancing up at Delpha with his mournful eyes. "Nothin' worse'n a dull blade."

Delpha scowled. "I know that. I just ain't had the chance to do it lately, that's all."

"'Course, 'course," Clement said, clearing his throat and bobbing his head. "Didn't mean nothin' by it. You prob'ly keep real busy with school, I reckon."

"I whittle lots to help make ends meet, actually," Delpha blurted. *Why did she say that?* Her blasted pride was throwing her off track.

Clement frowned hard. "It ain't too bad, anyway. I can tell you take good care of it. Real, real good." He worked for a couple of minutes in silence, moving from the whetstone to a smoother ceramic stone, and finally a worn leather strop. Delpha tried to look uninterested, but she watched his expert movements like a hawk, making a mental note to save up for her own ceramic stone. *Someday.* Clement picked up a half-carved wooden bird from his worktable and tested the carving blade for sharpness. For a minute, Delpha forgot about the zombies and magic and the Hearn well, mesmerized as a sparrow evolved from the pine in Clement's hands. Finally satisfied, he closed Delpha's knife and handed it over. "Sharp as a razor. She's a real beauty."

"Thanks," Delpha muttered gruffly.

"You can take the bird, too, if y'like. Or come back sometime again with Tyler, and I'll show you how to carve your own."

If I survive the zombies today and get my magic in order, maybe Mama an' me really can have enough money for me to take lessons, Delpha wished.

"No charge. It ain't any trouble," Clement added, like he'd read her mind.

"Maybe. Now about the water-witchin' . . ."

"Right. I can teach y'all to dowse."

He loped toward the door, leaving Delpha to run after him. Outside, Clement busied himself with collecting a Y-shaped tree branch. Delpha crossed the circular yard to the place Tyler and Katy sat munching granola bars with tired faces.

"Hearn, how are your hands?" Delpha whispered, glancing over her shoulder nervously.

"They glowed while you were in the barn," Katy admitted. Her lips were pale. "Liketa screamed bloody murder they stung so bad."

Tyler nodded in concern. "Her face went white as chalk."

Delpha smelled their food, and a wave of hunger hit her. She'd been so distracted by the workshop, she hadn't realized how dizzy she was.

Tyler dug around in his messy bag. "Want a box of raisins or a Pop-Tart?"

"Yes!" Delpha yelped. She snatched both and bolted the entire box of raisins like a starved animal. Halfway through devouring a sleeve of Pop-Tarts, Delpha heard Clement call out that he was ready. Tyler gazed at the dowsing rod wistfully. Delpha crammed the other pastry into her mouth.

"Katybird should rest," she observed, spewing crumbs. "I need to keep eating. Nimble, you're up. Go learn to dowse."

Tyler beamed, leaping up and bounding over to Clement.

"That was nice of you," Katy said, dimples sprouting in approval.

"It's not nice," Delpha grumbled. "It's delegating." But behind the box of Pop-Tarts, she found herself smiling, too.

"All right," Clement instructed in a reedy voice. "First, cut you a forked tree limb, like this. Then . . . you wanna grip the two handles with your hands"—he demonstrated with a fresh green hazel bough—"and let the end of the stick pull you along."

Tyler scrunched his face. "Huh?"

Clement squinted at the sky. "You ever been fishin'? You know the feelin' when a fish nibbles at the line? The dowsin' rod feels kindly the same when it's found water. You follow the bite."

After several tries, Tyler seemed to catch the hang of it, eventually navigating his way across some rotting boards that covered a hole in the ground. His foot went through. He yanked it out and shook a foul, gray goop from the bottom of his tennis shoe. "What the heck?" he howled.

"Well, Tyler, you dowsed and found my kitchen cesspit," Clement praised.

"You mean I'm standin' in . . . you know what?"

Delpha tried not to laugh. "*Kitchen* cesspit, you peckerwood. It's runoff from the sink. Old houses have 'em. Looks like you're a pro, Tyler. Time to go."

Clement put a hand on Tyler's shoulder, serious. "Underground pipes can trick you. Best to fix in your head which water you want to find."

Before Tyler could respond, a grating *BEEEEEEEEP* sounded from the radio in the barn, signaling the city's emergency alert system. Delpha and Katybird exchanged looks, then raced into the workshop to hear the message that followed. A tinny voice buzzed from the speaker in announcement:

"The Pisgah National Forest issues the following warning to Howler's Hollow residents: Evidence of unusual large predator behavior has been found on several hiking trails, including Memorial Gap, Skip to My Lou, Woven Branch, and Murphy's Pass. Citizens are advised to stay close to main streets or public areas. If you see wildlife, do not approach it. Be safe, and feel free to enjoy our yearly Spring Fling."

Delpha and Katy exchanged glances. "The zombies are spreading out," Katy whimpered. Her hands plunged deep into her hoodie pockets, but the light peeked out at her wrists anyway.

In her mind, Delpha traced a straight line from the Wise Woman Cemetery to the Hearn farm, then to the hiking trails mentioned on the radio. They were just several miles north of Main Street. "They're working closer to downtown," Delpha agreed. Her throat tightened.

The girls dashed outside. When Clement wasn't looking, Delpha mouthed to Tyler, *ZOMBIES*. Tyler's forehead wrinkled, then he said something to Clement. The gangly man beamed broadly and clapped Tyler on the shoulder, then walked into his house, a spring in his step, whistling. The smile looked out of place on his worried face, but like his nephew's, it was huge and infectious.

Tyler stumble-ran across the yard, calling, "Okay, let's go! Do your thing with Puppet, fast!"

"What'd you tell him?" Delpha asked.

"I told him your mom was picking us up at the bottom of the driveway, and I'd see him later this afternoon." The way Tyler's cheeks flamed, Delpha could tell it was killing him to lie to his uncle. Delpha felt bad, too, but they didn't have any choice. She decided she'd come back for a whittling class someday to make up for it. *No charge*, he'd said. Delpha found her heart feeling lighter.

The late-morning sun filtered through the trees and warmed the back of Delpha's neck as they ran. Halfway to Puppet, Katybird doubled over, gasping. Her hands sparked. Delpha's insides churned as she watched Tyler try to comfort Katy, whose face had turned unnaturally pale. Delpha squirmed. She hated watching people in pain.

"C'mon," Delpha barked, reaching to grab Katybird by the elbow. "We have to keep going!"

"Delpha, let her rest!" Tyler shouted.

"She can glow in Puppet same as here. We've got to beat the zombies to town." Delpha leaned behind Katybird's back and mouthed, "And her magic fits are getting worse." As if in agreement, a wave of helter-skelter energy radiated from Katy's hands, making Delpha's skin crawl.

"I think y'all need to ask your mamas for help," Tyler muttered, hazel eyes flashing.

"Not gonna happen."

"You ought to ask them, Delpha," Tyler said louder, his chin jutting. "This is dangerous!"

Cold, stubborn anger shot through Delpha, and she felt herself go stony inside. Her mama would blow a gasket if she found out. Besides, Delpha hadn't even wanted to be tied to Katybird Hearn in the first place. Working alone made a person less vulnerable. Other people meant one of two things: Either they tried to stop you and tell you what you couldn't do, or they wound their way into your heart, only to rip themselves out later on. Either way, asking for help meant other people meddling with your peace.

She leaned in close to Tyler's freckled face. "That," Delpha repeated, voice calm, "is not going to happen. There is a plan. We stick to it."

Tyler's fists clenched. "Fine. Be as stubborn as you want. But I'm staying here with Katy till she's ready to walk. Why don't you go start Puppet, and we'll catch up."

Delpha started walking and braced herself for the awful headache that seemed part and parcel of being a puppet maker.

As she raised her wand, faraway demon shrieks echoed through the hills behind her. *Maybe it's only hawks*, she told herself. But Delpha knew better.

CHAPTER 20
KATYBIRD

KATYBIRD WIPED FINE ROAD DUST FROM HER hands with a wet wipe, courtesy of Tyler's bag. Static whined from the portable radio in Tyler's lap as he tried without luck to tune it to a Forest Service frequency.

Delpha walked ahead to wake Puppet with magic—magic Delpha seemed to be mastering by the minute.

Meanwhile, Katybird remained a pointless good-for-nothing. The more Katy thought about this, the worse the ache in her stomach got. Strange screeches like giant eagles sounded through the forest, and Katy kept picturing poor Podge being snatched up by sharp talons, wondering why his girl didn't come save him.

Cleaning her hands felt the tiniest bit useful, so she kept at it until Tyler cleared his throat.

"Katybird? Doesn't it . . . seem a little irresponsible, not asking your parents for help? I mean, even if we find the well water and figure out what the heck a 'bond' is, we still might be too late. Folks could get hurt."

Katy clammed up, hating to admit Tyler was right. *Even if I am a failure as a witch*, she thought, *I could save people by telling Mama and Nanny.* But their disappointed faces jumped into her mind, like always, and her heart locked up with fear.

Tyler frowned and pressed harder. "'Sides, I don't really love the idea of turnin' into Big 'n' Ugly again. Threatening folks ain't really my style. Help . . . oughta look like being kind."

"Are zombies really folks?" Katy asked, nose wrinkled.

"Guess not," Tyler admitted. "Still. Seems like we might be in over our heads."

"Maybe. It's complicated." Katy struggled to her feet and they began walking toward Puppet.

Tyler bit his lip. "I mean, unless you think we can really do it. Are you pretty sure you can do the hex, once we find the well?"

Katy's heart thudded. "Tyler? Can you keep a secret?"

"Sure." Tyler scratched his ear. "I've had a lot of practice, I guess, with the whole Snarly Yow thing."

Katy drew a ragged breath. "Okay, here it is. I'm not sure my magic can be fixed. Hearn magic travels from mother to daughter, woman to woman. And I have something called androgen insensitivity."

Tyler's face fell. "Are you . . . you ain't dying, are you?"

"No, silly. I'm not sick. It's just . . . I have XY chromosomes, where most girls have two Xs. And even though I like myself fine, I think maybe I've confused the magic. Like it might not work for me. Ever." Saying it out loud was a relief, but now, her worry felt more real.

"Oh. Huh. Cool."

Katy raised an eyebrow. "I don't think having goofed-up magic is very 'cool.'"

"I meant . . . the other thing. You're unique!"

"Yeah. But that's why I'm worried."

"So why not ask your family to help you?"

Katy jutted her chin. "I still want to try to do it alone. I've got to. I don't want to disappoint Delpha. And my family will feel sorry for me, or worry about me, and I don't want that."

Tyler's eyebrows furrowed. "But if folks see the zombies, they'll start asking questions. Don't you reckon they'll trace it back to your family?"

Katy walked faster. They'd almost caught up with Delpha. The dark-haired girl stood with shoulders drooped, struggling to animate Puppet. Katy lowered her voice.

"Probably. If the zombies don't kill them first."

"Maybe if we figure out what a 'bond' is, that'll help," Tyler offered. He smiled, but his eyes stayed clouded. *He's trying to be hopeful for my sake*, Katy realized. Even though his optimism was just a kindness, it made her want to fight for her magic.

"My cousin's ghost said 'my fur' right before she disappeared. I think that might be a clue to what my 'bond' is. What could 'my fur' mean?"

"Fur coat? Maybe she was super attached to it and misses it."

"That ain't it. Fur . . . furniture? Fertilizer?"

"Furby?"

Katy giggled. "Furbies are not magical. They're creepy."

Puppet groaned, coming to life. Delpha wiped her nose on her sleeve, then spat red into the dirt. Katy winced. "You got more food in that bag?" she whispered. "Delpha'll be hungry as a bear again. Doing magic turns her into a food furnace."

Tyler unzipped the backpack. "We're down to baby carrots, Vienna sausages, and broccoli."

Katybird wrinkled her nose. "You brought broccoli? Even my mama's plant magic can't make broccoli taste good."

Tyler wiggled his eyebrows. "But it's good for you! And d'you know the scientific name 'crucifer' comes from the same Latin root as 'crucify'? Guess the ancient Romans thought broccoli was pure torture too."

Tyler laughed at his own joke, then kept chattering. But the phrase "pure torture" stuck in Katybird's mind like a song on repeat. Pure torture, *pure torture*. Katy had heard that recently, but when? Her forehead puckered. The words felt important. She tried the trick of thinking of something else instead, but nothing popped into her head.

"C'mon, y'all!" Delpha called. She sagged inside Puppet's doorway, wand raised. Katy and Tyler climbed inside, as anxious as Delpha to get going.

Puppet lurched down the hill, jarring Katy's bones. Tyler settled cross-legged on the floor, still fiddling with his portable radio. "Too bad your cousin couldn't have been clearer about the whole 'bond' thing."

Delpha snorted. "Seeing as she's dead, I'd say she did her best. Anyway, you didn't help much, Nimble. Next time, knock," she spat.

"Oh, I'm sorry, I'll knock the next time I'm risking my neck to warn you that your pet zombies have escaped—"

Katy wished they'd both shut up, because her thoughts were confetti in a whirlwind. "Pure torture" still plagued her. She absentmindedly picked some of Podge's shed fur from her sleeve. Katy's thoughts gathered into a single idea. *Podge!*

"That's IT!" Katybird exclaimed, grabbing Delpha's sleeve. "I think Echo was sayin' it was pure torture being parted from Fatso, her cat!"

Delpha shook her arm loose. "Don't touch the driver! What do you mean?"

Katybird turned to Tyler, heart racing. "What do all the Hearn zombies have in common?"

"Poor skin care?"

"Pets! They all have animals! When Echo said 'my fur,' I think she meant her fur baby—her pet! She was talking about Fatso!"

"You think Fatso was Echo's bond?"

"Yes! And if Fatso is Echo's bond, that means I need a bond, too. It's my raccoon, Podge. It has to be. He's like . . . my heart!"

"This is turning into a wild-goose chase, Hearn," Delpha groaned. "Are you sure you can't just try harder to make your magic work? We're cutting it close here."

"I'm doing the best I can!" Katy protested. She swallowed the fat lump in her throat. "We can't all be you. Now, will you help me find Podge, or not?"

Stomp, stomp, stomp went Puppet's legs. After several tense minutes, Delpha let out a frazzled sigh. "All right, Katy. After we find the well."

"Thanks," Katy whispered.

Tyler resumed messing with the radio dial like nothing had happened, but Katy suppressed a smile. Delpha had used Katy's first name. And she'd agreed to help Katy find Podge. A friendly, warm sensation—hope, Katy realized—spread from her heart outward.

Maybe we'll make it to town before the zombies get there. Maybe Podge isn't dead, after all. Maybe we won't all die.

Doubt tried to whisper in Katybird's ear, same as always.

To drown it out, Katy kept right on maybe-ing herself to the rhythm of Puppet's running, like a prayer.

Maybe we'll find the well water, then find Podge, then fix my magic.

Maybe we'll undo the curse, and I'll make my mama and nanny proud, after all.

Maybe I'll be a nature talker.

Maybe I'm a real witch.

Maybe, maybe, maybe.

CHAPTER 21
DELPHA

BY THE TIME THEY'D SKIDDED TO A STOP ON THE
edge of town, Tyler looked green from Puppet's frantic side-to-side
rocking. He looked crabby, too, as he fished through his bag and
pulled out a bag of carrots and a container of herb capsules, yanking
on the zipper harder than strictly necessary. "Here," he said, thrusting
the carrot bag into Delpha's hands before swallowing one of the capsules. Delpha wiped the blood from her nose and raised an eyebrow.

Katy was quieter than normal, too. She was twisting her friend-
ship bracelets on her wrists nonstop, looking nervously around every
few seconds.

Delpha's muscles felt like she'd been hit by a falling piano. She grimaced in the blinding midday sun and crunched a carrot. No sign of the zombies.

They left Puppet hidden in a stand of cypress trees behind the hardware store with the McGill spellbook inside—it was a hair conspicuous looking—then quietly trudged toward the quaint congregation of buildings that was downtown Howler's Hollow.

The tantalizing haze of pit-style barbecue smoke drifted through the air along with the clingy odor of fresh-cut grass. An employee from Sadie's Kitchen clanged the bell in front of the restaurant to announce they were now serving an early lunch of fresh sweet tea, fried catfish, and shrimp 'n' grits. Microphone feedback shrieked from a large gazebo stage as a voice boomed, "Test, one-two-three, a-hey-and-ahidey-ho!" Soft flapping and *ting, ting, ting* sounds filled the air as a breeze teased its way through dozens of canvas booths tied onto metal frames, providing relief to the craftspeople as they sold their wares in the midday heat. Katy plastered a cheerful smile on, and Tyler bounced on his heels, apparently buoyed from the sudden rush of chatter.

Main Street was crammed to the edges with folks scarfing fried plantains, fish, and boiled peanuts. Delpha's head swam with hunger, and she stumbled in her boots, crashing into a balding man holding a funnel cake. The man brushed off his shirt and snarled at Delpha,

"Watch it, young'un!" Delpha apologized, but the man only eyed Delpha suspiciously.

Katy's breath was hot on Delpha's ear as she hissed, "For mercy's sake, Delpha, your wand!"

Delpha snatched the wand from behind her ear and thrust it into her back pocket.

"What are you young'uns playin' at? Wizards?" A tense smile settled on the man's face. "Ain't you . . . Kathleen McGill's girl?"

Fear pierced through Delpha's chest. She shook her head stupidly. Her brain was so tired, it wasn't working right. Katybird slid in and winked. "Hi, Mr. Bell. Delpha's working on a top secret whittlin' project for the museum, but we'll let you in on it since you're a patron. She's tryin' her hand at making full-sized Irish whistles."

Delpha bobbed her head in agreement. *Bless you, Hearn.*

Mr. Bell's wife joined him. "Well, Katybird Hearn! Your mama's been worried sick about you all mornin', baby. I heard her askin' around for you down at the museum booth."

"Thanks, Miz Imogene. I'll go right down and see her," Katy replied politely. Out of the corner of her eye, Delpha saw Katy pull her hands into her jacket sleeves.

The couple wandered off, whispering as they went.

"That was close," Katybird muttered. Her bottom lip wobbled. "My mama's worried about me. She's right to be, too, Delpha."

"Don't get off track," Delpha snapped. The world around her spun in a tilt-a-whirl of food smells, bright sun, and crowd chatter. One of her knees buckled. She reached into her pocket for the familiar comfort of her knife, but her fingertips brushed nothing but grit and lint. *Gone.* Where had she lost it? She groaned inwardly. Probably jostled out while she was driving Puppet. They'd covered miles of mountainside, and now it was probably lost for good. *It don't matter*, she chided herself. But it did. Delpha felt sick.

"You need somethin' besides rabbit food," Katy observed. "You're a mess. Your magic is liketa kill you if you don't slow down!"

Several heads nearby jerked in their direction.

"Ix-nay on the agic-may!" Tyler muttered through a fake grin.

"I'm going to get you some nachos," Katy huffed.

Delpha's stomach vetoed her objections. "Don't be gone longer than five minutes," she snapped. "Tyler and I will keep at it."

Katy nodded and scurried off into the crowd.

"This is it," Delpha said without turning to Tyler. "You got your dowsing stick?"

Tyler nodded. He pulled out the dowsing rod and drew a deep breath.

"Remember what Clement said," Delpha reminded him. "Picture the old Hearn well in your head."

Tyler winced as families streamed around them with foil-wrapped sausage biscuits and steaming coffee in their hands, oblivious to the impending zombie doom. "This is weird-lookin', even for me."

Delpha grunted. "Better weird than dead."

"Here goes nothin'," he muttered, closing his eyes and taking a deep breath. "I'm dowsing for the old magic Hearn well." The hazel-wood branch jerked sideways so powerfully, it nearly pulled his arms clean out of their sockets. He stumbled forward on the pavement. "Whoa! We shouldn't have ANY trouble finding this well," he said, grinning.

Delpha's pulse quickened. "Good. Keep going."

They weaved through the crowd and past the tents, ignoring quizzical looks and glares as Tyler was pulled along like a drunken go-kart driver, sometimes bumping into people or strollers. "Sorry, sir. 'Scuse me, ma'am." Delpha winced at the trail of whispers and looks that followed them, but there was no helping it. She hoped to goodness they'd write it off as Tyler being, well, Tyler.

Finally, the two of them circled the massive gazebo stage that sat halfway down Main Street, where a troupe of traditional cloggers stamped out a rhythm to a live bluegrass band. The gazebo was raised several feet off the ground on stilts, with the space beneath covered in latticework. After several times around the structure, it was clear the dowsing rod was determined to lead them underneath the gazebo.

"What're we gonna do?" Tyler moaned. "There's lattice. And probably eighty people here watching the cloggers!"

"Let's go around the back," Delpha replied, scanning the crowd. "Where's Katy?" Tyler shrugged. "C'mon, then." Delpha and Tyler shuffled through the audience, then circled behind the gazebo. There, they found a narrow gap in the lattice for electrical maintenance and wiggled through, crouching to avoid hitting their heads. The cloggers' feet pounded a deafening cadence above, and Delpha had to shout in Tyler's ear.

"We'll have to dig," she hollered.

Tyler unzipped his bag and produced a tiny, fold-up shovel, used for digging latrines while camping. Delpha stuck out her bottom lip and nodded in approval. They took turns digging up the packed red clay, pausing here and there to wipe sweat onto their sleeves. About a foot deep, when Tyler's wrists had begun to ache and a small pile of dirt had accumulated beside the hole, the shovel hit something with a dull *thunk*. Delpha's heart jumped.

They uncovered the object with shaking hands. It turned out to be a rotting wooden box. Nestled inside it was a petite antique glass bottle of murky brown liquid. The label had long disintegrated, so Delpha gently worked out the cork and sniffed. "Ginseng tincture," she said, wrinkling her nose and replacing the cork.

The cloggers stamped offstage, and a fiddle began to play a soft reel overhead. Tyler dropped his voice to a whisper.

"What's that?"

"It's made from one of the most valuable plants in this region. Folks have harvested it till it's endangered." Delpha tilted the old bottle, swirling the liquid. "That's what this is."

"You can't know that!"

"I do. My mama's no stalk witch, but she does make tinctures. It always smells like armpit."

"All right. Well, toss it and let's keep digging for the well!"

"Hold up," Delpha grunted, handing Tyler the dowsing rod. "Dowse for Hearn well water again."

Tyler frowned but obeyed. This time, the dowsing stick didn't react to the spot where they'd been digging but went nuts when it got close to the tincture bottle in Delpha's hand. Tyler groaned. "Dang it. I flubbed it, Delpha. I coulda sworn I had my mind focused on the Hearn well!"

"I think you got it right. Some Hearn witch prob'ly used her well water to make a tincture, then buried it away for a rainy day, lucky for us."

"But Katy can't drink that! It'll kill her!"

"Nah," said Delpha, pursing her lips. "Tinctures keep forever. The ginseng won't hurt her. It's the water that's important, an' maybe she'll only need a drop or two. It's our best shot. Besides, we can't waste no more time."

Tyler frowned, studying her for a long minute, like he was deciding something about her. Finally he sighed. "You look awful tired, Delpha. You don't have to take care of everything yourself."

Delpha wanted that to be true. "So help me, then. Please?"

Tyler bit his lip, then nodded. "Okay. Let's go find Katybird."

CHAPTER 22

KATYBIRD

KATY HELD HER BREATH INSIDE A SMELLY port-a-john, indecision swirling in her chest. This day was literally stressing the whizz out of her. She'd caught the tiny approving smile on Tyler's face just as she'd left. He thought she was going to get her mama for help. And Delpha thought Katy was coming right back with nachos. Katy herself thought she'd rather be anywhere but here, caught between two rotten choices.

Maybe I'll let fate decide, she worried. She'd get the nachos. Then, if she ran into Delpha first, she'd keep trying the Reverse-Curse. If she ran into Mama and Nanny, she'd ask for help. *Either way, you're a disappointment*, Doubt told her.

Angrily, she slimed her hands with sanitizer before charging down the sidewalk, the noon sun stinging her neck. She kept her eyes peeled for Mr. and Mrs. Bell, too, not wanting another run-in with them after they'd seen Delpha's wand. Katy shuddered. Folks in the Hollow would be sweet as pie to your face, but they could hold on to gossip and grudges long enough to put the archangels to shame. *Not that they're wrong about us doin' magic*, she thought.

When Katy reached the end of Main Street without finding the Flores Family Taqueria stand, she doubled back between the two long rows of booths, deciding Delpha could make do with a burger from Moo and Chew. Katy's nose tickled with the smells of tooled leather, lavender-sage soaps, and the mouthwatering aroma of chili and mustard from Hot Diggity Dog. She sped by them, not stopping to chat with the folks who waved and greeted her by name. As she passed the face-painting tent, a little girl in line pointed at Katy and piped, "Mommy! I want them to paint me pretty hands like hers!" Katy glanced down in dismay to see her fingertips glimmering green.

Panicking, she pulled them into her sleeves and hurried away before the kid's mother looked up. Katy jogged behind the booths and onto the sidewalk, hurrying away from the hubbub.

Pent-up magic raged like fireballs in her knuckles and seared its way up to her elbows. Katy gasped to keep herself from hollering impolite words. She needed to be alone. All the shops would be locked, but the church was always open. Katy darted across the grass toward the brick building with a cross on it and yanked the glass door open.

The lights in the foyer were off, and Katybird stumbled inside, relieved to be alone. She curled up on the cool tile beneath a table of bulletins and wondered where Podge was. She hummed softly to herself in a shaky voice, only realizing halfway through that she'd picked "This Little Light of Mine." Katybird was too stressed to think of another song, so she decided to go with it.

Don't let magic blow you up, I'm gonna let it shine.

She'd not been in the church for ages. Her mama had stopped making her come when, after the girls from the slumber party kept praying for her "condition," Katy was forced to explain to her well-meaning youth leader that she was intersex. When they'd offered prayer for *that*, Katy had decided to stay home and watch cartoons with Podge, who appreciated Katy's awesomeness. 'Course, not showing up had meant a few elderly members had badgered her mama about whether the Hearns were backslidin' into their old ways, which was polite old-people code for witchin'. If those people could see her now, hands sparklin' with tangled-up magic, wouldn't their tongues wag? Her family would never live it down.

We'll find Podge, she decided. *We'll find the well water. Things'll be fine. If Delpha can be brave, then so can I.* The glow died down to a buzz that numbed her fingertips.

Katy headed for the front door, ready to rejoin Tyler and Delpha. Just before she grabbed the handle, a shout echoed down the long hallway leading to the fellowship hall. Someone was back there. "It's prob'ly nothing," she whispered. But she found herself moving toward the long, dark hallway anyway, sneakers squeaking on the tile.

Katy shoved open the door, then froze.

Over a dozen people stood slack-jawed around rummage sale tables, their hands clutching kitchy junk in terror. Five decaying witches stood at the center of the room with moldy wands raised. The tallest McGill zombie twisted all the way around, hissing at a tourist nearby, its eyeless sockets yawning with menace. The young woman blubbered, clutching her little purse dog protectively against her chest. Her sobs bounced eerily around the quiet room—everyone else had gone mute with fear.

It took a moment for the unthinkable to sink in: Katybird and Delpha had failed to beat a handful of cursed McGill zombies to downtown Howler's Hollow. The monsters had found their way to Spring Fling.

A wet, guttural growl made everyone jump.

"Which ones of you dawties is Hearns, then?" the zombie rasped, twirling its wand up and down its rotted fingers like a coin.

Do something, Katybird, she told herself, stomach churning. Her pulse drummed in her ears. She had no magic. No powers. But these poor people were just as defenseless, and they didn't know what they were up against. Katy looked around for a familiar face, to see who was in charge. But there was no one she recognized.

A balding man beside her took up a ceramic chicken as a weapon and moved to strike the zombie. If the man hit the zombie, he'd just make it angry. Without thinking, Katy yelled, "Stop!"

Everyone turned to look at her. Katy swallowed hard, then stepped farther into the big room and squared her shoulders. "It's part of a play rehearsal," Katybird cried, voice cracking. People's eyes flicked toward her in confusion, then back to the zombies. *Sell it, Katy*, she told herself. Sweat trickled down her back.

"But their makeup ain't done yet. It's not nearly creepy enough. Rummage sale's closed for an hour, folks. Bye!"

The shoppers relaxed. They grumbled as they filed out the door, shaking their heads. "Hillbillies!" one of them muttered.

She gulped.

The five McGill zombies turned in unison, gazing at Katy. Acid rose in Katy's throat. The nearest one lunged. With a rattling snarl, its bony fingers snatched at Katy, missing her face by a foot as Katy screamed and leaped backward. The zombies gathered around her in a slow half circle, seeming to savor her predicament. Katy was a mouse, and they were toying with her. She was dizzy with panic. She couldn't fight zombies with snarled-up magic. She glanced around the room for ideas. The zombies inched even closer, hissing. Could she distract them? They only cared about defeating the Hearns. Maybe Katy could play that against them and buy herself some time. But what might appeal universally to every old person, dead or alive?

"Th-the Hearns are on their way to this rummage sale," Katy blurted, her voice squeaking. "An' if you don't get the good stuff first, they'll snap up everything here faster than you can blink." Katy shuddered at her word choice. These things didn't have eyes to blink with. "They'll . . . they'll beat you at rummaging!"

The zombies exchanged dark looks. Katy held her breath, sweat rolling.

All at once, the undead witches attacked the rummage tables like a pack of wolves, with a savage rage that made Katy shake. The zombies shattered and shredded as much as they pocketed. One set a pile of socks on fire with her wand, filling the room with smoke. Plates smashed and silverware bounced, clanging across the floor.

Trembling, Katy scurried to the edge of the smoky room, grateful she wasn't the one being ripped to tatters. What next? The rummage sale would only keep them occupied for so long before they turned their creepy eye sockets toward the festival outside. *What would Delpha do?*

Her eyes landed on the baptismal tank at the far end of the room. The thing was, in essence, a deep bathtub on a raised platform, with walls built around it so little kids wouldn't topple in. The rectangular tank had a clear Plexiglas window on the front, so people could watch their friends and families be baptized by submersion—more or less a spiritual dunking booth. The act was meant to symbolize resurrection from death.

A wry smile played on Katy's face. It might work as a zombie jail, and there was a certain poetic irony to it. Skirting around the ransacking McGills, Katy stumbled to the baptistery and tried the big metal door. It was unlocked, but the lock mechanism was *inside* the tank, not outside. She couldn't trap the zombies with the lock like that. Rats.

The zombies smashed and ripped their way through another row of tables. Katy crawled to grab one of the fallen butter knives from the floor. When she'd gotten it, she hurried back to the baptistery door.

Katy licked her lips in concentration. Once, when Caleb was three, he'd accidentally locked himself in the bathroom while her dad was out for milk. Katy had undone the screws holding the doorknob to get Caleb out. Now she planned the same for the baptistery door.

She undid the screws with the flat knife, then yanked her half of the doorknob loose. Once that was done, she pushed the other half through, so it fell away in a clatter. Katy used her index finger to open the inside latch, swinging the door open. Then, hands shaking with fear and excitement, she replaced the handle halves backward, with the lock on the outside.

Katy glanced at the zombies, and her heart slid to her shoes as she realized not *every* innocent person had escaped the rummage sale.

The town's oldest, sweetest citizen, Mrs. Hattaway, who was mostly blind, had been manning the cash box. How had Katy not noticed? Now the tiny lady stood in the middle of the room, mistaking the zombies for actual people. "Precious saints," she warbled, "please don't do the dishes that-a-way!" She squinted at the zombies through thick glasses, clutching the money box with gnarled fingers. "I'm afraid y'all will have to pay for whatever you break!"

"Oh no, Mrs. Hattaway—!"

But Katybird wasn't fast enough. The tall McGill zombie's leathery face cracked as a smile split—*actually split*—its face. With insect-like speed, it raised its wand and landed a hex on Mrs. Hattaway's frail chest before Katybird could even scream.

It wasn't pretty magic. The old woman moaned as she slowly went gray and rigid from toe to head, like stone. Katy held her breath in horrified silence as Mrs. Hattaway's watery eyes went dull. Timidly, Katy reached with one finger to poke the old woman's arm, then leaped back, shuddering, when she felt cool granite. They'd turned Mrs. Hattaway into a tacky lawn ornament!

Katybird couldn't stop shivering from shock. Mrs. Hattaway was as much a part of the Hollow as Sadie's Kitchen or Spring Fling or the church itself. She couldn't be *dead*-dead. This couldn't really be happening. A guttural growl from one of the witch zombies assured her it really was.

The creatures turned toward Katy. She stumbled back, slipping on ceramic plate shards and slicing her elbow open. Chest tight, she jumped to her feet and screamed with all the ferocity she could muster. "The Hearns are in there!" She pointed at the baptistery door. "After them!"

All five zombies erupted with snarls and bloodthirsty squeals, hiking up their skirts and charging the door. Katybird followed hot on their heels, praying her plan would work. The first granny zombie screeched to a halt at the doorway, sensing something was fishy. *Too late.* Her zombie sisters slammed into her full throttle from behind, and four of them fell like ugly rag dolls into the baptismal tank.

The last granny teetered on the threshold, arms flailing. Katybird lifted her purple sneaker and kicked the thing with all her might. The zombie toppled forward, and Katybird slammed the door and locked it, breathing hard.

The trapped witches snarled and cussed and beat their hands against the walls, trying to escape. One who'd been born in a century without clear plastic headbutted the Plexiglas and fell back dazed and confused. A wretched chant arose: "Kill the Hearns! Kill the Hearns!" The undead witches' crazed faces contorted with a blind hatred that sent cold dread down Katybird's spine.

"Not this Hearn, you hateful old bats!"

Katybird turned, crestfallen, at the statue that had been Mrs. Hattaway. Her eyes welled with tears. What must the poor woman have felt? Without warning, the trapped magic in Katy's hands surged, and the stinging knocked the breath from her. For a few minutes, she knelt on the glass-strewn floor and felt sorry for herself. *If only I were like Delpha or Tyler or Mama or Nanny*, she thought. *If only my magic worked, I might have saved her . . .*

But everything was so wrong. Her magic. The zombies. Every bit of it was cattywampus, crooked, wrong. Katy wished she could reach out and straighten it all, like a picture frame on the wall.

Then, bolting upright, Katybird realized she could. Tyler was right. Katy had plenty of power at her disposal—her mama and her nanny would do anything in the world to help her if she asked them. Her own fear of disappointing her family was the only thing stopping her. She hadn't wanted to fail Delpha, either. But those worries seemed so small now, compared to what had happened to Mrs. Hattaway.

Heart quickening, Katybird fished a hair elastic from her pocket and yanked her curls into a ponytail. Folks in the Hollow needed protection, and she could help by telling her family the truth. Katybird sprinted for the outside door, shoes crunching and slipping their way across the wreckage of the rummage sale. She blinked hard in the harsh afternoon sun, then tore across the street toward her family's festival booth.

CHAPTER 23
DELPHA

DELPHA AND TYLER RAN THE LENGTH OF MAIN
Street a second time, searching the bustling street for Katybird.

"Let's split up," Delpha suggested, mopping her forehead. "You check by the port-a-johns on that side of the street, and I'll go look up by the Hearns' museum tent. Meet back at the welcome booth in five minutes."

"Okay," Tyler agreed before threading through the crowd.

Delpha squeezed the bottle of tincture in her sweaty palm. She hoped she'd find Katy first so she could give her the tincture right away. Then they'd see about finding the girl's silly raccoon and doing the Reverse-Curse. They were close now, and Delpha's heart fluttered in anticipation.

She swiveled right, toward the row of tents where the Hearns set up their museum info booth every year. Delpha squeezed past strollers and slow-walking folks, huffing with impatience. A flock of balloons bobbed a hundred yards ahead, marking the Hearns' booth. Almost there . . .

A woman nearby let out a bone-chilling scream. The festive chatter died for the length of several booths, replaced by worried whispers. Delpha tensed, hand shooting to her wand pocket. She stood on tiptoe to get a glimpse of what was going on, then stumbled back with a gasp as the canvas tent nearest to her erupted into flames. The crowd parted and people shrieked, littering the ground with snow cones and boiled peanuts in their frenzied press to escape. One man elbowed Delpha, and she lost her balance, crashing sideways onto the asphalt. When she got her breath back, she gasped.

Four wizened witches with cadaverous cats and foxes winding around their legs sauntered through the screaming crowd. Black smoke rolled from the burning tent behind them, and they cackled as the flames licked toward the neighboring booth.

Delpha coughed and scrambled to her feet, still clutching the tincture bottle. "No," she whispered. She and Katy had been solving this—they'd been *fixing* it!

"Where's them cursed McGills?" a Hearn zombie snarled through a mouth of crumbling teeth. The eyeless owl on her shoulder screeched and flapped, shedding mildewed feathers.

But before Delpha could run, a deafening explosion from the other side of the street shook the ground. Delpha swiveled long enough to see the far wall of the church collapse into rubble, and a handful of bedraggled McGill zombies crawled from the gaping hole in the wall. One of them snapped an arm back into place before raising a splintered wand. She led the little group in a limping charge to meet the Hearn zombies head-on.

The whole festival dissolved into chaos as fear rippled down Main Street. Some people tried to be heroic. A trio of men from the Howler's Hunting booth volleyed over their table with bolt-action rifles, firing off several shots before an undead Hearn calmly melted the guns' barrels into puddles with a flick of her withered wrist. *The curse demands the zombies murder whoever gets in the way of their feud*, Delpha remembered. "Don't try to fight 'em!" Delpha shouted, but her voice was tiny in the pandemonium.

In the middle of the road, a sandy-haired boy stood bewildered, clutching a balloon that read *Hearns' Appalachian Culture Museum*. A McGill zombie caught sight of the balloon from behind, and its face contorted in a horrible grin. It began stalking toward him like a cat. Delpha's heart liquefied. It was Caleb Hearn, Katy's little brother, all alone.

Delpha stuffed the tincture into her pocket and pulled out her wand. She was shaking, and she had no idea what to do, but she began to run toward Caleb anyway. *I can't let them hurt him!* she thought. Delpha tried to use her puppet magic on a tent, but a tourist ran into her and knocked her wand from her hand. After a quick search, Delpha couldn't find it, and she kept running for Caleb anyway.

Caleb signed something over and over, looking around. Then he yelled out, "Daddy? Daddy?"

Delpha stumbled. It felt like she was falling through space. For a second, she couldn't remember where, or *when*, she was. A lost memory bubbled up inside her, and a bright wave of pain pierced her chest. Her hand gripped her shirt over her heart, and she couldn't make her legs work.

"Daddy, don't leave without me! Daddy, the cake!" She was standing in her gravel driveway, watching their family's blue pickup rumble away. Her birthday. Delpha clutched a box of cake mix in one hand and a wire whisk in the other. They'd been fixing to make cobbler together. He shouted "I love you!" through the open truck window, but he didn't come back. It got dark. Cicadas had sung for a long time while she waited. There'd been no birthday dessert. Mama had locked herself in her room, and Daddy was gone. He left his best

girl, his little cricket, and he didn't come back for her, even though Delpha had slept out on the gravel and waited all night.

CRACK. Delpha startled, then leaped toward Caleb, but it was too late. The stone hex hit his tiny back so hard, he flew forward several feet and landed in Delpha's arms. Delpha hugged him tight. Caleb wheezed painfully for several breaths before his small body finally went still and rigid. The balloon floated off into the sky. Delpha's tears dotted the concrete.

Smoke stung Delpha's lungs. Her throat filled with a leaden lump of grief. She clutched Caleb's cool, stony hand and wept. "I'm so sorry, sweetie. I'm so sorry." He was so helpless, and Delpha had failed him. None of this made sense.

"You favor the McGills, wee one." The hot, foul stench of the McGill zombie's breath against her ear made Delpha's skin crawl, and she squeezed her eyes shut. Leathery, flaky skin scratched Delpha's cheek.

"Are ye one of us?"

"I . . . I am Delpha McGill," Delpha whispered, voice shaking.

"Trust no one, bairn! Hate and kill!" The zombie hobbled off, cackling to itself.

They'll keep killing folks until we unmake them, Delpha told herself. *Katy and I still have to do the Reverse-Curse.* Delpha planted a kiss on Caleb's stone cheek. "I'll find a way to fix you," she promised him. Then Delpha was up and running, screaming Katybird's name into the chaos, dodging running bodies.

"Delpha Storm McGill!"

Delpha froze in place, her stomach a block of ice. Only one person would call her by her full name. She turned stiffly to see Mama furious and pale as she strode through the confused crowd to snatch Delpha's arm. "What in mercy's name are you doin' here?"

Delpha stared like a deer in highlights, and Mama didn't wait for an answer. She kept right on scolding, lowering her voice to a hiss.

"Someone's been messin' with strong conjure, and we're gettin' out of here before folks start remembering our family used to do magic, and pointin' fingers. I've told the Hearns that secret magic is still breaking the rules . . ."

Delpha couldn't breathe. When Mama was like this, fussin' non-stop, it felt like the world was closing in on Delpha. She couldn't even think to form an excuse. Mama yanked her down the street by the arm with one hand, furiously texting on her cell phone with the other, giving Delpha no choice but to stumble along after her.

"I came home from a birth at seven this mornin', and you were gone. An' I told myself, I can trust my daughter! She's stayin' between our house and the museum trailhead, like a good girl. And here you are, in this mess. Where've you *been*?"

"J-just. Around. With Katybird Hearn and Tyler Nimble, s'all," Delpha stammered, blinking back terrified tears. If Mama found out . . .

"Since when do you spend time with those two?" Mama snapped, still texting, ignoring the screams around them.

"We were just . . . up at the old workshop on Graystone Mountain, gettin' my knife sharpened."

Delpha's mama whirled, eyes wide, and gave Delpha's arm a good shake. "You went *where*?"

"I know it's far, Mama. But it was just to see Tyler's uncle." Delpha looked back helplessly toward the woods behind the hardware store, where Puppet was hidden.

Mama's lips went tight, her face chalk white with rage, and she parked Delpha on a bench outside the diner. "You're goin' home. I've got to drive out to the Lawsons' and catch a baby. Mrs. Miller'll pick you up right here in one minute and carry you out to the house. Stay there and lock the doors. Pack your suitcase up, too." Mama shook her head as she walked toward her beat-up old Buick, muttering, "S'high time we hightailed it outta this godforsaken Hollow."

Delpha opened her mouth to protest, but what would she say? *This is all my doin', Mama. But don't worry, I might could get it under control, I think?* That'd go over with Mama like a fart at a funeral. But Delpha had no intention of going home with Mrs. Miller, Mama's midwifery partner. The ruckus on the other end of Main Street got louder. Delpha waited, trembling, until Mama's taillights bounced out of sight.

Then Delpha sprinted for all she was worth. Lungs screaming, she raced back to Main Street to find Katybird Hearn.

CHAPTER 24
KATYBIRD

KATY WAS HALFWAY TO THE MUSEUM BOOTH WHEN the shouts began. She glanced over her shoulder. Smoke snaked upward across the street, thick smoke that *wasn't* from the annual barbecue pit. She doubled her pace. At last, she skidded to a stop in front of her family's tent. Her mother stood peering out over the frantic crowd in confusion, shielding her eyes from the sun.

"Mama! Nanny!" A lump of dread welled in Katy's throat. Her ears went hot, but there was no going back now. Mama startled at Katy's voice, then latched onto Katy's shoulders with both hands, looking her up and down for signs of injury.

"Katybird Hearn, where have you been? What do you mean, leaving a note saying you'd walk to the festival?"

"Yes, ma'am, I'm sorry, but there ain't time!" Katy cried. "Me an' Delpha McGill . . . we did something stupid. Delpha cast a spell in the cemetery, and these—these bodies came up out of the ground. And now they're killing folks, and there's a Reverse-Curse from Delpha's spellbook to fix it. But my magic won't work, and I can't do my half of it. You or Nanny has to do it."

"What?" Nanny screeched.

An explosion from the direction of the church rattled the tent's poles, and a fresh wave of screams traveled down the street. Katy gasped. The McGill zombies had escaped the baptismal tank. "Oh no! Mama, it's them! I tried to trap 'em in the church, but . . ."

"Don't you worry," her mother said, then turned to Nanny. "Mama, find Caleb! Katybird, take me to Delpha. Let's run."

Relief flooded Katybird as her mother hustled around the table, hips swinging in determination. Mama held out her hand to Katy— but as Katy reached to take it, her mother's eyes widened, and she shoved Katybird down hard onto the sidewalk. A split second later, there came a deafening *crack!*

Katy watched, helpless, as her mama slumped sideways against the table, gasping for air. The tall McGill zombie from the church shrieked in triumph several feet away. Katy's nanny toppled, too. Katy caught her mama's head in her arms before it hit the ground, cradling it in the crook of her elbow. Katy heard a growl. Tyler Nimble rounded the tent in his Yow form, tackling the zombie to the ground and pinning her wand hand with his foot.

"Mama!" Katybird sobbed, burying her face in her mama's hair. Katy half hoped she could push the stone hex back with love alone. She tried, too, but the awful death-gray color snaked across her mama's pretty skin anyway. *"No! No!"*

"I love you, baby. Don't . . . forget," her mama gasped.

"Mama, no, please!"

"There's only one Katy . . ."

Her mama's hair didn't smell like her mama anymore. Katy caught the sob in her throat before it could escape, unwilling to believe that her mama was really gone. *There must be a way to fix all this*, she decided. She stood, numb, and gazed over the table. Nanny's body lay stiff and gray, just like Mama's.

The world was a blur of tears, but Katy ground her teeth stubbornly. The McGill zombie pinned beneath Tyler's foot wheezed, then gave a vile, throaty chuckle. Tyler growled at the cackling zombie, struggling to keep it still. Katy's belly became a furnace, melting her fear. She whirled, fists clenched, then ran over and jammed the heel of her sneaker into the side of the witch's grisly face with all her weight.

"Ye cannae hurt th' dead, Hearn bairn," the zombie rasped, clucking. "All my sisters will descend from yonder hills soon. It's a war we'll be havin'. Ye cannae stop it!"

Katy snatched the zombie's wand and broke it with a dusty crack. "I can burn your wand, you nasty hunk of—"

"Take my wand, aye. But it won't help ye," it teased with a rotten-toothed grin.

"No, *you'll* help me," Katy demanded, kicking it hard. "Tell me how to get my family back, or Tyler will rip off your head! I'll burn it along with your wand. That *would* be the end of you, I reckon." The McGill zombie wheezed with laughter, taunting Katy.

"We cannae be burned. We cannae be stopped. We are the Curse. Ye'll only git yer folk back after you've gubbed us. Eye fur eye, hair fur hair, death fur death, fair is fair!"

Tyler's eyes widened in relief. "Your family can be turned back, Katy! They're not really dead!" He smiled a little and relaxed his grip just long enough for the zombie to twist violently out of his grasp, giving him one last malicious look.

"I go tae collect my sisters. Daylight is just for havin' a wee bit of fun! Prepare for full war at midnight!" she spat, before scampering away.

Tyler glared after her as he shrank into boy form, drenched in sweat and heaving for breath. Then he gazed toward the Hearn booth with a sober expression. Katy knelt beside her mother. Mama couldn't help Katy now. If anything, Katybird had to do the helping.

"The zombies are *strong*," Tyler admitted, voice shaky.

"The only way to get 'em back in that cemetery is to do the Reverse-Curse," Katy whispered through dry lips.

"So, that means—"

"I'm out of choices. I do my half of the Reverse-Curse myself." Despite the late-afternoon sun, Katy shivered. "Or I don't ever get my family back."

CHAPTER 25

DELPHA

"KATYBIRD!" DELPHA'S THROAT WAS RAW FROM hollering, but she kept running and shouting anyway, hand clasping the tincture bottle. The street emptied around her as people gathered into town hall, seeking shelter. A massive Snarly Yow rounded up the dozen or so zombies, both McGills and Hearns, and herded them with fierce growls and snapping jaws, skidding and lunging, until finally the undead witches made a cackling retreat for the forested hills outside town. They almost seemed to be enjoying themselves, taunting him and wearing him out with their endless curse energy. *Let 'em run, Tyler*, Delpha thought. *They're too many to fight.*

"Katy!" Delpha shouted again, feet tearing across the pavement. She spotted Katybird's mop of hair, burrowed into Tyler's shoulder.

Tyler was pale and Katy was sobbing, and then Delpha saw why: On the ground behind Katy lay Mrs. Hearn, statue-like and gray.

Delpha frowned sharply. Her head jerked toward the forest. The Snarly Yow chasing the zombies doubled back toward Main Street, loping toward her. If that wasn't Tyler, then who was it? The Yow began shifting like she'd seen Tyler do, going from great dog to a lanky, tall man with red, curly hair. Delpha's mouth fell open in surprise as she recognized Tyler's uncle, Clement.

"You're a . . . Snarly Yow, too," Delpha blurted. "I thought you didn't like crowds."

Clement ran a hand over his face, catching his breath. "Don't reckon I do. But I heard the emergency announcement on the radio after y'all left. An' when I walked to the end of my drive to get the mail, I saw a big ol' path of broken tree limbs cuttin' clear down the side of the mountain. Hard to miss. I had a funny feeling ya might be in some sort of trouble, with y' bein' a witch and all. So I followed you." He stepped closer.

Delpha narrowed her eyes. "I'm . . . I'm not a witch," she lied.

"Of course you are. You're your mama's girl," Clement said softly.

Delpha's stomach clenched, and she stared at Clement. His eyes flickered between Delpha's face and the ground several times, like he was deciding what to say.

Then he reached into the pocket of his worn denim jacket and pulled out a pocketknife—Delpha's pocketknife with the howling wolf on it—and held it out to her. "I found it on the ground in my driveway. It used to be mine, a long, long time ago."

Delpha's fingers closed around her pocketknife. It was warm. She drew it to her heart, squeezing hard, trying to understand what Clement was saying. That knife had been her daddy's. She scowled into his earnest face, confused.

"I hoped it was you the minute you stepped into the workshop, but I thought maybe that was wishful thinkin'," Clement said in his gentle Hollow twang. "But when you pulled out your pocketknife . . . Well, I ain't seen that in years." Her mind became a jumble of discarded snapshots. Christmases. Lazy Sundays on the porch. Walks in the woods, hand in hand.

Clement swayed, studying Delpha with hopeful eyes. She gazed back at him, his face merging images of past and present: one young and happy, and the other older and sadder. A flash of pain shot through her head. For a fleeting moment, Delpha thought she recognized her father. "Daddy?" The word slipped out, and the sound of it made her feel young and homesick. A tear crawled down her face as she took a timid step closer. She had the strange urge to hurl herself into his arms and let herself feel . . . what? Safe?

But this was Tyler's uncle Clement, for goodness' sake. The two versions of him ripped apart again, pulling Delpha's heart apart with them. It felt like a thousand scabs ripped open at once, leaving her raw and skillet-hot with anger. He had left, and nothing could undo Delpha's pain now. It was fresh again, and Delpha's heart hardened around the ghost of her grudge.

Fool me once, shame on you. Fool me twice, shame on me, Delpha thought. Doors inside her slammed shut on *all* her feelings: her anger, her loneliness, her pain, and especially that tiny seed of long-buried hope. The only thing left now was duty, and getting the job done. *Doin' the job right*.

"Thanks for the knife, Clement. Now go chase a car."

"Delpha!!"

She turned to see Tyler standing behind her, jaw slack with shock.

"How long have you been standing there, nosey?" Delpha snapped, wiping her face with her sleeve.

"Long enough to hear you be rude to my uncle!"

Delpha rolled her eyes and ground her teeth. "Where's Katy?"

Tyler's chin wobbled. "Her mama and nanny got turned to stone. She needed a minute to . . . to . . . Aren't you going to apologize to my uncle? He saved our butts!"

Delpha started to walk away, then stopped and spun to face Tyler. She blinked as sudden realization set in. Clement was Tyler's uncle. They were chummy, even. They'd probably done things like cooking and fishing together, and the jealousy of it hit her chest with the force of a freight train. Fighting to breathe, she pushed the pain away. Anger was simpler. Anger at the wrong person was even more effortless, and it latched onto poor Tyler without Delpha's permission.

"Uncle dad-gummed Clement," Delpha drawled in a flat voice. "This day gets better and better. An' he's a wolf, too. Why not?" She flailed and stormed off, dragging Katybird along with her.

Tyler ran up alongside them, shoulders tense. "Listen, witch girl, my family may be ugly and hairy sometimes, but we've sure as heck helped keep the crazy zombies *you* raised from killin' you. You could at least be grateful!"

Delpha gave a brittle laugh. "S'that what you think?"

"Darn straight it's what I think! At least we're not a bunch of coldhearted necromancers, carryin' on and breathin' life back into a blood feud! Yeah. Don't look shocked. I know what necromancer means. I can read big words!"

Delpha yanked open the door to the unscathed side of the church and shoved Tyler through ahead of her, shocking even herself with her roughness. Tyler pitched forward, then whirled around to gawk at her. He caught his glasses before they slid off his nose. Before he could say a thing, Delpha snarled, "I will never, ever thank your uncle for saving me. I could never appreciate a . . . *thing* like that! He's a lowlife. A monster! And I. Don't. Need. His. Help. I couldn't care less what he thinks of me!"

Tyler blinked as if he'd been slapped. He gazed at Delpha for a moment, fighting tears. At that moment, Katybird arrived, swollen-eyed and sniffling as she stepped through the church door. She put a hand on Delpha's shoulder, her eyes darting in between Delpha and Tyler.

"What's going on here? I could hear you yellin' from the side-walk outside."

The rage fog lifted from Delpha's thoughts, replaced swiftly by shame. She'd shoved Tyler. She stared down at her boots, ears hot. How could she begin to explain? "Tyler, look, it's just that—"

Tyler held up a hand to cut her off. "Don't. Just don't, okay? Let's . . . get through this afternoon. I'll keep my monster self under control, and then I'll leave you alone forever. Let's just help Katybird do her danged spell." Without waiting, he turned and stumbled down the hallway, leaving Delpha lagging behind for once.

Katybird gazed after Tyler, then gave Delpha a reproachful look. "What was that about?"

Delpha bit her lip, not even sure where to start. *Coldhearted*, Tyler had said. Maybe it was true. She wished she could call him back, but her voice wouldn't work.

"Never mind," Katybird said in a sharp voice. Her eyes were red from crying, but they had a new steel to them, too. "You got that well water? I'm ready to try the Reverse-Curse again."

Delpha nodded. She looked back to see Clement, sitting outside on the church's doorstep, shoulders stooped. She wished he'd leave. Delpha wanted to tell him so, too, but that meant talking to him again, and her heart couldn't take that. Katy studied her. Delpha clenched her jaw.

"Let's go fix your magic."

Delpha ducked into a Sunday school room after Tyler, her chest tightening. Her heart hurt. She was hemorrhaging decency and left only with anger. Even her anger hurt.

She was a mess on the inside, a jumbled tangle of feelings and half-remembered days spent with her father, fury at her mother for not understanding Delpha's need for magic, and rage at Clement for leaving in the first place. The agony of it—past and present—was unforgivable. She was even mad at herself for wanting to run back outside and just . . . stare at him. Why hadn't she recognized him? Delpha had a memory like an elephant. *So how on earth had she forgotten his face?*

She tried to focus as Katybird explained how her mama and grandma had been hit with a stone hex, and how it could only be undone by defeating the zombies. "That awful hag said they'd just been havin' fun, and the real war starts at midnight," Katy sniffed bitterly. Delpha's stomach was a stone sinking to the bottom of a creek bed. She couldn't bring herself to tell Katy that Caleb was petrified, too. Tyler pulled out a little plastic chair for Katybird to sit down, and then he and Delpha sat cross-legged on either side of her, neither looking at the other.

Tyler's eyes swam with a raw pain that Delpha didn't understand, but she knew darn well she'd put it there. She'd been so scared and lost, her words had tumbled out like razors. She couldn't even recall what all she'd said to Tyler. Feelings were dangerous things. Delpha imagined herself locking hers away somewhere dark and far, far away. *Be in charge, Delpha*, she told herself. *Get ahold of yourself.*

"Here's the tincture." She held out the brown bottle to Katybird.

"I thought you said you had water from my family's old well," Katy sniffled, peering at the murky liquid.

"Delpha thinks it's an old ginseng tincture made from Hearn well water," Tyler muttered, hugging his arms across his chest. "But I don't know, Katy—it looks sketchy as heck."

"I'll drink it." Katy grabbed the bottle, unscrewing the cap. She gagged at the smell, then squeezed her eyes shut and chugged. Delpha's hand shot out to slow her down.

"Easy there, Katy."

Katybird coughed and made a face. "It tastes like armpit." She replaced the cap and sighed. "Okay. Let's do the Reverse-Curse."

"Are you sure you don't need a minute?" Tyler asked.

Katybird nodded, chin brave. "This is my family's best shot."

Delpha lowered her eyebrows into fierce lines. *"With cunning mind an' strongest will, I call the hex of war to still,"* she began.

"Love like hearth with coals aglow, my open heart makes magic grow," Katy responded. Her hands began to sparkle green, but if she noticed, she seemed determined to ignore them.

Delpha mouthed *with feeling*, and both girls recited fiercely, *"These balanced pow'rs make evil quake! Together, watch the curses break!"*

The cotton-and-paper clouds suspended from the Sunday school ceiling began to sway, then burst into flames. Their strings burned away in an instant, and Delpha and Katybird dove to the side as the clouds fell from the ceiling like comets.

Tyler yelped and dashed into the hallway in search of a fire extinguisher. He pried one off the wall just outside the door, coughing. Smoke billowed from the Sunday school room's doorway as Tyler ran back inside.

Delpha beat at the flames with a naptime mat as they licked their way across the melting carpet. In a corner, Katybird growled in pain, clutching her greenish arms to her body. Tyler yanked the extinguisher pins, aimed the nozzle, and swept the foam across the flames. In a frenzied few minutes, the carpet stopped smoldering. Katy's luminescent arms dimmed through the haze. Tyler waved smoke away from his eyes and wheezed loudly. Katy stamped her foot in frustration.

"On the bright side, *something* happened, Katybird—" Tyler quipped weakly.

She scowled, and Tyler bit his lip. Katy was bein' so fierce and brave. Tyler was tryin' so hard to have a good attitude. Delpha pretended not to notice all these feelings flying around. *If you want to keep them safe, stay focused, Delpha.*

"We'll assume the Reverse-Curse didn't work, then," Delpha snarled. "We're going out to find your dumb skunk."

"Raccoon!"

"Whatever. Once you have your bond, we'll try it again." With that, Delpha shouldered her satchel and stalked down the hall toward the back exit, leaving Katy red-faced.

Tyler gasped for air behind her as the toes of his sneakers nipped Delpha's heels. *Puff, puff* went his inhaler. "Or, wild suggestion here, how 'bout you call your mama, Delpha? And keep"—he inhaled deep and exhaled—"whatever just happened from happening again?"

"Snap your trap and let me help Katy!" Delpha spat. She pushed the door open and stomped across the tiny vacant parking lot of the church to where Puppet hid in the brush behind the hardware store next door. With a quick yank-grab-*SLAM!*, she retrieved her spellbook, then marched back to where Tyler and Katy waited by the church's rear door. There, she planted her boots on the crumbling asphalt and opened her book, flipping until she found a page that seemed like it might do the trick. Ignoring Tyler's glare, she raised her wand.

Tyler tensed suddenly. "The air smells wrong."

"Hush, Nimble."

"Delpha McGill, listen. Something ain't right."

"Is your tongue hinged in the middle?"

"No, really, it—" Without warning, Tyler shifted into Yow form. It happened so fast, he yelped in surprise and staggered, disoriented. Then his eyes locked on something darting out from behind the church's rusted dumpster. Delpha shivered, following his gaze. It was a skeletal cat.

A Hearn zombie followed a split second later. Cackling, she aimed her withered hands straight at Delpha's chest. But somehow, Tyler was faster and sprang at the undead witch with teeth bared. He growled as they both slammed into the side of the dumpster. Katybird screamed from behind them, and Delpha ducked, instinctively curling her body around the McGill spellbook.

The zombie popped from her back to her feet like a click beetle, then spun to the ivy-draped fence behind the dumpster and hissed something to the plants. Green tendrils shot out toward Delpha, winding up around her legs before she could run. Twisting around and around, the vines encased her arms and chest so tight, Delpha yowled in pain. *My ribs are gonna pop*, she thought, panicking.

Tyler exploded in rage, snapping and growling. He lunged at the zombie again, but she was quicker this time and shot an arc of electricity through his left leg. He slammed into the ground so hard, his head bounced with a sickening *thwack*. When he tried to get up, he cried out in agony, unable to get his clumsy foot beneath him.

"Help!" Delpha hollered, clawing. The zombie chuckled and hobbled toward Tyler menacingly. *If I could just get free and use my wand . . .* The edges of Delpha's vision began to go dark. "Somebody help me!"

Katybird shouted orders at the ivy in vain, then resorted to kicking and ripping at it with her hands, but it was no use. As soon as Katy tore one tendril loose, another vine grew in its place.

A streak of gray rushed past Delpha's face, then tackled the zombie to the ground. *Clement.* He and the zombie became a blurred tangle, both moving too fast for Delpha to see, hissing and snarling and ripping. Tyler managed to struggle to his feet just as Clement clamped his teeth around the nape of the Hearn zombie's neck.

"It can't be killed," shrieked Katybird. "You have to trap it!"

Tyler limped to the dumpster, still in Yow form, and heaved at it. The dumpster groaned and tipped easily. "Throw 'er in here!"

Clement flung the zombie into the dumpster with a grunt, and Tyler slammed the lid shut. He and Clement flipped it again, so the opening rested against the ground. The zombie banged and howled, and the two Yows jumped back from the dumpster as the metal sides buzzed with electricity. But it held. Tyler and Clement whipped back into human shapes, gasping for breath.

"The ivy!" Katybird yelled, still clawing away at the vines. Delpha felt her face going numb and cold, and her body seemed to be floating away from her.

Clement scrambled to help. The ivy had stopped growing, but it still wound tightly around Delpha's neck.

"She's got a knife in 'er pocket. Can you reach it, Katy?" Clement's hoarse voice said.

Strong hands yanked hard to create a gap in the tangle by Delpha's leg, and Katybird squeezed her hands between the vines, slowly working out the knife.

"Give 'er here."

A blurry mop of red hair and a worried face appeared, and the tightness around Delpha's neck lessened, strand by strand.

Finally, the feeling rushed back into Delpha's face. Then Clement yanked her away from the hungry ivy, and settled her gently on the church's back steps. Katy threw her arms around Delpha's shoulders as Tyler took out his tattered T-shirt from earlier and handed it to Clement to staunch blood from a nasty gash in his head.

Delpha waved Katy off and brought her knees to her chest, wheezing.

"She's got asthma," Clement announced softly.

Tyler lowered himself gingerly to the ground next to Delpha. Under torn jeans, his leg was an angry web of red welts. He didn't look happy with Delpha, but at least he was actually looking at her now. That was something. He pressed his inhaler into her hand. "Use it. I wiped off the Yow cooties for you."

Delpha breathed in the medicine, nostrils flaring, then handed the inhaler back.

"Didn't know you had asthma, too," Tyler muttered.

"Only when I'm being strangled," Delpha answered hoarsely, gazing hard at the red streaks on Tyler's leg. "Hey, Tyler . . ." she whispered finally.

Tyler's shoulders tightened, and he looked away. "I'm good. Don't get me wrong—this has been as fun as lickin' a bug zapper, but I could use a minute to myself now." He crossed his arms. Delpha frowned but didn't blame him. The kid was sweet, but he wasn't a saint.

She shot a glance at Clement. With blood all down his jaw and neck, the guy looked like a barbed-wire victim. He'd showed up again. Well. Delpha put a dead bolt on her feelings. She pressed her lips together tightly, then opened her spellbook.

"All right, Katybird. Time to find your bond." Delpha straightened her shoulders and read a charm that sounded newer than the others. It rocked in the comforting, singsong mountain rhythm that was as familiar to Delpha as cornbread and honeysuckles.

"Come up you critters from the valley,
Crawl down from yonder mountain brow
Jump out from bresh and tree and fl'ar
Y'all be my puppets for a spell."

After this, Delpha closed her eyes, trying to picture Podge, and muttered, "But just the raccoon."

Delpha's hands shook instantly. A squeak of concentration escaped her lips without permission. This spell was hard. Harder than driving Puppet. Blood began trickling from both her nostrils, and she grimaced in pain. Her head felt like it was being popped like a blister of bubble wrap.

"Delpha, what are you *doing*?" Katybird demanded.

Delpha ground her teeth and grabbed Katybird's shoulder for support with her free hand. Clement hovered at her side, but Delpha was too focused to shoo him away.

Suddenly, Katy's raccoon chirped behind Delpha. And in front of her. Then from every direction. Down the alleyway and out of the woods poured dozens of raccoons, chittering in protest. Waddling, trash-fed raccoons scampered in step with scruffy, wiry-looking ones. They encircled Delpha, their number growing by the second. Katy's face twisted in dismay.

"Delpha, stop this! Your puppet magic is workin' on animals! This can't be good for them!" Katybird hollered, her face reddening.

Delpha ignored her and spat out penny-flavored blood onto the ground—the last straw for Katybird, apparently.

"And it's not good for you, either!" Katy cried, knocking the wand from Delpha's hand. Delpha staggered, then wiped her mouth on the back of her hand and blinked in shock.

"Puppet making is the magic I've practiced the most," Delpha protested, clutching her throbbing head between her hands. "Can you tell which one is Pudgy?"

"Podge," Katybird called. "Come find Mama, baby!"

The ground was a moving carpet of black-and-gray fuzz, and Delpha could barely tell where one animal ended and the next started. Clement let out a low whistle of admiration. Tyler looked at Katy doubtfully. "Don't get too close! They could have rabies!" To Tyler's dismay, Katy ignored him and waded right into the chirping mass.

"Podge, *come*!" Out of the squirming crowd of animals, a fat raccoon scurried up to Katy's jeans leg and climbed onto her shoulder. Katy burst into a laughing sob. She buried her face in Podge's fur, sighing and gibbering in baby talk. The raccoon sniffed all around Katy's face, licking away tears and touching her cheeks with its tiny bandit hands. Podge nosed through the colorful strands of Katy's hair, making her laugh. Even Tyler couldn't help but turn his scowl into a grin.

Delpha picked up her wand, then relaxed as the remaining tide of little bandits receded and scampered for the hills. She teetered at the church's back door and pressed her forehead against the crook of her elbow. She looked up to see Katy whisper to Clement, "Delpha needs food. Like, a trucker's worth. Can you get some?"

Clement gave a quick nod. "Y'all go in the church, though. Better lock the door, and don't come out again."

"Not a problem," Tyler muttered, limping inside.

The red evening sun hung low. A crow cawed, and Delpha jumped, heart racing, before realizing it was just a normal bird.

Katy stood close to Delpha, nuzzling her face into Podge's fur.

"I don't like how you did it, but I'm proud you found him. Thanks." She squeezed Delpha's arm gently.

Delpha shifted awkwardly, a crack of emotion threatening to widen.

"Let's go see if the Reverse-Curse works now you've got Pork."

"Podge."

"Whatever."

CHAPTER 26
KATYBIRD

IT'S NOW OR NEVER, Katy told herself as she settled cross-legged facing Delpha inside the little wooden chapel. She glanced around and winced, worrying over how flammable all the polished maple pews might be. A distant guttural shriek filtered through the stained-glass windows along with the bloodred sunset. Katy shuddered. She was glad to be inside.

In the hallway outside, Clement paced from window to window as he monitored the surrounding hills and street. Tyler hobbled into the chapel with two monster-sized bags of animal crackers and several cold barbecue sandwiches.

Wordlessly, he dropped one of each beside Delpha, and handed a sandwich to Katy. Podge darted over to snatch a cracker, then reclaimed his place on Katy's shoulder. She nuzzled her face into his fur.

"I'm ready. Let's try it again."

Delpha gulped down an animal cracker and gave a weary nod.

"With cunning mind an' strongest will, I call the hex of war to still," Delpha murmured.

Katy hated how defeated Delpha already sounded. *Believe in me, Delpha! I can do this*, Katy thought. *Mama and Nanny need me!*

Then Katybird had a terrible thought. "Caleb's still out there," she yelped, jumping to her feet. Her head spun with the realization. "I have to go look for him!" Delpha grabbed for Katy's arm and shook her head. Delpha's tight-pressed bottom lip quivered.

"You're crying. Why are you crying?" Katy demanded, heart pounding.

"He . . . he got hit. With a stone hex," Delpha whispered, staring at the carpet.

"What? How do you know?" Katy cried, voice mangled.

"I saw it happen," Delpha said slowly, chewing her lip. "I didn't wanna to tell you, 'cause you were so upset already."

As if on cue, another faraway zombie screech made Katy jump. Through the stained glass, automatic streetlights flickered on, announcing the arrival of nighttime.

So that was it. Katybird's whole family was depending on her broken magic. Katy steeled herself. Podge hopped into her lap, and Katy cleared the tears from her throat.

"Love like hearth with coals aglow, my open heart makes magic grow," she intoned.

The buzzing in her fingers started before she'd gotten the last word out. Searing light erupted in her hands and raced up her arms . . . and didn't stop there. Her entire body turned a shocking, translucent green, and for an eternal minute, Katy was certain her skin would split away in all directions. She couldn't even scream. Her jaw simply locked in agony as Tyler and Delpha hollered somewhere far away.

Work, she willed her magic. *Don't let everyone down*, her head begged her soul. But the magic wouldn't yield. As the light subsided, she realized she'd been holding her breath.

"Podge?" Her hand fumbled for her pet. A whimper escaped her lips, and the weakness of the sound made her mad. She clamped her mouth tight.

"He's still here," Delpha told her. Her face was stricken as she dragged Podge out from under a pew. "He hid. I think you scared 'im."

"He wasn't hurt?" Katy demanded through clenched teeth.

"No, but *you* were," Tyler retorted hotly. He glared at Delpha for some reason. The two of them had been waging a silent war of dirty looks since Clement had arrived, and it didn't take a detective to recognize there was some sort of connection between the two events. Now Tyler seemed happy to blame everything on Delpha, even things that weren't her fault. Delpha sat stiff as an ice statue.

"ENOUGH," Katy spat, jumping to her feet. "THAT'S ENOUGH."

Delpha and Tyler startled.

"I can't think with the two of you feelin' in my space. Go over to that pew." Katy pointed across the chapel. "And sort out whatever your trouble is. It's got something to do with Clement; I ain't blind. Open your mouths and talk about it and *let me settle myself*!"

They both started to protest, but Katybird gave them the look she often gave Podge when he'd knocked a glass off the table. They shuffled away, brooding. *Fine*, Katy thought. *Sulk. But do it over there.*

Katy slouched to the floor and shut her eyes. She couldn't even pray without worrying she was letting God down. So, instead, she skimmed her fingers along Podge's coarse fur and let her mind go blank. *There's only one Katy*, Mama had whispered. It'd been their special goodbye since Katy was small, to remind her to take a break from other people's needs and think of what *she* wanted, too. *What do I want right now?* she asked herself.

I want to be a witch. But what did that mean to Katy? She wanted good to win. But what was good? Katy thought harder. *I want to put my two feet on the ground and walk in a world that gives everybody a fair shake*, she realized, *and not just the "normal" folks. I'd like to feel safe to be myself.* She wanted balance between give and take so nobody claimed more than their fair share of things. She'd use her power to help it happen, if she could control it. If she could nudge the world into being better, she reasoned, that would be enough.

Tyler and Delpha's voices mumbled from across the room. They were talking. She'd accomplished that, at least.

Katy's eyelids were so heavy. It was her second night without sleep, and every time her hands glowed, every time she tried to do the spell, it pulled a little more strength from her. She fought to blink her eyes open, and when she did, Delpha and Tyler stood above her, shuffling their feet.

"We've been talkin'. We'll agree to work out our differences if you agree to sleep. N-not for long! Just, like, fifteen minutes," Tyler said. "It's just you keep trying the spell, and it's not working, and . . ."

"No way! I can do this!" Katy whimpered, tears brimming. "I'm so close!"

"You look like roadkill, Katybird," Delpha muttered. "Last time you tried the spell, your face went pale as Death eatin' a saltine. Just rest long enough to recharge your batt'ries. Then we'll try it again."

Katy's shoulders sagged. She opened her mouth to protest, but her vision was already blurring, and her traitorous head was lolling back against the wall, muzzy with sleep.

CHAPTER 27
DELPHA

"IS SHE ASLEEP?" TYLER WHISPERED.

Delpha studied Katy's face. "Out like a light."

Without that earnest mother-hen expression on her face, Katybird looked so young. Awful guilt weighed on Delpha, and she settled onto the floor beside Katy. Her head felt like split firewood since she'd done the spell to find Podge—fat lot of good that it had done. She choked down a bite of sandwich.

Tyler lowered himself to the floor, wincing as his sore leg bumped the pew. "She'll keep tryin' that spell until she hurts herself bad, you know."

"I know," Delpha said. "That's why I've got no intention of wakin' her up again."

"You lied to Katy? But you told her . . ."

Delpha felt a door inside herself crack open, spilling a bit of her heart. "I said what I had to. If we let her try the Reverse-Curse again, I'm scared it'll kill her." The thought made Delpha sick inside. "I want the zombies gone, but I ain't a monster."

Tyler's lip snarled. "No, that's me, ain't it? *I'm* the monster. Nasty ol' Snarly Yow, just like my uncle."

Delpha's heart opened a little more. *Oh boy.* She took a long breath. "About before. I wasn't talking about you bein' a Yow, Tyler."

"I don't want to hear it."

"I'm tryin' to tell you a thing, if you'll close your lid a second." Delpha wiped her sweaty palms on her shorts, heart pounding. "Clement is . . . my father." The word "father" dropped out like lead. Not Daddy. Not Dad. *Father.*

Tyler's jaw dropped. "What? Why didn't you say something?"

"I didn't know until he showed up at Spring Fling."

"But how—"

Delpha's chest tightened. "I can't talk about it. I'm only tellin' you this because I can see you're hurtin', and there ain't a point to it. I like *you* fine. You're a good person. Bein' a Yow is cool. I just— Your uncle . . ."

Tyler blushed, then grinned. "Whoa. But we're, like, cousins!"

Delpha studied Tyler's face. Behind his smudged glasses, the stormy hurt had faded, replaced by his usual goofy wonder. *How do you forgive folks that easily?* she wondered. Delpha smiled a little. Tyler's mouth twitched with a thousand questions. Finally, it settled into a grin. "Do you want a hug?"

"Nope. Back to work."

"Okeydokey. How will we fix the zombies, if we're not waking Katy?"

Delpha reached for her spellbook. Her heart hitched as she studied Katybird's pale lips and Tyler's red-streaked leg.

They'll keep tryin' to help me until it kills them, Delpha realized. All the fight withered inside Delpha. What was worse? Folks causing your plans to fail, or losing folks for the sake of your plans? She suspected this must be what dying felt like. *There was no way to keep from getting hurt.* But if she had to choose . . .

"I'm going to use the phone."

Delpha started walking and didn't look back. She checked door after door until she found the church office. She located the phone, yanked up the receiver, and dialed her mama's cell phone number. No answer. She punched in her home number, and after two quick rings, her mama's voice spoke in an urgent whisper.

"Delpha McGill, this better be you, calling to say you're safe!"

"Yeah, it's me," Delpha blurted, voice cracking. "I . . . I lied before, an' I'm in a mess. I found Mamaw's spellbook, an' I used it, an' the zombies downtown are all my fault." Delpha held the phone away from her ear, bracing for yelling. But Mama's voice stayed deadly low and quiet.

"Oh, Delpha. Please tell me that's not true."

Delpha felt a flare of annoyance. "I could tell you that, but that won't help me, now will it? Truth is, Mama, I need you to come help me do this spell right. Katy can't—"

Mama wasn't about to move on yet. "After everything I've done! After everything I've given up, Delpha. I did it all to keep that nonsense out of our lives!" Mama was shouting now, voice boiling with rage.

Delpha ground her molars, angry tears pricking her throat. If Mama had her druthers, blackberries wouldn't thorn, baby birds would stay bald forever, and the summer clouds would never scatter hail. But you can't control the nature of a thing. "This is part of me. You can't just . . . hack everything out of your life that makes you scared!"

There was a long, long pause on the other end of the phone. Then, finally:

"Baby girl, I can't even get out of the house. You stay safe! There's zombies outside, trying to break into the cabin. I'll figure out somethin'—" The line went to static for a second, and Delpha yelped in panic.

"Mama?"

Her mother's voice broke back in. "—can't get the police. If you're safe, you stay put, you hear?" Delpha could hear muffled shrieks over the phone line.

The world stopped spinning for Delpha. She dropped the phone. There were zombies up at her cabin. Her mama couldn't get out. *Her mama.* Delpha started for the back door to get Puppet, but her knees buckled, and the walls whirled. She wasn't strong enough to work the puppet magic again, not yet. There was only one person left to ask. Her heart hammered. She steadied herself against the wall panels, then doubled back down the hallway.

"CLEMENT!"

She stumbled into the foyer as Clement whirled from the window in alarm, his face craggy with worried shadows cast from the orange streetlight outside. Delpha choked back a sob. She had one last piece of her pride to give up, and her mama was the only person in the world she was willing to trade it for.

"I need your help." Delpha clenched her teeth to stop herself from angry-crying.

Clement nodded, eyes wide.

"Drive to my cabin and bring my mama here. Some zombies have got her trapped, and I can't do this spell without her."

Clement's shoulders sagged. "Delpha, I can't," he whispered hoarsely.

Flames erupted in Delpha's heart. "What do you mean, you can't? You danged well better! You get in your truck, you drive up the pass, and you be a decent human being for once in your life!" she yelled, brandishing her wand without thinking.

Clement flinched. "I wish I could!"

Delpha shook from head to toe, filled with anger. Couldn't he see how difficult this was, just asking for his help in the first place? "You're not talkin' sense! It's not hard! Just *do it*!"

Clement's face crumpled, and he sank to the floor with his head between his hands. "Don't you see?" he wept, sides heaving. "I've tried to go back. I've tried over and over, but every time I do, I get turned around. It's like home moves. I've charted maps and trails. I've tried to remember the address. I've even tried to ask for help, but every time I do, I can't remember what I'm asking for."

Delpha curled her lip, not understanding, not wanting to understand. But something tickled the back of her mind, and she had to ask it. She had to know.

"It was my birthday," Delpha whispered. "We were supposed to make cake."

Clement's face contorted again. "I know. I'm sorry."

"Why, then?" Delpha choked.

"Your mama and I were out picking blackberries. Your mamaw was mindin' you while you napped. We startled a bear and her cubs out in the woods, and it started chargin' your mama. I'd never used Yow magic in front of her, and when I did—she was like a different person. She was scared t' death. We argued. When I wouldn't promise to never do it again, she hexed me. My body had a mind of its own, and I couldn't stop it from drivin' away. Then when I tried to come home—"

"Mama doesn't do magic," Delpha broke in icily. "She hates it. She's scared of it." But her heart pounded, because she'd seen the hex Clement was describing in her own spellbook. It was the "Getteth Lost" hex. It thwarted all the hexed person's attempts to contact someone. She'd seen the "Forgit a Face" charm that could wipe a person's face from your thoughts, too.

"Yeah," Clement chuckled sadly, rubbing his whiskers. "She don't use it. But she did that day. And she's a danged good witch, turns out. She'd do 'bout anything to protect you, Delpha. I couldn't even go into town and ask about y'all. I'd try to write letters, and my hands plumb forgot how to write. But it wasn't enough. I shoulda found my way back, Delpha. I shoulda found a way."

Delpha stared. Cold wind whistled through the hollow of her heart. All those years, wasted. She'd thought magic would protect her from ever getting hurt again. But here was Clement, telling her it was much, much more complicated than that. Now what?

Now nothing. Delpha felt numb inside, and she hoped her feelings wouldn't come knocking again anytime soon. Her mama was in danger, and Delpha had problems to solve.

With a mechanical wave, she told Clement, "Follow me."

In the church office, the receiver still dangled and swayed, and her mama's voice yelled her name. Delpha snatched it up and pressed it to her ear. She talked fast. "Mama, I know what you did to Clement. He's here with me, and he's comin' to get you."

Mama hollered something that made the phone speaker buzz. She was upset, but there was nothing for it. "First, you gotta undo that danged 'Getteth Lost' hex, and don't tell me you didn't do one, 'cause I saw it in the book."

Delpha squeezed one eye shut as her mama protested loudly on the other end of the line.

"Calm down, Mama," Delpha pleaded.

"Don't you see, Delpha? You come by trouble honest. Magic's our family's curse. First the feuds, then my own flesh and bone when I was a girl, and now this. I cut my own heart out when I hexed your daddy. To keep you safe. Because the magic can't have you. I can't stand to lose you, too," Mama's tinny voice pleaded.

Delpha's pulse hammered. Her daddy leaving had always been a can of worms Delpha was terrified to touch, but now that it was open, she surprised herself by having plenty of things to say. "What about Clement, Mama? What about me? Don't reckon I'd call us safe. And anyway, magic doesn't have me, cause I think it *is* me. I am it. And I can't cut my heart out, Mama. I love you, but I can't do that."

A deep sigh hissed in the receiver. "Saints preserve us." Delpha gripped the phone harder and wiped her eyes on her sleeve. Mama was stubborn as a mule, but she only said "saints preserve us" when she knew she was at the end of her rope. Delpha was making headway.

"Undo the hex. The 'Getteth Lost' is pointless now, anyway. He's foundeth. You have to let him come help you. 'Cause I need your help!"

There was a long pause on the other end of the line, then finally: "All right."

Delpha looked up to tell Clement that he could go home now, but he was already running out the door, footsteps pounding down the hallway and toward the parking lot.

CHAPTER 28
KATYBIRD

KATYBIRD LET OUT A LONG GROAN AND TRIED to sit up. Everything was dark in the chapel, every muscle in her body hurt, and a pounding rhythm beat inside her head. "I think I've been hit by a Mack truck," she wheezed. The warm press of Podge's coat against her face made her sneeze, and every one of her ribs wailed in protest.

"What time is it?"

"Easy there, Katy. It's about ten at night," the shadow sitting beside her said. The voice was soft and brittle, and Katy jerked away from the stranger and squinted. *Pound, pound, pound* went her head. Then she caught the silhouette of a long braid with a wand stuck through it.

"Delpha?"

"My mama's on her way. She'll help us. Rest now." Delpha sighed hard, then leaned her head back against the pew.

"You asked for help?"

"Had to. I was scared you'd break yourself."

Katy's mouth popped open. She hadn't realized much mattered to Delpha but getting the spell done. It hurt a little, too, that Delpha had given up on Katy's magic, but Katy couldn't exactly blame her. Truth be told, it felt good to have all that pressure off. *It's better this way*, Doubt whispered.

Thunk thunka thum thum, thunk thunka thum thum. Katybird realized the pounding noise wasn't inside her head. It was coming from outside the church.

And it was getting louder.

"What's that noise?" she whispered to Delpha.

"Drums, I think."

Katy strained to listen. Delpha was right. Now Katy could hear the pattern clearly—Celtic skin drums, just like the recordings in her family's museum.

An eerie dread spidered its way across Katy's shoulders, and she staggered to a window. Flickers of light winked in and out of trees as the torches wove their way down the ridges of the surrounding slopes. There appeared to be two big groups on opposing hills: the McGills and Hearns, no doubt. Katy remembered the evil McGill zombie's promise of war at midnight. Unearthly shrieks and howls cut Katy straight to the bone. "It's the zombies! They're . . . they're coming downtown. By the looks of all those torches, it's the whole graveyard of them!" Katy cried.

Delpha sat up straight, shadows zigzagging across her worried brow. "That's just a couple miles away."

Tyler called from one of the opposite stained-glass windows, swaying and fidgeting. "Um, guys? There's folks gatherin' inside town hall. They're carrying guns. I think they're organizing a hunting party for the zombies."

"What if your mama doesn't get here in time?" Katy demanded. "All those people are going out after the zombies with nothing but piddly guns!"

Before Delpha could answer, a rasping chuckle echoed from the church's hallway, startling all three of them. Dull bootfalls echoed along the walls, slow and heavy. "Weeee Hearn," a ghastly voice scraped through the darkness. "Come 'ere, wee Hearn. I've got somethin' fur ye." Katy thought she recognized the gutteral voice as one of the McGill zombies from the basptismal tank. Maybe it had gotten trapped in the rubble? Delpha and Katy exchanged looks of fear.

Tyler bristled and flexed, but Katy shook her head wildly. *Run*, she mouthed. Delpha was on her feet now, crouching as she tiptoed around the pews to one of the smaller windows along the length of the chapel. A tiny squeaking noise made Katy cringe. Delpha was opening the unoiled crank-style window. Katy and Tyler rushed to her side.

"I kin heaaaar yooooou, silly lass. Got ears like a cat."

The hand crank squeaked faster, and cool night air poured through the partly opened window. *C'mon, c'mon.* When the crack was big enough, Delpha waved at Katy to go first. Exhaling, Katy slithered through the gap and dropped several feet to the ground outside. Tyler passed Podge into her waiting hands, then motioned for Delpha to go next. Tyler tried to squeeze through the opening last but groaned halfway through. Katy's breath caught. He was stuck!

"Tyler, the crank!" Delpha yelped.

The zombie cackled inside the chapel, and Delpha tried to clamber back up the outside wall of the church. "Move, Tyler, move!" she hollered, clawing at the bricks. Katy grabbed the heel of Delpha's boot and boosted her up to the sill. "Leftie loosie, Tyler! Leftie loosie!"

The window widened, and Tyler scraped his way out, just before the pane above his head turned to stone as a hex hit the glass. He dropped to the ground, panting. "What now?"

"Puppet," Delpha said uncertainly. "Maybe . . . maybe we could draw the zombies away from downtown before people try to fight 'em."

A chorus of shouts reverberated across the street from town hall. Inside its windows, folks raised their rifles and fists as they ginned up courage for a fight. A voice bellowed through the windows: "Are we gonna tolerate conjure in this valley?"

"NO!!" came the answering chorus.

"Are we gonna sit still while monsters and abominations threaten our loved ones?"

"NO!!"

"What'll we do?"

"TAKE 'EM OUT!!"

A small flock of mud-splattered ATVs and Jeeps littered the parking lot. Katy winced. "We can't yet. These people will follow the zombie torches into the hills, tryin' to fight them. They're gonna get themselves killed."

"What are we supposed to do?" Delpha growled.

Katy's heart pounded. Why was Delpha asking *her*? But the answer was on her lips already. "We have to try to warn everybody inside. It's the right thing to do."

"How're we gonna do that without announcing we're witches?" Delpha snorted. "We'll have to explain how we know the zombies can't be killed."

Katy gave Delpha a sad smile. "'Fraid you're the only witch here, Delpha. And, anyway, we'll think of something to say."

Delpha grimaced but nodded. "Fine."

They ran to town hall, and Katybird pounded on the massive

wooden door. "It's three kids," she hollered. "Let us in!" The door yanked open, and Katy, Delpha, and Tyler were pulled inside. As the door slammed shut behind them, Katy studied the room. More than a hundred people were gathered there—folks from the Hollow, mostly, plus a couple dozen tourists—some seated and others gathered around a raised lectern at the front of the room, rifles in hand.

"Rock slides have made our mountain roads impassable, and the cell towers have been blown apart, so it's up to us to defend ourselves. Everyone will hunt in pairs," the deputy's voice blared from the lectern, making Katy wince and cover her ears. "If you see one of the evil critters, shoot to kill." Shouts of agreement erupted.

Delpha elbowed her way to the stage and climbed the steps, with Katy and Tyler following close behind her. The deputy cast them an annoyed glance and waved them off the platform with his bullhorn, but Delpha stalked forward anyway, scowling at the crowd.

"Y'all don't know what you're up against," Delpha hollered. "Y'all are gonna get yourselves killed!" She was met with a chorus of boos and shouts to sit down and mind her elders. From behind, Katy saw the tips of Delpha's ears flush and her shoulders tense. "Don't be stupid! You can't fight this magic with bullets!"

"Is that the McGill girl?" a voice nearby whispered.

A man below with a beet-red face shook a finger up at Delpha.

"An' how would you know, young'un?" he yelled loud enough for the whole room to hear.

A wave of uneasy whispers traveled around the edges of the room, and Katy only caught snippets of hushed words as wary eyes studied Delpha. The phrases "great-great-granddaddy warned us" and "the old feud" and "devil worshippers" drifted to Katy's ears. A crawling dread filled her, as decades of cheerful politeness and the fragile trust her family had built with their community unraveled. Folks had written off old witch stories as tall tales before, but in their panic they latched onto any old dusty gossip, even the nonsense.

Delpha even looked the part of a dangerous witch as people showered her with suspicious looks. Her wand hand inched toward her pocket. Katy grabbed Delpha's elbow and squeezed it, but Delpha didn't relax.

"Don't be idiots!" Delpha yelled, but people were shouting over her now. The deputy moved to grab Delpha.

As he seized her arm, Delpha kicked and fought, howling in fury. Tyler lunged forward, his eyes wild and defensive, a guttural snarl erupting in his throat. Katy shrieked as several men leaped onto the platform to help restrain Delpha.

Look, Katy told herself. *Look at all those gun barrels in so many jumpy hands.* Across the platform, Delpha struggled against the men, trying to reach her wand. Beside her, Tyler's fingernails grew long and sharp. *Click-click, click-click*, the men's rifles answered.

Everyone around Katy swam in their own personal swamp of panic, but in that moment, Katy's heart floated above it all. She understood what was happening better than anyone else in the room. Fear birthed suspicion, and suspicion created fear, around and around in an endless dance of confusion. She'd had a whole life to spend pondering why folks feared "different," which left her with a more clear-headed kind of anger.

Through a window, Katy saw the two zombie armies start descending from their separate hills, east and west of town. Her eyes caught, too, on a gray boy statue sprawled in the street outside. Her heart lurched. *Caleb.*

Delpha screamed in anguish as a burly, shaking man aimed his rifle at Tyler's chest. *Click-click.* Katy felt she was watching a tragic play where the heroine had forgotten her cue. *That's me*, Katy realized. *It has to be me, because there's nobody else.*

She climbed atop the lectern, sending Podge scurrying from her shoulder to the floor. Katy studied the ivy outside the windowpane, swinging placidly in the breeze. *Ivy*, she considered, *doesn't give two hoots about people's silly imaginary boundaries and boxes.* It could climb anything. Overcome anything, with a clinging, tenacious love of life and desire to thrive. No matter who tried to cut it back and erase it, ivy stubbornly thrived, because it belonged in the world as much as any other plant. It didn't apologize for claiming space. That was its nature. Katy understood its essence, maybe, because that's part of who she was meant to be, too.

She cupped her hands over her heart. She knew what to do. The universe had left a perfect, Katybird-shaped hole in its fabric, and Katybird decided to step right into it. There was no room for Doubt. She could sense the universe smiling at her, too, big and smug, because Katy was exactly the sort of girl it needed, and it had known all along.

"Magic, I'm your girl," Katy whispered. She smiled at the ivy. "Come on, then! Let's talk!" she said—no, commanded—because she wasn't taking no for an answer anymore. Her head tilted with the authority of a queen.

Green light burst outward from Katybird's chest, and she wobbled to keep her balance. For a minute, she thought she might be exploding, but when she looked down, magic poured freely from her fingers, too. People ducked and screamed as a deep green cloud collected in front of Katy—*sweet, respectable Katy Hearn.* Oscillating forms of trees and ferns and animals formed and faded within it, as if the timeless ideas of forest things had been conjured inside the mist.

From the cloud's roiling center glided a shimmering emerald form. Its body was composed entirely of dew-covered leaves, and its glowing eyes winked at Katybird in feral curiosity.

"Aye?" came a melodic voice. "What is it thee wants with the ivy spirit, daughter of witches?"

Katy shook her hair. "We need to protect these folks. Keep 'em in town hall until Delpha and I can put things right. An' keep em' from shootin' each other by accident, would you?"

"Whatever thee asks." The thing wheeled backward and dissolved into a comet of light shooting for the door. Katybird jumped from the lectern and scooped up Podge in her arms as she ran. The slack-jawed deputies loosened their grips on Delpha and Tyler, who wriggled away and wasted no time tearing after Katy.

Once the three were outside, Katy slammed the heavy door behind her with a clunk, then screeched to Tyler and Delpha, "Stand back!"

Thick vines of ivy and kudzu exploded from the ground, weaving together with mind-boggling speed, encasing town hall in a wall of green. From inside the thicket of vines, Katy saw a glowing yellow eye wink at her, then vanish.

Tyler thumped Katy's shoulder, whooping. "That was . . . so much whoa! Your hands were all *skkkshhhh*, and the vines were like, *whoooosh*! How'd you do that?"

"I just did it, I guess," Katy said, heart floating. She didn't explain how she'd understood what it meant to be ivy, or about finding her Katy-shaped space. She wanted to hold that treasure inside for a while, just for herself.

And now, I bet I can do my half of the Reverse-Curse, Katy realized. *Love like hearth with coals aglow.* But as she rolled the now-familiar words around in her head and envisioned herself saying them, something about the picture felt wrong. Something didn't quite fit. Katy frowned hard. Was she doubting again?

Before she could ponder it further, screeches ripped through the night. The three of them turned, wide-eyed, to find the army of Hearn zombies at the foot of a hill to the west, preparing to mount their attack against the McGills, who charged from a hill to the east.

"We gotta get out of here," Delpha hollered, already dashing down the street toward the back lot of the hardware store, where Puppet sat waiting. Heart climbing into her throat, Katybird joined Tyler as they chased after Delpha through the darkness.

Katy glanced over her shoulder, heart in her throat. Glimmering torches of the opposing zombie clans converged at the head of Main Street like swarms of lighting bugs. Just ahead, Tyler and Delpha rounded the alley between the church and the hardware store, jumping the chain-link fence and tearing up the grassy hill to the cedars where Puppet waited.

Delpha slapped her pocket with a horror-stricken look. "My wand's gone!"

"Your hair!" Katybird pointed to where the carved stick was jammed into Delpha's thick braid.

Delpha yanked it free and leveled it at Puppet. The shed sprang to life faster than Katy had ever seen before, and Delpha staggered forward, her face beaded in sweat. "C'mon!" she barked, crawling into the doorway.

Katy and Tyler clambered in after her. All three jumped as a streetlight below exploded in a shower of sparks as one of the Hearn zombies hit it with an arc of lightning. A chorus of hyena-like howls made icy dread collect in Katy's middle. There were *so* many zombies. A dozen of them already swarmed the vine cocoon around town hall like hungry yellow jackets at a picnic.

"We gotta draw 'em off," Katybird gasped.

"Sounds fun," Delpha quipped, face pale.

"How do we hold their attention?" Katy whimpered.

Tyler hesitated, then dug out a handful of flashlights and emergency flares from the bottom of his bag. Katy winced and thought of the old saying: "Don't trouble Trouble, and Trouble won't trouble you." This was lobbing a stick of dynamite at Trouble, and there would be no going back. And what happened then? They couldn't run forever.

Tyler passed the girls each a flashlight. "This is such a bad idea," he muttered, "but here we go."

"Hey, you ugly old buzzards!" Tyler hollered hoarsely toward the street. He pushed a cartridge into the flare gun and locked the barrel, then cocked the hammer, aiming high. The flare lit up the sky like a meteorite. For an awful second, the night fell completely silent. They had the zombies' undivided attention.

"You're up, Katybird."

Suddenly, Katy felt almost too excited. *I called up the ivy spirit,* she reminded herself. *I can do this, too.* "I'm Katybird Hearn!" she screamed into the darkness, clutching Podge in one hand and waving her flashlight beam around with the other. "And I've got Delpha McGill with me! Catch us if you can!"

It was like Katy had pressed a detonator. The night filled with the sound of footfalls and guttural shrieks that hurtled in their direction.

"Run!" Tyler yelped. "Go, Delpha, go!"

Delpha raised her wand, and the woodshed jerked into violent motion, throwing Tyler and Katy against a wall. Tyler fumbled to hold the door open so Delpha could steer better in the dark. Puppet galloped its way toward the rim of the valley outside of town, with the zombies swarming behind them in the distance.

"Slow down, or you'll lose them!" Katybird hollered.

Delpha grimaced, but Puppet slowed to a trot. The zombies tore up the hill after them, closing the distance faster than Katy thought possible.

"Speed up, *speed up!*"

They whizzed all the way to the opposite end of town, up the hill, and into the forest, slowing and speeding up again as they tried to keep the zombie clans at their heels.

"Where are we going?" Tyler asked.

"To end this," Delpha said with a jerk of her chin. "To the Wise Woman Cemetery up yonder."

Katy waved her flashlight at the trailing zombies, whooping like a maniac, and they screeched in response.

In the moonlight, Katy saw Delpha's eyes were a little too wide. A tear track etched its way through dried blood and grime on her cheek. *She's scared spitless*, Katy realized. It wasn't until earlier, in the church, she'd realized Delpha was capable of crying, but she'd seen it then, too, after she'd fought with Tyler in the church. If you blinked, you'd miss the signs of Delpha's need for people. But if you watched close for them, they were everywhere.

Katy wracked her brain for helpful words. It was hard to know how to be there for Delpha. Delpha didn't love nicely. She wasn't huggy. But Delpha loved hard, and she'd worked herself ragged, when it came down to it, making sure everyone was safe.

"Don't know how we're gonna do the Reverse-Curse with these zombies right on our tails," Delpha grunted, swallowing hard.

Tyler reached over and gave Delpha's hand a squeeze. "When we get to the graveyard, I'll take care of all the zombies. You and Katy, y'all just do the Reverse-Curse. Don't worry." His madcap grin seemed a hair forced to Katy, and his voice cracked. "I've got a plan."

"I don't like the sound of that, Tyler. What sort'a plan? You can't fight off both zombie armies at once!"

"Yeah, but I can outrun 'em, at least as a Yow."

Katy frowned. "But your leg . . ."

"Almost right as rain. It looks worse than it feels."

"No, Tyler. Just . . . no," Delpha barked through clenched teeth.

"Trust *me* this time, Delpha. I just need to keep 'em distracted until y'all get your spell done. Katy's got it in the bag this time!"

Katy started to protest, then realized he was right. She *could* do her part. She had to. She gave a quick nod of agreement.

Delpha's eyes brightened, still staring out the door. Her mouth relaxed into a tiny smile. "Okay." Delpha rolled her shoulders, and Puppet sped down into the lonely crook of the forest that held the graveyard.

White tombstones loomed ahead as Puppet stomped to a stop in the familiar clearing. Katy vaulted to the ground, butterflies in her chest, and then Delpha followed her, tumbling from Puppet's doorway in exhaustion.

The two girls ran to the center of the grassy circle, to the exact spot where Delpha had cast the "Wend-to-War" hex the night before.

Katy glanced at Tyler with worried eyes. Tyler nodded and gave her a double thumbs-up, even as she saw his knees wobble in fear.

"Hold my glasses?"

"Give 'em here. And run fast," Katy whispered, hugging Podge tight. "Don't let 'em catch you." A lump of worry squeezed her throat.

Eyes wide, Tyler gave a quick nod, then tore off into the dark forest toward the zombies' winking torches, howling.

CHAPTER 29
DELPHA

DELPHA TRIED TO FOCUS ON WHAT NEEDED TO BE done, but her body wouldn't stop shaking. *Did Clement make it to Mama in time? Were they both all right?* The thought of the zombies hurting her mother had her stomach in knots. And there were so many things she wanted to say to Clement still. What if she never got the chance?

A dog yelped somewhere in the forest surrounding the graveyard. Delpha lurched toward the sound. *Tyler.* Why had she agreed to let him distract an entire zombie horde? *Stupid*, she berated herself.

"Delpha, we've got to focus," Katy whimpered.

"Right," Delpha muttered. Soon, everything would be right again. She flipped her braid over her shoulder and tried to clear her head.

"Ready?" Katy asked.

Delpha tried to swallow, but her throat was too dry. *"With cunning mind an' strongest will, I call the hex of war to still,"* she croaked.

Katybird bounced on the heels of her sneakers. *"Love like hearth with coals aglow, my open heart makes magic grow."*

They glanced at each other, then chanted: *"These balanced pow'rs make evil quake. Together, watch the curses break!"*

Cicadas droned, and the cries of the zombies loomed even closer. Delpha's eyes skittered across the tree line in confusion.

"Why ain't it workin'?" Delpha shouted, turning on Katy. "I thought you got your magic sorted out!"

"Don't freak out, Delpha! Let's just try it again—"

"No! I've done everything right! Why am I stuck doing this with you in the first place?" A whirlwind of feelings rose in Delpha's chest. Sobs clawed up her throat, and she clenched her wand until her fingertips went tingly and dead. "None of this is fair. None of it! I've . . . done . . . *everything.*"

Delpha couldn't think straight. She was crazy with worry for her mama. For Tyler, and for herself and Katy, too, if they didn't get the spell right.

Katybird chewed on her lip and stared at Delpha, fidgeting. "I been thinkin'. Someone told me once that cunning folk sometimes tricked people into fixin' things they didn't realize were broke. Maybe the witches that wrote the Reverse-Curse were being crafty, too."

"What's that supposed to mean?" Delpha demanded.

"It's a little nutty, but hear me out," Katy said, eyes shining. "Let's say when you curse someone, you have to really mean it. When we did the 'Wend-to-War' hex that made the zombies, we were both spittin' angry at each other. The curse got its power from inside us"—Katy tapped her chest—"and went outward. We were all gnarled up inside, and the curse just took the hate further."

Delpha frowned. "Okay. So?"

"What if the Reverse-Curse has to go all the way in reverse? What if it's meant to fix *us*?"

Delpha snorted. "This is sillier than when you thought Puppet was a tree, Katy. We don't have time for nonsense! Besides, I ain't messed up inside!"

"Well, *I* was!" Katy countered. "I wasn't sure of myself. But I think bein' around you changed me," she insisted. "Your nerve made me jealous at first, but kind of in a good way. It made me try harder. Then in town hall, I had to find my 'strongest will'!"

Delpha crossed her arms. "So?"

"So, maybe we've had it wrong this whole time! What . . . what if we traded our parts of the spell, Delpha? What if *I'm* supposed to do that first line, 'With cunning mind an' strongest will'?"

Delpha's pulse raced in excitement. If Katy was onto something, they could finally work the dad-blasted Reverse-Curse. But when Delpha thought about the second line of the spell—*Love like hearth with coals aglow, my open heart makes magic grow*—her mouth went dry as dust. "Nope. The second part ain't me."

"Why not?"

"I don't love *love* the way you do." Delpha didn't add that she could hardly bring herself to say the words of Katy's half of the Reverse-Curse without breaking down into tears. If Delpha went around letting people in all willy-nilly like Katy did, how would she survive when they left her? Her stomach clenched. *What if Clement leaves again?* Delpha hugged herself tight around her ribs. *And why do I care?*

"If what you're sayin's true," Delpha said, "and I have to mean it when I say it, then we'll never break the danged curse."

"I guess the zombies are just gonna kill me, then," Katy snapped, eyes flashing. "They'll get Tyler, too. And my family will stay stone, and your mama and Clement will get killed . . ."

"Why are you sayin' all that?" Delpha cried through gritted teeth.

"'Cause you're actin' selfish! I nearly killed myself trying to do the Reverse-Curse. Aren't you going to at least try?" Katy demanded.

Delpha dug her fingers into the damp grass. Why couldn't Katybird understand? Love ruined you from the inside out. Delpha knew what was behind all those shut doors inside her heart. Inside, she was like Echo's haint, all fragile down and feathers. If she pried herself open, where would those pieces fly off to?

The zombies were close enough now that Delpha could hear them screeching curses as they crashed through the trees just outside the graveyard clearing.

"Love lets people smash you like a bug," Delpha choked, squeezing her eyes tight.

"Love puts you back together again when that happens," Katy insisted.

"I'm a lone wolf."

"Ain't such a thing. There's always a pack."

"I don't have a pack."

"You're the leader, silly goose."

Delpha's head jerked up, and she met Katy's eyes in surprise.

"And we need you."

A dog howled in the forest, and frightened tears spilled down Katy's freckled face. Delpha couldn't deny it. She *did* care for them.

Love had always felt like a rug about to be yanked from under Delpha's feet. *But what if it's more like bones?* Delpha thought. *What if it's inside you, like steel, giving you the strength to carry the people who need carrying?* Delpha hated that she couldn't control the way other people loved her. She hated that a thousand things could go wrong in their heads, keeping them from seeing the Right Thing to do, even when they cared. But Delpha McGill could control Delpha McGill, and right now, she could see clearly how to do right by Katybird and Tyler. And even if it meant opening each door in her heart and having everything inside it blow away in the wind, she reasoned, at least she'd know she'd done the right thing.

"All right," she whispered. "I'll try."

The deafening crack of a lightning hex sounded a few feet away, and a young tree shuddered as it hit the ground beside them. Both girls scrambled away, and the heavy tang of ozone clung to Delpha's nostrils.

Two gray Yows tore into the clearing, heading off a McGill zombie who brandished a smoking wand. Tyler was still alive! And Clement had come for them! Through the trees, Delpha thought she caught sight of her mama, too, throwing rocks at a skeletal Hearn owl that swooped at her, talons extended. *Mama, fighting off zombies*, Delpha marveled. *Maybe I can do this*.

"Now?" Katybird gasped.

"Now."

Katy raised her chin. *"With cunning mind an' strongest will, I call the hex of war to still!"*

Delpha hesitated, then grasped Katy's hand. *I'm sick of being alone*, Delpha marveled. *I like Katybird having my back*. Maybe

Katy was right. Maybe the two of them were stronger together. It was a wild sliver of trust. *"Love like hearth with coals aglow,"* Delpha chanted in a low voice. *"My open heart makes magic grow."*

The air between Delpha and Katy went electric, a summer storm ready to rumble its way across the mountains. Delpha's eyes widened, and Katy gave a quick nod.

"These balanced pow'rs make evil quake! Together, watch the curses break!" they shouted up to the stars. A wave of calm mushroomed in a translucent ripple from Delpha and Katy's clasped hands. Even the crickets hushed, and all Delpha could hear was blood rushing in her ears.

Then peaceful, rasping hums from a hundred zombie throats mingled together and whispered through the spring leaves, gathering into a single, lilting melody. Ragged forms limped into the clearing toward their crumbling headstones, and Katybird and Delpha tensed, jumping out of their paths. But the corpses walked and hummed peaceably all the way to their graves, yawning and adjusting their moldering bosoms and bonnets for a long eternity's nap. They lay down, ladylike, in front of their respective grave markers, where, without a fuss, they sank back into their dirt, and unending sleep reclaimed them.

Katy and Delpha stood breathless, staring, until the rightful sounds of the forest resumed. A single whoop of joy went up from the woods, and a few seconds later, Tyler loped out from between the trees, disheveled and beaming. "Yes! Yes!" he howled, limping across the clearing, alive and well. When he reached them, he grabbed his glasses from Katy and shoved them crookedly onto his nose.

Delpha felt the corner of her mouth slide upward. "Looks like we did it," she whispered to Katybird.

Katybird's face crumpled with relief. "Then the stone hexes are undone. I've got my family back."

Delpha hugged Katy fiercely, trying to ignore the tight lump gathering in her own throat. *That makes one of us*, she thought.

Moments later, as Tyler doubled over to catch his breath, Clement staggered from the forest with Delpha's mama close behind, her gauzy blouse flapping around her open arms as she gathered Delpha tight to her chest. Her eyes were so red and swollen, the blue parts shone like spring bluets. Delpha crumpled like a rag doll.

"I'm sorry I lied to you, Mama. And I'm sorry about the zombies," Delpha's muffled voice croaked.

"Hush, now. I'm just happy you're all right," Mama crooned. Then she whispered into Delpha's ear: "I'm sorry, too. We . . . got a lot of things to talk about, but this ain't the place. I'm real proud of how brave you were. Mamaw would've been real proud, too."

Delpha pulled back in surprise, too stunned to do much except nod.

Katybird and Tyler shuffled awkwardly.

"Y'all all right?" Mama asked them sharply, grabbing their arms and checking them over. Delpha wiped her eyes.

Katybird shrugged. Tyler beamed, making the cuts on his face bleed faster. "I prob'ly need stitches. Muzz and Honey are gonna kill Clement when they find out he took me zombie hunting while they were on their anniversary trip," Tyler quipped to his uncle, wincing at the sight of the antiseptic spray Clement was pulling from his knapsack.

Clement chuckled, but the laugh didn't reach his eyes. The ghosts of tears tracked through the forest grime and blood on his cheeks. He kept stealing glances at Delpha and Mama, eyes full of the same questions Delpha wanted answers to: *Who are we now? What happens next? Are some cuts too deep to heal?* Delpha felt small and shy, suddenly, and even though she wished she knew how to make things right, she was a far piece off from knowing how. Someone grabbed Delpha's hand and squeezed.

You ain't alone, Katy's hand said.

Delpha swallowed hard and squeezed back.

Thanks.

A glint of copper on Clement's finger caught Delpha's eye. It was familiar as sunshine, because Delpha had seen its twin every day on Mama's hand since . . . forever. *Wedding bands.* Well, then. Folks didn't go around wearing old wedding bands unless they still had some feelings about them.

"M-mind if I help?" Mama asked, motioning to Tyler's swollen leg.

Tyler shrugged.

"May I borrow your wand, Delpha?"

Delpha nearly dropped her teeth. "To use?"

"Well, I'm not gonna eat it."

Delpha handed it over, astonished and curious. Tyler and Katy exchanged *Are you seeing this?* glances. Mama took a deep, juddering breath, raised the wand, and gently swished it over Tyler's injured leg. Cool mountain mist snaked around Tyler's leg until the angry red streaks shrank away to nothing. Just like that.

"Th-thank you, ma'am," Tyler stammered. When Mama turned to give back Delpha's wand, Tyler mouthed to Delpha, *Oh. My. Lanta!*

Delpha stared at her mother, bug-eyed.

"It's been a while since I used my healing magic." Mama sighed, inspecting Tyler's healed leg with a critical eye. "Not too shabby." She looked like a person who had been on a diet far too long, finally eating pineapple upside-down cake again and remembering how nice it is. Tyler grinned at her and handed her a tin of Vienna sausages.

"I better sit down a minute, though. Forgot how much conjure wears you slap out."

Mama walked over to the rotting log where Clement sat, and the two of them began talking in hushed tones. After a minute, Mama timidly raised the wand and began to heal the wound on Clement's head. Delpha squirmed and pretended not to notice, climbing into the battered wreck that was Puppet, where she made herself busy thumbing through the spellbook while Katy and Tyler rolled pine cones for Podge to chase. She leaned back against the worn wooden walls, relishing the peace and quiet.

After a few minutes of searching, a lopsided smile crawled up Delpha's face. "Hey, Katy. C'mere." Delpha waved Katy over to Puppet, feeling almost bashful, spellbook dangling beneath her arm. Tyler trailed behind Katy, eavesdropping as usual.

Katy hugged Delpha. Delpha let her . . . for three whole seconds.

"You okay?"

"Yup. I found a spell I thought you might like in the spellbook. It's another two-parter."

Katy pulled a face. "I think I've had enough magic for one night. I want to get back to Mama an' Nanny an' Caleb, soon as we can."

"No rush. I think we'll need to practice a few days for this one, anyway. It's heavy-duty nature magic."

Katy raised her eyebrows. "Nature magic?"

Delpha's smile broadened. "Tree magic, specifically."

CHAPTER 30
DELPHA

A WEEK LATER, IN THE CHEERY APRIL SUNSHINE,
a small procession of pickups and Jeeps wound through the blossoming cherry trees to Wise Woman Cemetery.

Soon, a circle of people gathered around a dilapidated shed.

Tyler Nimble stood flanked by his mothers, who had grounded him through the end of eternity (and were very proud of him).

Beside them stood Katybird Hearn, along with her entire family, who had also grounded Katy for the rest of her natural life (and were also very, *very* proud of her).

Delpha, Mama, and Clement completed the circle. Delpha's family wasn't quite a *family* yet. On Katy's Nanny's advice, Delpha was giving her parents time. But Clement was spending all his spare hours quietly fixing things around the McGill cabin and admiring Delpha's woodworking, and for now, that suited Delpha perfectly. It was a quiet rhythm.

The rest of the Hollow seemed eager to forget about all the trouble with the zombies, especially since Mama had helped their amnesia along with a "Don't Worry Yer Head About It None" charm from the McGill spellbook.

Delpha opened the spellbook and winked at Katybird. Katy grinned and joined her next to Puppet. They'd been practicing on dead saplings every afternoon, and now they were ready.

"Go on, Hearn," Delpha grinned, holding the book out for Katy to read. Delpha raised her wand. Katy tucked back her newly purpled hair and raised her chin before chanting with Delpha:

> *"Boards be unhewn,*
> *Nails undone—*
> *Rev'rse the course of time.*
> *Let rootlets crawl.*
> *Let branches sprawl.*
> *Up to yonder sky thee climb!"*

In a flurry of motion, Puppet's boards took the vague shape of a tree. Delpha held her wand steady as pulp grew around the worn planks. A thick skin of bark spread over the tree's surface, and gnarled roots plunged deep into the earth, rippling the dirt beneath their feet. Green-tinted light filtered through leaves overhead and danced across the girls' faces. Their families oohed and aahed at their handiwork. The tree was a little lopsided, branches dipping low to the ground on one side—a feature Tyler was cheerfully taking advantage of in a clumsy attempt to scale it.

"It's a little cattywampus," Katy whispered behind her hand, giggling.

Delpha wiped her nose on the back of her hand.

"It's perfect."

Acknowledgments

To Lauren Spieller, for your tenacity, honesty, and tireless feedback, and for believing so hard in this story, and to the entire family at Triada US Literary Agency.

To Jenne Abramowitz, for your editor's eye and for your love of Howler's Hollow.

To the many wonderful individuals on the team at Scholastic, for your hard work and support, and to the amazing marketing and publicity teams.

To the brave souls who read early iterations of this book and gave feedback behind the scenes; I am so grateful for you. You know who you are, and I am so grateful for your encouragement and honesty.

To my beta readers and long-suffering critique partners; thanks for wading through the tears and notes with me. May your tea mugs stay hot and your joy be great.

To the dear friends who forbade me from giving up or feeling sorry for myself; you know who you are. I promise to return the favor.

To InterACT, for your tireless advocacy and for making a wealth of solid, generous information available to me, I am humbled and grateful.

To my lifelong partner-in-adventure, for countless cups of coffee, therapeutic arc-welding sessions, and late-night processing walks; I love you.

To my granny ancestors, actual and inherited, whose names are sprinkled liberally throughout the book, thanks for working your fingers to the bone to get me here. It's never far from my mind, and I'm grateful.

My kind, indomitable children: This book would never have existed without you.

My Gnome, for being wickedly good at playing the "what if" game. The zombies are for you.

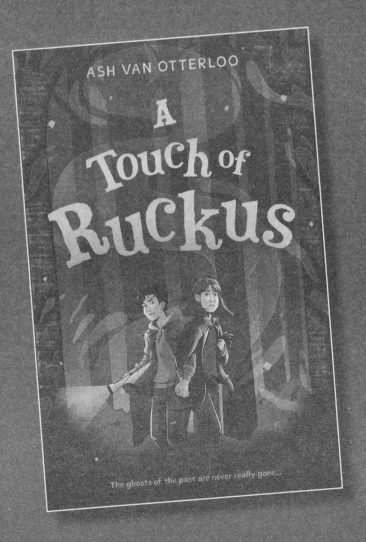

Every time Tennessee Lancaster

visited the Hollow, it got harder to tell where she stopped and where the forest began. Mist swirled across the back roads, dancing wild outside her half-lowered van window. Tennie's stomach did odd little cartwheels, as if the rippling fog squirmed inside her, too.

She jutted her chin closer to the opening. Damp air rushed over her freckled skin until her nose went numb. Autumn—Halloween especially—was her favorite time of year. She was determined to enjoy it properly, even if her family was moving. But as the trees whizzed by in an orange-and-ruby fury, Tennie's nerves couldn't settle.

Her family's new apartment—the one they'd just left all their moving boxes in—was a two-bedroom rental too small for all six of them. So they were making a pit stop at her grandmother's town an hour away. Her older brother, Birch, would stay with Mimsy for a month, while the rest of them crammed in like sardines.

"When we get there, I'll do the talking," Mama barked from the front seat, as "Monster Mash" blared on the radio. Her hyper fingers strummed the steering wheel. "Mimsy don't need to know about the housing mix-up."

Tennie didn't point out they'd all already been over this a dozen times. "Yes, ma'am."

"So here's the plan. Last week, she asked me to come help clean out Poppy's old things, which I'm not going to do. That woman can't ever stop complaining about my daddy, even now that he's passed. But Birch can go instead, as a favor to her. Problem solved."

Sadness at the thought of Poppy's things getting thrown out gripped Tennie, followed by a pang of jealousy. She'd have loved to be the one staying over at Mimsy's.

"Not as a favor to *us*?" Dad joked in a road-ragged voice from the passenger's seat. "If she says no, we're up a creek without a paddle here."

"Absolutely *NOT*. I won't have my mother fixin' my life like one of her dusty antiques," Mama muttered. "I'd never hear the end of it."

Tennie's legs clenched. She hated this ongoing pride war between Mama and Mimsy. "You know Mimsy loves us, Mama! And she always brags on what a good paramedic you are."

"That won't stop her from being proud as peas if she thinks she's saving Birch from sleeping on a couch. So stick to the story, got it? *Birch, d'you hear me?*"

THWUNK. Tennie's eyes narrowed when Birch's unnaturally long, cave-cricket legs knocked the back of her seat for the hundredth time as he shifted in his sleep. He wasn't even *listening*.

"We hear you, Mama—" Tennie said, covering for her brother. Her mom's shoulders loosened, and Tennie congratulated herself. She was the family's parent-whisperer. Once Birch was dropped off, and Mimsy was good and hoodwinked into thinking the Lancaster finances were fine, everyone's feathers would unruffle. Then, Tennie could relax, too, and enjoy her spooky fall season properly, with *Corpse Bride* marathons and candy corn.

But as Tennie imagined Birch lounging around Mimsy's picture-perfect front porch, the restlessness in her gut grew wilder. Why did Captain Earbuds get rewarded for being a lazy pain, while Tennie worked hard to help everyone get along?

So, ask Mama and Dad if you can go instead, a rebellious flicker suggested for the hundredth time. *That way, you get a whole room to yourself. Finally.*

Tennie's fingers tensed in her rainbow-striped gloves, curling up like threatened spiders. The thought of opening her mouth to ask Mama to change her plans was unthinkable. Especially while Mama was this keyed up. "I can't be selfish," she whispered, fogging the glass by her nose.

Five-year-old Shiloh, the drooling mirror image of her sleeping twin, Harper, snuggled her head into Tennie's side, hugging her clown-faced Raggedy Andy doll—an antique Mimsy had gifted her, and who precocious Shi had renamed "Mr. Fancy Pants." Tennie sagged and smooched the top of her sister's sweaty auburn head. Both twins' French braids fuzzed out like halos, making them look more angelic than they were. *If I go to Mimsy's, these little monsters'll wear Mama slap out. Birch won't help, and she'll start getting blue again*, Tennie worried.

But the fire in her stomach wouldn't quiet. *Think of Mimsy's fireplace! A soft, giant bed, all to yourself! Hot breakfast every day!* The flames crackled. Tennie pressed her lips. Time to give it an ice-cold drenching. She peeled her left glove from her hand, slipping her bare fingers into her hoodie pocket. She grazed them across a shard of plastic she kept there.

Tennie inhaled sharply. Her own magic always unsettled her.

The van around her dissolved into smeary smoke, and a blurred memory from five years ago replaced it.

Her old living room fluttered with orange streamers and homemade ISN'T IT GREAT? TENNESSEE'S EIGHT! banners. Memory-Tennie twirled and walked tiptoe in a ruffled pumpkin-print dress. She pestered Mama, who balanced a cake on one arm and crying baby Shiloh in the other.

"Stop grabbing, Tennie!" Mama snapped. The scent of apple shampoo from her still-dripping shower hair tickled Tennie's nose. "Guests will be here any minute, and the kitchen still isn't clean! And you know how sanctimonious Mimsy gets about that!"

Birch trotted into the room holding a jar of spiders, then wrinkled his nose. "Ugh, what smells like toilets?"

Tennie gasped. She pointed at baby Harper in her playpen, who had just strewn the contents of her diaper in unthinkable places. "Ewwwww!"

"Gross!" Birch hollered, dropping his spider jar and yarfing onto the floor. Tiny spiders fanned out from the broken glass in a skittering shadow, sending chills up Tennie's neck. She shrieked. Dad rushed in with paper towels as Mama tried to stamp the spiderlings with squeaking sneakers.

The doorbell rang. Mimsy let herself in and started fussing hard over the mess. Mama yelled that she didn't need Mimsy's help. A sour feeling filled Tennie's mouth at the sound of their arguing.

Everything was wrong. Fury rose in Tennie. Her family had ruined her birthday party before it began! Tennie hollered then, too. She yelled ugly, hateful words at her whole awful family. She snatched the party tiara from her head and snapped it into bits. Mama's face crumpled. She cried in the bedroom for hours, and Tennie cried in hers. Dad turned guests away, making up a story about a stomach bug. Mimsy cleaned the living room, then left, never bringing it up again.

Tennie yanked her trembling fingers from the shattered plastic. Her vision spun like a ceiling fan until the van grew solid around her. She pulled deep breaths through her nostrils and fixed a chill expression on her face, just in case her parents glanced in the rearview. The memory slowly fell asleep again, but the guilty feeling stayed in Tennie's gut, like the sore spot you got on your arm after a booster shot.

It worked like a charm. Tennie's anger fizzled. But that was no surprise. She'd smothered it this way a hundred times, and she had to admit, she felt a little smug over how good she'd gotten at it.

The first time she'd discovered her ability, it had been by accident. She'd clutched her shattered birthday tiara and forced herself to picture Mama's tears as her guilt coiled around her like a hungry snake. The memory had grown more and more real, until suddenly Tennie wasn't just *remembering* her crappy party—she was *at* her crappy party. Presently, Tennie's heart rate slowed. *Eighty beats per minute.* By now, she'd probably relived this particular scene hundreds of times, and she recovered from it faster than when she woke a brand-new memory.

Reliving the party was her anchor when her feelings got out of control—helping her keep her promise to herself to never add fuel to her family's problems again. Over time she'd discovered her ability was good for digging through other folks' memories, too. When they really cared about something, their recollections would get nice and stuck in an object, and Tennie was free to take it all in. Sometimes she just caught a feeling, and other times she practically time-traveled into the past.

But stealing memories could be upsetting. Sometimes, she hated what she found. Hidden sadness, secret worry, and real pain were more common than folks let on, making her superpower feel more like a superburden. But that's what the gloves were for. They kept the memories out.

Everybody's hiding something, Tennie thought, eyeballing the back of her parents' heads as the van hit a bump. She hadn't snooped through their stuff with her gloves off in a while. What sort of things were they not telling? Tennie pursed her lips and pushed the thought away.